A.S. FENICHEL

TAINTED BRIDE

FOREVER BRIDES

Tainted Bride

A
FOREVER BRIDES
NOVEL

Only trust can save her...

Sailing to London, Sophia Braighton only hopes to escape
certain ruin. But when she arrives, her Great Aunt Daphne has
other plans for the American-born beauty. Determined to
marry off her niece to a man of means, she propels Sophia into
London society, not knowing that the young woman's trust in
men is shattered. In fact, Sophia never expects to ever feel
anything for a man. Then again, she never expects to find
herself in the company of the dashing earl of Marlton...

From the moment he sees Sophia, Daniel Fallon feels alive in a
way he has not since his broken engagement. Though the
vulnerable beauty shies from the passion burning bright
between them, Daniel is determined to court her and make her
his bride. And when he learns of the painful secret she harbors,
he is equally determined to take revenge on the man
responsible.

But will the quest destroy him—and his future with his
beloved?

Edited by Penny Barber

Cover design by KaNaXa

This book is dedicated to those of us who have lost our better half.
One day the sun will rise again.

For Dave Mansue, who is my sunrise.

Acknowledgments

Books like this one are from the heart and therefore need a lot of help to see the light of day. I wrote Tainted Bride as part of a healing process. I wanted to let people know that finding happiness after tragedy, any tragedy, was possible. Because my own journey has many turns, I want to acknowledge the people who kept me going and helped me along the way. Eleanor Fenichel (Mom), Harvey Fenichel (Dad), Lou Fenichel, Linda Tugend, Amy Fenichel, Kenny Tugend, Lisa Brown, Debra Kaplan, Clinton Haldeman, Lorraine Mannifield, Bill Kaplan, Keith Mannifield, Stacey Carton, Denise Ragolia Ayers, Dave Mansue, Karla Doyle, Karen Bostrom, Shelly Freydont and NANOWRIMO.

Chapter One

After six weeks of seasickness, Sophia's legs wobbled on the gangplank. She searched London's crowded dock for her aunt and uncle. A shame her aching muscles kept her from running to dry land and finding them. She wasn't above kissing the solid ground.

Her maid, Marie, and footman, Jasper, hadn't left her side since Sophia's mother charged them with her care on the journey.

People from every walk of life bustled around the docks, unloading stores and loading supplies for the next journey. A woman in a serviceable dress hugged a young man as he exited the ship from steerage. The mother and son reunion stuck like a knife and she turned away as a child's screaming pulled her attention to the baby who had also endured the long voyage.

At the bottom of the walkway, an older woman in a perfectly tailored burgundy morning dress glanced at something one of her impeccable footmen held. She took the object and pursed her lips. Brown spots marred her tapered hand as she smoothed her bun, though not a hair dared go askew from the perfect coif. She evaluated Sophia down the length of her narrow nose and her frown deepened tightening the profound lines of someone who wore the expression often.

When Sophia reached the dock, one of the woman's footmen approached. "Miss Braighton?"

"Yes. I'm Sophia Braighton."

A touch of sympathy in his eyes, he nodded. "Follow me, please, Miss." He walked her to the woman.

Handing Sophia a miniature portrait of herself, she spoke with a deep, formal air of authority. "I'm Lady Daphne Collington, your great aunt on your father's side. You will be in my charge. Your things may be loaded into the carriage."

Jasper ran off with her ladyship's footman to load the trunks. Dressed in navy blue livery, he looked better than Sophia, but shabby in comparison to the Collington servants in turquoise and bright white.

Sophia handed her miniature back and covered her dismay with a pleasant smile. Taking a deep breath to quash her nausea, she hoped the carriage loading would take some time. The thought of being closeted into another moving vehicle had her in knots. "Lady Collington, where are my Aunt Adelaide and Uncle Cecil? I was given to believe they would be fostering me for this season."

Lady Collington harrumphed.

She would never survive the season with her notorious aunt. Unable to go back to Philadelphia, she held her tongue and hoped for the best. No. There was no going back, and with Lady Collington as her chaperone, there would be no hiding away.

"I'm not accustomed to being spoken to so frankly by one so young. You are far too direct, a consequence of being raised in the Colonies, to be sure. In addition, you are emaciated and we shall have to do something about those ill-fitting clothes." Lady

Collington scrutinized her. "I have no idea how we will get you married. Skin and bones are not at all the fashion this season. And that hair, blond is much more in style. Is it always so stringy or is it the salt air?" She climbed into her carriage.

There was no help for it. She should be happy anyone would have her after her banishment from home. "Marie, will you be comfortable in the carriage with my trunks?"

Footmen were loading her trunks into the coach behind the elegant carriage with terrible efficiency.

"Of course. The question is, will you?"

Sophia forced a smile and leaned toward Marie. "Mother is very fond of Aunt Daphne, but she did warn me that she can be a bit harsh at first blush."

Marie raised narrow eyebrows, bobbed, and strode toward the other carriage.

Sophia stepped into the carriage and sat opposite Daphne.

Lady Collington straitened the crisp white lace at her collar. "My niece and her husband have gone to the country. The child is ill again."

Sophia's chest tightened. Best to drop the subject. She would learn more from the servants regarding her cousin than from Lady Collington. "I'm not usually so thin. I'm afraid the voyage was uncomfortable for me.

Lady Collington's eyes widened before her stern gaze returned. "Seasickness is a matter of the mind. You should be stronger-minded than a common girl and have been able to overcome such a disturbance."

Sophia hoped she didn't look as stunned by Daphne's announcement as she felt. Otherwise, she was gaping at the woman. "I see. Have you traveled much abroad then, Lady Collington?"

"Why would I ever wish to leave England?"

Sophia's parents had told many stories about her great aunt

over the years. The dowager countess was a widow of an earl who had died before Sophia was born. Every time Sophia's father received a letter from his aunt, he would read it to the entire family. The contents were always severe, but the Braightons found the messages amusing. In a recent letter, she had disclosed that her son, the current earl, had married but chose to stay most of the time in the country. A circumstance the dowager found quite vexing.

Sophia hid her amusement. "I cannot imagine. May I call you aunt?"

"If you wish, but only in the confines of family and close friends. I assume you have been taught proper etiquette."

Sophia forced a smile. "Oh yes, Aunt. Four years at Mrs. Mirabelle's School for Young Ladies."

Lady Daphne's piercing blue eyes narrowed. "This Mirabelle, was she English? I hope your mother did not send you to some Italian to learn manners."

"Miss Mirabelle was very much English, Aunt Daphne." The carriage began moving, and she tried to ignore her nausea. "I was under the impression that you quite liked my mother. She has always seemed very fond of you, whenever she speaks of England."

"Of course, I like your mother. She is a delight and I regret my nephew chose to take his family to America. I advised him strongly against it. That does not mean I would wish your manners to be in the Italian style. It would make my work much more difficult. English men have a certain expectation of a wife, you know."

"Yes, Aunt." Looking forward to a bed that didn't move while she slept was her only solace.

Daphne gave her a hard look. "Do you not wish to find a husband?"

"I'll do as you tell me, Aunt." It was a strain, but Sophia

was too tired and sick to argue with a woman who'd never understand.

"Of course you will." Daphne ran her finger under her collar where the satin and lace caused an angry rash.

They traveled the rest of the way to London's Grosvenor Square in silence, though she felt Aunt Daphne's gaze on her the entire time.

As Sophia stepped down onto solid ground, she covered her giggle with her hand. There would be no more rocking of boats or carriages for a while. The thirty-foot ceiling in the foyer was capped by a crystal chandelier glittering like a crown. Polished to a high shine, the wooden railing of the curved staircase enrobed the space.

"This is your home? No one else lives here with you?" Even with the massive sitting room on the right and library to the left, the walls closed in on her. It was all as grand as her father's stories had indicated.

Daphne cleared her throat. "Upon his father's death, my son, the Earl of Grafton, gifted me this townhouse, since it had long been my home in London. He purchased another for his new wife."

"It's so big." How would she, Sophia Braighton from Philadelphia, ever fit in such a place? She stepped across the white marble with grey veins. Black accent tiles formed geometric shapes in the floor and walls of the entry.

"There will be plenty of time to explore the house, Sophia. You must be exhausted, and I would like to rest as well. Mrs. Colms, the housekeeper, will show you to your room."

A large woman in a gray dress and white cap stood off to the side. "Tonight, I'll have your meal sent up, but in the future, I expect you will prefer to dine with me. We shall not accept any invitations for balls or dinners this week, while you recover from your journey. However, we do have a picnic in three days, which we will attend."

"Thank you, Aunt Daphne. I am tired." She took a few steps then turned, overcome by a sudden feeling of guilt for all the trouble she would likely cause Aunt Daphne. Exhaustion and the idea of resting in a bed that didn't sway with the waves of the ocean might have had a hand in her emotional state, but she hated to be a burden. "I'm sorry to have been foisted on you in such a way. I do appreciate your willingness to sponsor me this season." She threw herself against her Great Aunt Daphne and wrapped her arms around her.

Lady Collington gave Sophia's back one quick pat before dropping her hands back to her sides.

Sophia ended the awkward embrace. Her face warmed over her impulsive show of affection for a woman she had never before met.

Lips tight and eyes wide, Daphne cleared her throat.

She kissed Daphne's cheek and rushed up the steps with no idea where she was supposed to go.

From below, Aunt Daphne said, "Show the girl her room."

Mrs. Colms ambling footfall pounded up the steps and down the hall. She opened the door to a bedroom with sunshine filtering in and the scent of flowers. "If you require anything, ask me or one of the staff, miss."

"Thank you." Everything was clean and new in the room complete with fresh-cut flowers. Kinder thoughts of her severe aunt warmed her heart. Aunt Daphne had gone to the trouble of having new, cream-colored curtains hung and fresh linens purchased. A small writing desk appeared new as well and a supply of paper, quills, and ink sat on one side. The palest pink damask covered the walls and it too was fresh and new.

Already in the room unpacking gowns, Marie grumbled

over how they would all need to be taken in. She hoped for an under-maid who sewed tolerably well.

Her window overlooked orderly gardens. Every bush was groomed to perfection. Roses bloomed as if by command. Would she too be expected to do everything perfectly? Fear over how much she would disappoint Aunt Daphne tightened around her heart. Disappointing another family member loomed unbearably. Threatening tears stung her eyes. "Marie, leave that for now. I would like to nap a while."

Marie gave her a pitying look. "Shall I help you undress, my lady?"

"No. I'll just lie down atop the coverlet. Come and wake me in two hours, please. Oh, and when you chat with the servants, would you inquire as to the nature of my cousin's illness?"

With three gowns slung over her arm, Marie slipped out of the room.

Sophia leaned back against the mountain of expensive pillows. She missed her mother and father. She longed for home, but it was the home of years gone by, not the place recently left behind. Her father's house hadn't changed in that time, but she was different, and everything familiar was tainted.

Sophia cried in spite of her determination to be brave. Finally, exhaustion overtook her and she slept.

Someone pulled her away. A heavy weight covered her and a hand pressed over her mouth. She couldn't scream or even breathe. She smothered and struggled to free herself. Excruciating pain erupted between her legs. Her father's angry screams rose above a commotion of banging and her mother's crying. Mortified and afraid, she curled into a ball on the hard floor. Every inch of her body hurt. Then, mercifully, the world went black.

She woke from the same nightmare that had haunted her for the past three years. Perspiration soaked her dress and her heart raced as she gasped for breath. Hair stuck to her face and neck. Blinking the room into focus, she lay still while the worst of her terror passed.

The banging from the nightmare continued. Someone was tapping on the door.

"Enter." Sophia sat up.

Marie stepped inside. "I have ordered you a bath, Miss."

"Thank you, Marie. I would adore a real bath." She stood and stretched. The sun cast a blush over the manicured garden. The shadows of tall shrubberies, with their crisp shapes, stretched long across the walkways. She had slept far longer than two hours.

Marie supervised the arrival of the bath and buckets of water. "I spoke to her ladyship's maid. The air in London does not agree with your young cousin. They have taken her to the country, where she has less trouble breathing. That is all the staff here knows. I'll have a meal sent up when you are finished with your bath."

"Thank you." She sank into the bath. Warm, rose-scented water washed away the nightmare's effects. By the time she pulled herself out, she was too exhausted to eat much. Marie bundled her into the soft down bed, and sleep claimed her almost before her head hit the pillow.

Sophia woke gasping. Daylight pierced gaps in the window dressing. In times of great stress, the dream haunted her sleep with more frequency. Finding herself the ward of Lady Daphne Collington was certainly stressful. She struggled from bed and pulled the drapery back.

According to her parents, London weather was dreary, but the sun shone on the maze of shrubs below as if daring her to be grim. She readied herself to face the day.

In the breakfast room, Daphne sat tall and elegant. Her cheeks were high and her hair arranged into a neat bun. She must have been even more stunning when she was young.

"Good morning, aunt." Sophia walked to the sideboard and filled a plate with boar's head ham, oyster patties, and bread.

The room faced the street and was flooded with light from the high windows. The enormous table must have been a remnant from a time when many more people resided under the roof. She sat to Daphne's left.

"You are looking better, Sophia. I trust you slept well." Daphne spoke over her crisp newspaper.

"Oh, I feel fine. I couldn't ask for a more pleasant room. Thank you, Aunt Daphne."

Daphne waved a hand and kept her expression stern. "You may explore the house today if you wish. I generally take a walk in the park each day after calling hours. You may join me if you feel up to it."

"I would like that very much."

Daphne nodded and returned to her paper, while sipping coffee.

A cup of chocolate arrived via footman, and Sophia was grateful to Marie for thinking to inform the cook of her preferences.

"Stupid girl" Aunt Daphne muttered.

Sophia's heart raced. She had not chipped the fine china or even scratched one delicate flower from the edge of the plate. How had she managed to disappoint so quickly? "I beg your pardon?"

Daphne handed over the newspaper. "Elinor Burkenstock has ruined herself. Her poor mother must be beside herself.

She will never get that nit married off now. You should take note, Sophia. That type of behavior will not be tolerated while you are in this house."

Sophia breathed and read the article.

> *This reporter has it on good authority that the fine gathering at the Addison's Ball was marred by dreadful behavior. Sources say Miss EB was caught in a compromising position with Sir M, by none other than Lady P. This reporter is shocked by the blatant disregard for propriety displayed by Miss EB...*

The account went on, but it was so confusing, she stopped reading and looked at Daphne. "I don't understand all of this Miss EB, Sir M, and Lady P business."

"It is a rather silly code the paper uses to avoid being outright slanderous. Meaningless, really, since everyone knows everyone else, at least by reputation. Miss EB is, of course, Elinor Burkenstock. Sir M is Sir Michael Rollins, a man of questionable honor and, by all accounts, little means. Lady P is Lady Pemberhamble, the most outrageous gossip in all of England. It really is a shame. The stupid girl will be put on the shelf, or if by some miracle her father can force a marriage with Rollins, she will then be married to a libertine."

"I'm surprised this gossip interests you, Aunt."

Lady Collington's lips tipped up in what might have been a smile, but it vanished quickly. "I do not perpetuate gossip, my dear, but reading about it is part of how we get by here in London without being bored to tears.

"Besides, the girl's mother, Virginia Burkenstock is a particular friend of mine. Was it so different in Philadelphia?"

Three years ago, people she'd thought were her friends had abandoned her at the first sign of scandal. Sophia's father had squashed the truth, but still, rumors circulated for a season. "No. I suppose not, but I don't like the malice behind such rumors. For all we know, there might be little truth to the story. But because her family was unable to hush it up and it made it to print, she'll be ruined."

"What would you suggest, Sophia?" Aunt Daphne raised one imperialistic eyebrow.

Sophia smoothed the fine white tablecloth. "You said Mrs. Burkenstock is your friend. So, you know this girl. Is she worth helping?"

The second dark grey eyebrow joined the first. "She is a lovely little thing, if not the brightest of the season. She probably was lured away for a kiss and Lady P was waiting in the wings to catch them."

Sophia shivered with memories, and her skin roiled as she rubbed them away. A stolen kiss was minor compared to her experience, but this Miss Burkenstock would suffer, and Sophia's heart wrenched. "Would you be opposed to my helping her?"

"It is risky to associate yourself with someone whose reputation is soiled, especially since you have just arrived in town." Daphne looked out at the street and smoothed her hair from temple to chignon. "But, I believe this little misstep might be swept under the carpet, if she had friends willing to stand by her. I'll support your desire to help, as long as Miss Burkenstock does nothing else to embarrass herself or her family."

Sophia's heart leaped, not only because she would be allowed to help a stranger, but more so, because her stern aunt had shown a softer side. She jumped up, rounded the table, and kissed Daphne's cheek

"It is very uncommon, this constant show of affection, Sophia." Daphne's tone returned to its prior harshness.

Sophia's cheeks warmed. "I apologize, aunt. Would you prefer I did not kiss or hug you?"

"I did not say that." If Daphne had feathers, they would be ruffling. She pursed her lips, which drew her cheeks in severely. "I merely noted it is uncommon."

"Yes, Aunt." Delight warmed the rest of her. Her great aunt was exactly as papa and mamma had always described. "May we call on Miss and Mrs. Burkenstock this morning? It would be good to show immediate support, don't you agree?"

"Are you certain you are up to going into society today?"

"I would not want to attend a ball just yet, but I think a morning call would not be too taxing, and I should have an appropriate day dress."

"Very well. Get ready and I shall have the carriage brought round in one hour."

Chapter Two

Sophia's parents had said London would be damp and dreary, but so far, that was not the case. The sun warmed her and nothing was as wonderful as standing on terra firma. The Burkenstock townhouse stood only a few blocks away from Collington House and would have been an easy walk, but they took the Collington carriage emblazoned with the crest for all to see. Daphne informed her walking to pay a call was not done.

A stooped butler with bushy gray eyebrows met Sophia and Lady Collington at the door. Wide-eyed, he stared at them. "The lady of the house is not taking any calls today."

If they were left standing in the doorway, she was to blame for the embarrassment it would cause Aunt Daphne. Her stomach churned like she was back on the sea.

Lady Collington gave him a scathing look. "We will be admitted. Go and inform your lady I am here and don't you dare leave me standing on the stoop like some chimney sweep."

He turned sheet white, seized her card, and admitted them.

"Please wait in the red parlor, my lady. I shall inform Mrs. Burkenstock of your arrival." The home was not as ornate as Collington house, but it was charming and simple pieces made it homey. The red parlor had only one red chair amongst all the brown and green furniture.

Daphne sat straight as a tree with her hands in her lap, her face a mask of serenity.

Sophia tried to sit still, but it was impossible. She walked to the window. The house sat close to the street and the parlor faced only the side of another townhome. "Perhaps we should not have come, Aunt."

"Be still, Sophia. It is as if you are a rabbit caught in a trap. It is only a morning call, not the inquisition. Try to act like a lady."

The door opened and a woman with blond hair pulled back in a chignon trudged in wringing her hands. Red swelling ringed her blue eyes and flushed her cheeks, but Mrs. Burkenstock displayed a practiced smile. "Lady Collington."

Aunt Daphne remained sitting and nodded. "Mrs. Burkenstock, may I introduce my niece, Sophia Braighton?"

Sophia curtsied.

"How do you do, Miss Braighton? I'm afraid you have caught us on a difficult day." Mrs. Burkenstock said and her voice broke.

Sophia forced a smile.

"Virginia, sit down and call for tea. Tea always makes things seem a bit more tolerable."

Virginia sat near Aunt Daphne. Tea arrived and she poured. Virginia relaxed as if the tea had indeed made something better.

They sipped their tea speaking of the fine weather and people Sophia did not know until a girl arrived, her blue eyes and pert nose red and swollen.

"Miss Braighton, this is my daughter Elinor."

Elinor curtsied with the grace of a swan. "Nice to meet you, Miss Braighton. Hello, Lady Collington. It was nice of you to call this morning." With the same hair as Virginia, her skin was fair and bright.

Aunt Daphne nodded. "Sophia is my niece from America. I think the two of you will get along well together."

Taking a seat across the room, Elinor separated herself from the conversation area.

Sophia joined her on the settee. "I have just arrived from America."

"Yes. Your aunt said as much," Elinor whispered.

"I haven't any friends in London."

Elinor met Sophia's gaze directly. Her eyes narrowed.

The stare continued until Sophia found herself fidgeting. She clasped her hands together to keep still.

"Why have you come?" Her tone was politer than the question.

"Well, I have no friends, and it seemed you need one just now."

A weak grin touched Elinor's lips, but a tear escaped down her cheek.

"Shall we take a turn in the garden while my aunt and your mother chat?" Sophia asked.

Elinor nodded and blubbered an explanation of where they were going.

They rushed out of the room before her tears flowed uncontrollably.

The gardens were a bit unkempt, comforting, compared to the tailored gardens outside her new window at Collington House. They found a small bench. Elinor drooped down and wept into her hands. Golden ringlets bounced around her face as she shook.

Sophia patted Elinor's back. Crying wouldn't help the situation. "That will do, Miss Burkenstock."

"You should call me Elinor, if we are to be friends." Elinor gasped between sobs.

"Wonderful and you will call me Sophia. I understand you have had a difficult few days, but you can't sob the rest of your life away because some libertine stole a kiss."

Elinor blushed and turned her chin down toward her shoulder. "He did not exactly steal it."

"Oh? You like Mr. Rollins, then?"

Elinor sighed. "He is so beautiful, and charming, and he dances like a dream. Mother said to forget him, since his father squandered all their money, but I just thought to have one real kiss before I found a suitable husband."

"Do you have a dowry?"

Elinor sniffed and wiped her tears. "Yes. Why do you ask?"

"Do you think, perhaps, he is merely a fortune hunter?"

Elinor looked into the trees as if this were the first time, she'd considered the possibility. "I do not care. He has land and if he needs money, then why should he not marry into it? Women go about marrying for money and position all the time and no one faults them for it. For that matter, so do a lot of men. Perhaps he has a mind to build up his family fortune again? After all, it is not his fault his father was irresponsible."

"Perhaps he has a mind to gamble, drink and who knows what else," Sophia said.

Elinor frowned. "I wish I knew which it was. Then, perhaps, I may convince my father to let me marry Michael. I do not wish to be a fool in front of all of London."

Few fools worried about appearing foolish. Sophia liked her honesty in spite of all the dramatic weeping and fretting.

A young woman about Sophia's age stood a few feet away

listening to the conversation. She swept amber-gold hair off her brow. Intelligent green eyes didn't blink as she stared back at Sophia.

Elinor jumped up, threw herself into the girl's arms and began howling all over again.

Sophia sighed and stood. "I had just gotten her to stop."

She half-smiled as she patted Elinor's back. "Stop crying, dear. It will all be fine. Introduce me to your friend."

Elinor straightened and wiped her face. "Oh goodness, you must think me the worst hostess."

"Not at all."

"Lady Dorothea Flammel, Miss Sophia Braighton from America." They both curtsied, dipping their heads slightly.

Dorothea glared. "When did you arrive in London, Miss Braighton?"

"Yesterday morning."

"And how do you know Miss Burkenstock?" She smoothed her impeccable skirt.

"We have just met. You must have seen my aunt, the Dowager Countess of Grafton when you arrived."

"Indeed." She stood like a statue looking down her pretty nose at Sophia. "What brings you out today? You must be quite exhausted after your journey. Where did you say you were from, Australia?"

Elinor gasped.

"America, as I'm sure you heard a moment ago. May I ask you a question, Lady Dorothea?"

She nodded and waves of golden hair bobbed gently as if commanded to before settling back into a perfect frame for her heart-shaped face.

Elinor looked from one to the other with a mix of wonder and anxiety.

If Sophia had not been so focused on Lady Dorothea, she would have laughed. "Are you intentionally being rude because you are worried that I mean Miss Burkenstock ill will, or is this your normal disposition?"

"Would it make a difference?" The amusement in Dorothea's eyes didn't reach her lips.

"Of course it makes a difference." Sophia needed to make acquaintances, though she hoped she would find a friend or two. She'd found a friend and an adversary. Not a bad morning. London would be a forlorn place if she were friendless at every ball and picnic. "If your rudeness is only to protect Miss Burkenstock, then I'll make every effort to prove to you I mean no harm. I saw the article in the paper this morning, as I'm sure you did and felt Miss Burkenstock needed a friend. I spoke to my aunt, who told me she was a fine young lady and my aunt agreed to show her support."

"My goodness, that is so kind of you." Elinor's tears flowed again. Sophia and Lady Dorothea continued to meet each other's gazes.

Sophia pretended there was a spec on her white gloves. "However, if this level of rudeness is how you normally go through your day, then I have no time or desire to get to know you better. Therefore, I'll hereafter ignore you to the best of my ability."

"My, but you do make speeches, Miss Braighton." Dorothea smiled. "I think we shall attempt a friendship, if that would suit you. You are the first interesting person I have met in an age. I would be pleased if you would call me Dory."

"Thank you, Dory. I'm Sophia."

"Oh, thank heaven that is over." Elinor took a dramatic breath. "Now, what are we to do about my reputation? After all, I'm the one who is ruined."

"Indeed." Dory nodded. "Tell us exactly what happened, Elinor."

Her fair skin turned bright pink, but she spoke excitedly, as if she'd waited a lifetime to tell someone her news. "Well, Michael and I danced at the Addison ball two nights ago. Actually, we danced twice. I would have danced with him a third time—he is such a wonderful dancer and so nice to look at—but mother forbid it. It was quite hot in the ballroom and he asked me if I would like to go out on the veranda." Elinor's eyes glazed over with the memory of a man who had destroyed her chances of making a good match.

Sophia forced herself not to scoff aloud.

"Of course, I agreed. It was stifling hot, and I was feeling a bit overwhelmed by his closeness. I thought some air might be just the thing. But, when we reached the veranda, Michael said it was too crowded and there was no place for us to talk and wouldn't I like to have some quiet?"

Dory smoothed the already crisp skirt of her morning dress. "I'm surprised you would have agreed to this, Elinor."

"I knew I should have said no, but his eyes were so warm and sweet. He really seemed to like me, and I like him so much." She wrapped her arms around her middle and watched a butterfly settle on a pink rose. "We found a small parlor, which was empty. When he took me in his arms, I just couldn't bring myself to push him away. In truth, I did not want to. We kissed, and it was as if my entire world had been whittled down to that moment in time." She flung her hands up. "Then, that awful woman came in. She smirked at us and left without a word."

Sophia didn't understand how anyone could want to be that far out of control. Anger over being caught by Lady Pemberhamble, she understood. The part about not wanting him to stop and the world shrinking, bah, what bunk.

"What did Mr. Rollins do then?" Dory swatted at a mosquito.

"He kissed my nose and told me not to worry. He said everything would be all right, and I should trust him. Then he brought me back to my mother."

"Perhaps he intends to offer for you," Dory said.

New, louder sobs erupted from Elinor. "He left town. He sent a note and left town."

How such a grating sound emerged from such a pretty girl, was a mystery. "Stop crying!" Dory and Sophia said in unison. Suppressing giggles, they grinned at each other.

Dory rolled her eyes and pulled a handkerchief from her reticule. She handed it to Elinor who blew her nose loudly. "What did the note say, Elinor?"

"It said, 'I must leave London for a while. Trust me, Michael.'" She wept louder. "But, how can I trust him? Why did he leave town? What am I to do?"

Dory stood and put her hands on her hips. "First, you will stop this crying, as it is beginning to try my nerves. I know you like him, but he has little means, according to the gossip, so he is not really a good match. However, you have money, so it might work. The fact that he has left town puts you in an awkward position. Since we do not know his intentions, we shall proceed to repair your reputation without regard to Sir Michael Rollins. Are you attending the Watlington ball?"

Elinor gaped.

Sophia covered a giggle with a cough.

"I...I was supposed to, but now mother thinks it's best if we do not go out in society. I'm...to...be put on the...shelf." She gasped around her sobs, before screaming with renewed tears.

Resisting the urge to throttle her, Sophia patted Elinor's hand. "You'll not be put on a shelf, dear. You can't stay in this townhouse indefinitely. That will only confirm what the paper reported. I'll ask my aunt if we can attend the Watlington ball and you will convince your mother you should also attend. Then we'll begin to repair the damage."

Dory nodded and the three rejoined the women in the red parlor.

~

W ednesday, they attended a picnic in the park. Aunt Daphne introduced Sophia to a dozen people they met in a grassy space near the Serpentine. A gentleman with dark red hair, which beamed in the sunshine, approached her.

She steadied her nerves.

His sea-blue eyes and engaging smile warmed her skin more than she liked. However, as hard as she tried, she didn't recall his name. She prayed she would be able to carry on the conversation long enough someone would say it and save her an awkward moment.

"Would you like a glass of wine, Miss Braighton?" His grin made her smile back.

Of course he remembered her name, he only had one new name to memorize. She could just ask him for his name, but then everyone would know what a dolt she was. "No thank you, sir. I do not take wine."

"No? How very odd."

"Is it?"

"Most young women are quite anxious for wine rather than lemonade." He poured himself a glass of dark burgundy.

Sophia shrugged. "My mother is Italian, so wine was always on the table. I never acquired a taste for it. My mother would say—" She dropped her voice, softened her vowels, and rolled her tongue, creating a heavy Italian accent. "Bella, everyone drinks wine. It is good for the heart. Try it. Try it. You will learn to like it."

Lady Collington nearly smiled. "That is a very good imitation, Sophia. For a moment I thought your mother had joined us."

In a deep English accent, Sophia said, "Leave her be. It is no crime to be sober, at least not in America." Oh, how she missed Papa's warm smile and sage advice.

"Your father to a tee." Daphne clapped her hands and laughed.

Her admirer beamed at her. His teeth were white and straight, and he never took his gaze off her. "Can you impersonate only family members, Miss Braighton?"

She returned to her own voice. "Anyone whom I have heard speak."

Everyone turned toward her. She mimicked the German lady from the market and then Miss Mirabelle from her charm school. She demonstrated some other people from Philadelphia, whom she imitated well and everyone clapped.

"That's very good. Can you try someone we all know, your aunt for example?"

"People are often not fond of being mimicked." The idea of insulting anyone made her want to run and hide. She would be in real trouble if she alienated Aunt Daphne. Just get through the season without any scandal.

Daphne waved her gloved hand. "Go ahead, niece. I can take it."

Sophia sat flagpole straight on the blanket. She pursed her lips, pulled her shoulders back and clasped her hands. "Firstly, it is never proper to go into society before ten in the morning. I cannot countenance why anyone would wish to step out of doors before that hour."

Lady Collington hadn't said those exact words, but the tone, accent and vocal similarity was good and everyone applauded, including the subject of her impersonation.

"How did you learn such a thing?" he asked.

She shrugged and spoke in a facsimile of his voice. "It's something I have always excelled at." In her own, she said, "A silly game to amuse my brother."

"It is very amusing. Would you care to walk with me down to the river, Miss Braighton?"

She looked at Aunt Daphne, who nodded. "Thank you, I would like that." The butterflies returned. For the life of her, she still didn't remember his name. As they walked, she reviewed the earlier introductions and it was as if a blanket were drawn over her memory.

He waited until they were out of earshot of the picnickers. "May I ask you a question, Miss Braighton?"

"I believe you just have."

"I supposed that is true. Another, then?"

She nodded, but gazed at the water and prayed for divine intervention. "Do you have any idea what my name is?"

She spun toward him. Her heart leaped in her throat, and she tried but was unable to find words to respond.

He gently pushed her chin up closing her gaping mouth.

"I...I'm sorry. I cannot remember the names of anyone I met today. The introductions were made so fast. I was nervous and didn't pay close enough attention." She continued to ramble.

He offered his hand. "Shall we start again?"

She smiled and took his hand.

"Miss, may I present myself to you? I'm Thomas Wheel." He bowed deeply and formally removing his hat and sweeping it to the side.

"It is a pleasure to meet you, Mr. Wheel. I'm Sophia

Braighton. I hope we shall be great friends." She curtsied so low he might have been a duke rather than a rich gentleman.

"I suspect we shall be friends, Miss Braighton." They continued their walk along the Serpentine.

"Did you know all along that I didn't remember your name, Mr. Wheel?"

"I must admit, I suspected it from the first. Beside your gift for impersonation, you also have a gift for showing everything you feel in your expression. You are quite easy to read. I advise you never take up gambling."

She turned her head away. "Most wouldn't consider that a gift. It's more a curse, to have the entire world know what I'm thinking."

He shrugged. "Most people are not paying any attention to anything which does not relate directly to them. I think you have little to worry about here in London. You will find almost everyone is so self-involved they will barely see your face."

"You noticed."

"Ah yes, well, I'm one of the few people in London who acknowledges the fact that my life is terribly dull. Therefore, I spend all my time analyzing other people. Really it is an absurd vocation and I'm terribly ashamed." He didn't look at all ashamed. In fact, his eyes were alight with glee.

"I do not believe you." She giggled. "Perhaps my interest in you is unique."

"I'm not certain I believe that either, but it is kind, so I'll accept the answer and say, thank you."

After a short walk, they returned to the picnic.

The carriage rumbled along the road back to Collington House. Horses, carts and people going about their days filled the cab with noise, but Daphne's voice cut through. "Mr. Wheel might be an excellent catch. He comes from a well-respected family. His father made a fortune in shipping, and he has improved the family fortune with his new ideas. Since your family is also in shipping it would be a fine match. I would approve of you seeing more of him, if you wish."

The carriage jerked and pulled around a corner. Sophia grabbed for purchase on the cushion. Thomas Wheel had a nice smile and easy manner. However, he was tall and broad and could overpower her easily. She clutched the seat tighter to keep any shake from her voice. "He's nice, I suppose."

Daphne raised one eyebrow. "You do not like him. Most women find him quite charming. He holds no title, but neither do you."

"He is charming, and I really don't care about titles, Aunt. I'm sure he is a wonderful catch."

Aunt Daphne crossed her arms over her chest and pursed her lips. She sat straight as an arrow even as the carriage took another sharp turn. "Indeed, he is."

Perched on the edge of Sophia's bed, Aunt Daphne inspected as Marie pulled out dress after dress from the wardrobe. With each offering, she shook her head and waved the item away. "These frocks may be fine in the wilds of the colonies, but they will never do in real society. The Watlington ball is in a few days and none of your dresses will do."

"Well, they are all I have, aunt." Sophia kept her tone even.

"You know the United States is no longer considered colonies of England?"

Daphne waved a dismissal. "We shall go immediately to Madam Michard and see what can be done with the greatest haste. You will need a full wardrobe for the season, but perhaps we can get a gown or two rushed so you have something for the Watlington's. Then we must attend Fallon's, as well. The daughter is making her debut and it will be the event of the season."

A mere hour later, they were ensconced in Madam Michard's shop with yards of material draped before Sophia.

The proprietress had squeezed her curvaceous figure into a satin gown of red with black lace and the frock barely contained her. Lace strained at both her bust and hip but eased at her minimal waist.

Madam insisted the new French style, worn without a corset, was the only possible style to do the young miss's figure justice.

However, Daphne insisted a light corset would be worn at all times. She wouldn't have her niece traipsing around in the nude. The dress was revealing enough.

Doing away with tight corsets in favor of the light ones sounded rather wonderful. She tried on a pale green dress with a low neckline. The satin fell straight down from just below her breasts. Dark green ribbons hung in the same line and swayed with every move. The outline of her body was alluringly visible. She flushed with pleasure at the idea of going to a ball in such a gown.

Either Lady Daphne was not as old-fashioned as she pretended to be, or she was impatient to unload Sophia before the season was out.

Madam Michard smoothed her dark hair and smiled in the

mirror over Sophia's shoulder. Her thick French accent warmed her words. "Do you approve of the style?"

Sophia admired herself in the glass. "It's so beautiful. I have never worn a gown so stunning. I fear I can't possibly do it justice."

"It will do." Lady Collington told Madam Michard.

Madam Michard stood behind Sophia and met her gaze in the mirror. "You should look harder into the glass, mademoiselle. You would see the dress pales in comparison to the wearer."

Being attractive had only brought sorrow to Sophia's life. Still, it was a lovely compliment and the dress gave her confidence that she could get through her season in London.

Madam Michard suggested other colors of fabric and ribbon that would suit.

They ordered at least a dozen dresses and scheduled three for delivery the next day. It was a stroke of luck those three had just been finished as samples of the new style and needed only minor alterations. Madam Michard was probably paid handsomely to have the gowns ready with such unprecedented speed.

S ophia was gowned, coifed, and ready to leave for the Watlington ball. She barely recognized the woman staring back from the mirror. She wore the pale green she had modeled in the shop and her hair was intricately curled and braided with green ribbons and pearls twined throughout. Her color was high with the excitement of her first London ball and even if she were the only one to notice, she would say, she looked rather pretty.

Mr. Wheel had called that morning and agreed to come to

the ball. She was happy he had agreed, but only her vanity enjoyed the attention of a handsome admirer. She was flattered by his consideration, and she liked him but he didn't make her heart flutter or her stomach tighten in the way Elinor described. Perhaps that kind of infatuation would never happen to her.

Just as well.

As Sophia descended the staircase, Daphne beamed up from the bottom. "You are going to be a diamond of the first water this season, Sophia."

"Do you think so?"

"Mark my words. No man will be able to resist. You will have an offer of marriage before the month is out. We can only hope it is the right offer."

"Yes, Aunt Daphne." She was careful to keep her eyes downcast as she quietly accepted her wrap from Wells, the butler.

They arrived at the ball twenty minutes later in a crush of carriages. The Watlington butler announced, "Lady Daphne Collington, the Dowager Countess of Grafton and her niece, Miss Sophia Braighton,"

The room quieted as they descended into the ballroom, down a grand staircase. At eye level from the top of the steps hung a crystal chandelier as big as most parlors. She forced her mouth closed to keep from gaping at it.

"Do not stare, girl. If our hostess catches you looking at it, she will bore you for several hours with stories of where each and every crystal came from and how long it takes to light the hideous thing," Daphne's lips barely moved as she gave the warning. She patted the front of her silver hair though not one strand was out of place.

"I have never seen anything like it." Glaring light poured from the oversized crystal eyesore. It filled the entire ceiling and stretched as tall as the roof of her Philadelphia home. A very tall man would have been able to touch the lowest crystal. It was impossible not to stare at the thing even though it hurt her eyes to do so.

"Of course not. How could there be more than one of those monstrosities in the world? It's as if one took a horse and stuffed him into the upstairs parlor. It may be a beautiful horse, but once it's in the parlor, it's just a great beast that no one can take their eyes from."

Sophia giggled behind her hand and followed Daphne to meet their host and hostess. The Earl of Watlington and his wife were both rotund in the extreme, but pleasant enough. They smiled happily and the earl kissed Sophia's gloved hand.

Daphne walked over to a clutch of women sitting on one side of the room. Sophia joined Elinor and Dory on the other side of the ballroom.

Elinor's pale blue dress set off the color of her eyes and enhanced her milky skin. "No one will ask me to dance. No one will even talk to me."

"I forbid you to cry." Dory spoke through a grin and tugged on the lace sleeve of her lavender gown. Her golden hair hung in perfect ringlets and her eyes sparkled devilishly.

Elinor pouted. "Dory already has several dances filled and I have none. None."

"Have you seen Mr. Wheel?" Sophia searched the room.

Dory's eyes widened. "Mr. Wheel? You are not even in London a full week. Do not tell me you have set your cap for Thomas Wheel already. He is on the top of the mammas' eligible bachelor list."

"No. Not for me. For Elinor."

Elinor shrieked, "I do not want to marry Mr. Wheel. I don't even know him well. I met him on only two occasions and while he was respectable, he is not for me. I could never like him enough to marry him. He is always so clever and everyone knows his interests lie in music and business. He would suit Dory much better, but of course, he's untitled. The countess would never approve."

Sophia put up a hand. "You are not going to marry him. For goodness sake, Elinor. He will simply dance with you and that will make other men know it is all right to dance with you. Soon this entire thing will start to go away."

A young man with black hair and sweat dappling his fore head stopped and asked Dory for a spot on her dance card.

She waved her matching lavender fan over the lower part of her face and batted her eyes. It was an amazing transformation. The white lace around her color fluttered with the fanning.

As soon as the man bowed and walked away, Dory's smile turned genuine. "That is brilliant, Sophia. But how do you intend to get him to dance with her? Besides, he may not even come to this ball. He and his friends rarely come to these things. They do not like to be pushed around by all the mothers who want to marry off their darling daughters."

Sophia giggled. "Don't say it so derisively, Dory. The three of us are those very daughters."

Dory laughed also. "I know, but it does not make it less true. How do you know he will come?"

"I asked him to, and he said he would."

"He will not come." Elinor brushed a pale strand from her face.

"Of course he will," Sophia said.

"No, he won't." Now she was pouting.

"He has just arrived." Dory nodded at the grand stairs.

The butler introduced Thomas and the room erupted with chatter so loud she could not hear the name of the man next to him. He was the most beautiful man she'd ever seen. His hair resembled dark gold and that silly chandelier's light sent shimmers of firelight through his unruly waves. Both men wore black evening dress with simple white cravats.

Her stomach flip-flopped, her arms prickled with goosebumps, and she had trouble catching her breath. "Who is that with him?"

Dory grinned wickedly and spoke in a whisper. "That is Lord Daniel Fallon, The Earl of Marlton."

Chapter Three

"I cannot believe I let you talk me into attending this ridiculous ball, with that ridiculous chandelier." The Earl of Marlton blistered at Thomas.

Thomas smirked. "Don't point at the thing. We'll end up spending the entire night fending off stories of crystals from Austria. I have other plans for this evening."

"Yes, so you said, a goddess with a gift for humor. So, where is this icon of beauty and merriment? What did you say she does, juggle? Most unladylike."

"She is an excellent mimic, as I'm sure you remember. She is there." Thomas nodded toward the right. "Standing with Lady Dorothea and Elinor Burkenstock."

"The chit who was caught with Michael?"

"Indeed."

He nearly stopped in his tracks and forced his feet forward before anyone took notice of his awe. She was tall for a woman, with hair so dark it looked black, except the candlelight from the grotesque chandelier set off shimmers of red and gold. Her skin was like honeyed cream.

Completely out of sorts and out of character, Daniel clung to control before he made a fool of himself.

Thomas bowed to the ladies. "May I present Daniel Fallon, The Earl of Marlton. Marlton, I believe you know Miss Burkenstock and Lady Dorothea. This is Miss Sophia Braighton from America.

Daniel bowed, his heart racing. "A pleasure to meet you, Miss Braighton."

Her gown revealed the swell of perfectly round breasts as she curtsied. "My lord. It's nice to meet you."

"My friend has spoken of nothing else since meeting you." He ached to touch her and discover if her skin was as soft as it appeared.

"I'm sure he has exaggerated." She would not meet his gaze, the floor and her shoes seeming more interesting.

Daniel wanted to continue the conversation, but she excused herself and pulled Thomas aside. The two spoke in hushed whispers. Beating his lifelong friend to a pulp was not out of the question. He clenched his hands into tight fists, battle-ready.

Thomas frowned, but then adjusted his face to a gentlemanly smile and bowed before, of all people, Elinor Burkenstock. He asked the girl to dance. She accepted politely, and the two swept off to join the other dancers while the crowd whispered and twittered. No doubt over how the popular and wealthy Thomas Wheel had chosen his first dance partner of the evening, a girl ensconced in scandal.

Daniel hated these events. However, there was some symmetry in one of them cleaning up Michael's mess.

In spite of her American accent, her whisper near his ear set him on fire. "Will you also dance with my friend, my lord?"

He looked into eyes, golden like a tigress's. "Would that please you, Miss Braighton?"

"It...It would please me very much." Her voice was musical, low, and warm.

At least he wasn't the only one out of sorts. His palms itched to wrap her up and calm every worry until she was pliant in his arms. "Then I shall claim the next dance, if you will agree to add me to your dance card this evening."

She nodded and cast her eyes down depriving him of her gaze.

He ached to touch the rosy flesh and see if it was as warm and soft as it looked. He knew he was wearing a stupid grin. Waiting to hold her for the dance would be the death of him. Desperate to cover his ridiculous desire for the American, he turned toward Lady Dorothea. "Lady Dorothea. I have not seen you in years. You are obviously well. How is your brother?" A crooked grin brightened Dory's face. She looked from him to Sophia and back again. "Markus married while you were abroad, as I'm sure you've heard. He and Emma are happily ensconced in the country. They prefer the country house to London. I believe they will spend only a fortnight here all season and that is only because my mother insists. You should visit them. I know my brother would be happy to see you."

He nodded. "I will visit them as soon as I can."

She stepped closer. "You are also a good friend of Sir Michael Rollins, are you not?"

Her brother, Markus, and Michael Rollins were part of his inner circle of friends. They, with he and Thomas, had been inseparable throughout school. "You are aware that I am."

"Would you happen to know where he has taken himself to?" Dory asked.

"My lady, I'm sorry to tell you I do not. Even if I did, I would not divulge the information. If Sir Michael does not wish to be found, then we shall leave him in peace." His tone broached no argument.

Sophia said, "Your friend is a coward."

He stared her down, expecting an immediate apology from her, but the tigress only looked back at him.

"Miss Braighton, while you are by far the most beautiful woman I have ever encountered, I'll not allow you, or anyone, to slander my friends."

"It's only slander, if what I say is untrue, my lord." Something flickered in her honeyed gaze when he'd called her beautiful. Perhaps joy, but likely vanity. All women love a compliment.

He didn't know why he flattered her. He had no interest in the girl, or any other untried debutante, for that matter. She was beautiful, but they were all the same. Jocelyn had taught him that. He wouldn't be made the fool ever again. "Since you have only just arrived in London, you may not be aware the Sir Michael is a war hero. He is most certainly not a coward. I think it would be best if we changed the subject. I would not wish to argue on our first meeting."

She shrugged. "Next time perhaps? Or must one wait until the third meeting? I always forget that rule. There are so many here in London."

She was delightful, and he laughed.

Many in the crowd turned at the sound.

Lady Dorothea stepped a few feet away.

"Where in the Americas did you live, Miss Braighton?"

"Philadelphia."

He smiled. "I quite liked the city, and I did not notice a lack of rules to be found in society at large."

When she smiled, her face was so bright with joy he struggled not to stumble over his own feet. Part of him wanted to move toward her, but his brain signaled danger. She intrigued him, but he stood his ground.

"You're right. Rules, rules and more rules." Her voice lilted. "You have traveled to America?"

"I spent a year there. I was in Philadelphia for several weeks. I only arrived back in London last month. How I miss the open sea." He breathed deeply, recalling the smell of the ocean.

Her nose wrinkled and all the pleasure went out of her face. "You did not enjoy the voyage?"

"I'm afraid I was ill the entire time. I must have lost a stone during the crossing." She pressed her fist to her stomach and pulled a face. Though she was slim, her gown revealed curves.

"If this is the result of your illness, I think you should travel more often, Miss Braighton."

Her blush started in her cheeks and spread to the root of her hair and down until it disappeared beneath her intriguing gown. His mouth turned dry as a desert. "I must embarrass you more often, Miss Braighton. The effect is the most charming thing I have ever seen."

She touched her cheek. "I wish I could stop that. I'm out of practice, not being out in society much the last few years."

"No? How strange. Were you ill on land as well as at sea?" His gut tightened and not with lust as it had since first spotting her, but genuine concern for her health.

Thomas and Miss Burkenstock returned and Sophia let out a long breath. The stiffness of her stance eased as if she'd been saved from having to answer. Every thought in her head was clearly readable in those stunning eyes and kissable lips.

Daniel kept his word and asked Elinor for the next dance. Relief and longing washed over him as he walked away from Sophia.

"Will you grace me with a dance now, Miss Braighton?" Thomas asked.

She inclined her head, and they walked to the dance floor. It was a minuet and they had little time to speak. Sophia was glad for the time to think. What was happening to her? The earl walked in and her mind drifted toward thoughts of him. Her heart pounded and heat infused her cheeks. The dance ended too soon. She would have to dance with Daniel Fallon.

Escape seemed the only option. "Shall we get some lemonade, Mr. Wheel?"

"As you wish."

They walked to the refreshment table. "How long have you known the earl?" The heat of the ballroom or the fine weather would have been much safer subjects.

"Which earl do you mean, Miss Braighton? I know quite a few gentlemen with that title." He smiled.

"You know perfectly well which one."

"Have I lost you already? Well, it would not be the first lovely woman I've lost to Daniel, but perhaps, you will be the last."

"Don't be absurd. I barely know him. He was very gracious to dance with Elinor."

"I also danced with the silly girl."

"You did it as a favor to me and don't call her silly. She's a lovely girl and if your friend hadn't abandoned her, she would not be in this position."

From across the room, her eyes filled with fire and she gestured right and left as she spoke to Thomas. He shouldn't care about their conversation. It would be easy enough to leave the ball and go to his club as he and Thomas originally intended for the evening. Daniel wound his way through the crowd toward her.

As soon as she saw him, she frowned.

Seeing him displeased her, yet she was happy and animated with Thomas. Perhaps he had interrupted an intimate conversation. Friendship be dammed, he was going to pummel Thomas.

"Have you abandoned poor Elinor?" Her tone was like a mother scolding her child.

"Poor Elinor? Pardon me, Miss Burkenstock had a long line of dance partners awaiting her availability. Your plan seems to have worked." He accepted a glass of lemonade, choked on the sour libation and put it back on the table.

"Oh, how wonderful." She clapped her hands and smiled. His heart might explode.

"Now explain to me why your friend would leave in such a rush?" She looked from one to the other. "Does Mr. Rollins often make promises to young women and then run for the hills?"

"Never before that I'm aware of," Thomas said.

A waltz began. "I believe you have promised me a dance, Miss Braighton."

Her hazel eyes grew as large as saucers. She scanned the room. "I...I don't have permission to dance a waltz."

He followed her gaze to where Lady Collington sat amongst a group of dowager-aged women.

The Countess of Grafton watched with an unreadable expression.

He offered his arm. "It will be fine. I'm a great admirer of your aunt."

Once she was in his arms and spinning around the floor to the count of three, she quieted.

Most young unmarried women spent the entire dance trying to impress him with all of their accomplishments. Sophia didn't look up and bat her eyelashes or smile and try to press closer. Her warmth seeped through the thin fabric of her gown. The newest fashions left little to his imagination. He was on fire. She sparked in him feelings he'd sworn never to entertain again.

She cleared her throat. "What did you mean when you said you are an admirer of my aunt?"

"She is unique. I like someone who is not a sheep in the crowd and Lady Collington is an original. Some call her the cruel countess and perhaps they have some cause. She can be quite biting if vexed. She can also be a fierce and loyal ally. I quite like her."

"The cruel countess. I suppose I can see why she's gained that moniker."

"Is she unkind to you?" He had no right to worry over her wellbeing but he couldn't deny the spark of distress.

"No. Aunt Daphne has been very kind and thoughtful in her way. I just wish she would not have to be disappointed." Sophia sighed heavily. Her breasts swelled over the low neck of her gown.

"Why would her ladyship ever be disappointed in you?"

She shook her head and her silken curls swished from side to side. "You will not tell me? Then I'll guess. You are not the woman you appear to be. You are really the scullery maid from the Braighton house in America? No? You are her nephew, not her niece?"

She giggled.

He shook his head. "No, that cannot be it. You are already married?"

As he guessed, her mouth and eyes grew wider until she burst into a fit of giggles. She was adorable. "Enough."

The sound had his heart beating so rapidly, he might have an episode, as if he was one of those horrible characters from a bad novel.

"I'll tell you, if you promise to keep my secret."

The dance ended, Daniel took her arm and walked swiftly to the veranda. His hand on her elbow left only his white glove separating skin from touching skin. The idea of actually feeling her flesh was heady. The cool night air helped to cool his desire.

She breathed deeply, causing her breasts to lift dangerously close to the edge of her gown's neckline.

So much for the cooling effect of the night air.

She leaned over the veranda wall and looked out into the shadowy gardens, lit only by torches.

There were a few people lingering on the veranda—ladies getting away from the heat of the crowded ballroom and a few couples hiding behind Greek statues and Roman pillars.

"Are you cold?"

"No." Her voice was small and far away.

He yearned for her thoughts. "You were going to tell me a secret."

Heart-wrenching sorrow filled her eyes, and they glistened though no tears fell. She straightened her posture and raised her chin. This woman held herself as if she was a queen.

He wanted her more with every second spent in her presence.

She spoke for his ears only, but her whisper shook with intensity. "My secret is I shall never marry. I should have told my aunt, but my mother made me promise to try to enjoy the season and not ruin it with such thoughts." As she said the last words, her voice had dropped into a lush Italian accent.

He supposed the accent was her mother's. Thomas had said her mimicry was amusing, but there was no joke here.

Her face was open, and she absolutely believed she wouldn't marry. Of course, it was ridiculous. She was beautiful, smart, funny, and quick-witted. He had gleaned all of this in only a short time in her presence. She had the body of a goddess. She would marry and probably well. He was sure she would have offers before the end of the month, if not sooner.

"I think you will marry." Regret dripped from his voice.

"No." Her eyes filled with tears, and she moved away to hide in the shadow of one of the pillars surrounding the veranda.

His mind screamed at him to apologize and walk away, but his body disobeyed, and he followed her into the shadows. He tugged the glove from his hand and gently caressed the soft skin from her elbow to the cap sleeve of her gown. He dropped his hand.

She turned, only a breath away. The warmth of her body reached him though they didn't touch.

"Please do not cry." The soft tone hardly resembled his voice. She moved him in a way no one else ever had.

"I won't. I'm sorry to make such a scene." She dabbed at her eyes. Once again, the tigress returned, sad, fierce, and distant. The tears made her seem even fiercer, somehow making her even more perfect. This was no stuffy debutante, with little thought for anyone but herself. She was soft, emotional, filled with life, and he wanted nothing else in the world but to pull her into his arms, to watch her tigress's eyes close as his lips covered hers.

"I think I'm going to kiss you, Miss Braighton." He inched closer.

Her eyes widened, and she gasped as he rubbed his lips lightly against hers.

"No." The word was less than a whisper.

"Are you sure?" He asked, pressing his cheek to hers.

"I cannot like you." Her voice was tight and the pitch high.

He was curious as to why she believed such a ridiculous thing, but had no opportunity to press further. A feminine throat cleared, and he stepped away from her.

"Sophia, there you are. Hello, my lord." Dory Flammel stood only a few feet away. She pulled the Burkenstock girl behind her. "Lady Collington is looking for you. I believe she is tired and would like to go home."

"Of course." Sophia curtsied. "Thank you for the dance and the chat, my lord. Congratulations on a successful evening, Elinor. Dory, will I see you tomorrow?"

"I'll call in the morning and we can go riding in the park." Dory winked.

Sophia frowned at Dory, gave another hasty curtsy, and rushed into the ballroom to find Lady Collington. The Burken-stock girl chased after Sophia and they both disappeared in the crowd.

His stomach churned as he watched her go. She had said she would never marry and she specifically couldn't like him? Unacceptable.

When he looked away from the windows, he found Lady Dorothea Flammel watching him. He narrowed his eyes at her assessing ones. "What is it you're looking at, my lady?"

"I'm looking at a man smitten." Her directness was out of order and yet refreshing among members of the ton.

"You see too much for your own good, my lady."

"Some would say I see only what I wish to see, my lord. My brother, Markus, is quite fond of you."

Daniel smiled. "Markus, Thomas, Michael and I were

quite inseparable throughout our time at Eton. I still consider all three my closest friends. I do not see Markus much, as I have been away and he is happily settled, but I would bleed for him, should he ask it of me."

Dory cringed. "Let us hope it does not come to that. Will you break my new friend's heart? I have only known her for a few days, but I'm already quite fond of her. I would hate to see her harmed in any way."

"Are you asking me to extend my friendship with your brother to you, my lady?"

"I'll not ask you to bleed."

"I have no intention of pursuing Miss Braighton."

"I see." Her tone held just the right touch of doubt.

"As I said, you see entirely too much."

She smiled, but it didn't touch her eyes. The smile might have been for his benefit or the group of people who stepped onto the veranda. She waited for the group to move away. "Did you know Jocelyn was a close friend of mine? I know much of what transpired between you two was kept quiet, but she came to me after you broke off the engagement."

His body stiffened at the mention of the woman he'd once planned to marry. Rage replaced his earlier emotions.

She smiled more kindly at him. "She came to my home and cried out her story. When she was finished, I told her I was very sorry for her. I was sorry. Sorry she had been such a fool. Sorry she had such low character, she thought so little of herself, and she would give herself away with no thought of honor. Sorry I had misjudged her. I asked her to leave my house and cut off our friendship. She called me terrible names before my brother intervened. It was an ugly scene. Until that moment, I had not realized how important it was to be able to judge a person's character."

His anger ebbed. "A valuable lesson."

"Indeed."

"I had not realized anyone else was hurt by Jocelyn's behavior."

"We have something in common, my lord."

"I'm sorry," he whispered.

Dory waved a gloved hand and pushed back a wayward curl. "None of what transpired was your fault, my lord. You should forgive yourself and perhaps, find someone you can trust to marry." She turned and left him on the veranda, giving him no chance to respond.

White's Gentleman's Club was crowded when Daniel and Thomas arrived late in the evening. They found a small table in one of the parlors and ordered brandy.

"So, what did you think of my goddess?" Thomas's eyes twinkled with mirth.

Daniel lowered his glass and looked at his long-time friend. "I think I do not care for you calling her that."

Thomas laughed. "I suspected as much. You, my friend, are smitten. The question is, will you do anything about it, or will you continue to let that light-skirt you were engaged to ruin your life?"

Pure fury bubbled in his chest. His instinct still told him to defend his ex-fiancée, but he shrugged and steadied his emotions. It was, after all, the truth. "I'll marry eventually. I have to, but it will not be Sophia Braighton.

"I will find someone with whom I can have an agreeable marriage. I shall leave Sophia for someone else. I would just prefer if it were not you."

"You are a fool, Dan. I saw the way you looked at her and the way she looked at you. She is going to haunt you for the rest of your life as your one big mistake if you do not pursue your interest."

His gut tightened and a bead of sweat dripped down the side of his neck. "You may be right." He took a long swallow of brandy. "However, I should rather be a fool privately, than to have my stupidity displayed before all of London once again."

Thomas shook his head. "What do you suppose possessed Michael to leave London? You don't really think he would run because of being caught with the Burkenstock girl, do you?"

Daniel sipped his brandy. "I spoke to him a few days before the incident, and I had the impression he was going to offer for that silly chit. She is quite rich and not terribly hard to look at. I'm not sure why he ran. He did mention something about an opportunity with some grain he was going to buy, in hopes of raising enough money to do some work at his estate in Essex."

Thomas raised an eyebrow. "Maybe he wants to come to the marriage negotiations with more than empty hands and no prospects. He had better hurry. She is rich, quite pretty, and none too smart. She may find herself another before he returns."

"If she is so fickle, he is better off without her."

Tipping back his glass, Thomas finished his drink. "The girl has no reason to wait. From what I know, he left her no assurances. It's not at all the same as what Jocelyn did to you. You had signed a contract. She knew you would marry her. Hell, I think you loved her. She was not the kind of woman who would ever have been faithful, and she was not smart enough to be discreet. You are right about one thing—you are better off without Jocelyn."

"I did not love her," he said softly. "I thought I did for a moment, but it was only lust and desire. She was beautiful and charming. She might have been discreet, but I was just too diligent in my desire to see her. If I had kept away, I would never have discovered them. She claimed to be under the weather. I thought to surprise her and spend the evening in her company, even if it was playing backgammon in the parlor, anything to be near her. What a fool I was. When I arrived, I found her in the parlor, but she and Swanery were not playing backgammon. Their game has been played between men and women since the beginning of time."

"My God, man, you never said anything about having caught her red- handed. What did you do?"

Old anger boiled. He still saw his beloved under that sod on the chaise. "What any English gentleman would do. I bowed, punched Swanery in the jaw, turned and left the house."

"What did Jocelyn do?"

The ugly hatred he still harbored for the woman bubbled to the surface. "She screamed horrible names at me. She used words I had never heard a woman utter, even in the gaming hells from women of questionable virtue."

"I don't think there was much question." Thomas referred to the whores' virtue.

"No, and neither was there in regard to Jocelyn. She was every inch the harlot that those women in the gaming hells were. At least with a prostitute you know what you are getting. Jocelyn was a wolf in sheep's clothing. And you are correct, I'm much better off without her.

"Michael will turn up at some point, either to claim Miss Burkenstock, or to find a new chit with a fortune. He has no choice. He must repair the damage his father has done."

"You're right, of course." Thomas called for another brandy.

Chapter Four

Sophia was dressed and ready when Dory arrived the next morning for a ride in the park. Dory's rich velvet royal blue riding costume fit her snugly and showed off her curves. Sophia wore a similar outfit, though hers was in a dark wine.

"Sophia, you and I shall need crops to smack away the admirers. We are the perfect riding duo."

"You look lovely."

"Hello, Lady Dorothea." Daphne entered in a green morning dress ready to set out to make her calls.

"Will you be joining us in the park, my lady?"

"I'll follow in my carriage, but leave you once we arrive. I have several errands to attend to and a few calls to make. Two footmen and Sophia's maid will accompany you for the remainder of your ride."

"I have also brought a footman and my lady's maid, Countess. I feel we shall be very safe indeed." Dory's voice lilted with sarcasm.

Daphne pursed her lips. "Dorothea Flammel, I have always liked you. I think you are an original, but do not try to charm me as you do the dunderheads in the ton, or I shall change my opinion of you. You are smart and that is why I approve of the friendship emerging between you and my niece. Do not make me rethink my view."

Dory didn't flinch. She curtsied bowing her head. "I would never dream of insulting you, Lady Collington. I think you are also quite extraordinary. I'm glad you approve of Sophia's and my new friendship. I would hate to have to go behind your back to continue to see your niece."

Not even the countess resisted a chuckle. "Shall we go, girls?"

Once mounted, Sophia said, "You are too bold for your own good, Dory. She's not called the cruel countess for nothing. She can ruin your reputation if she chooses."

Dory shrugged her straight shoulders. She sat a horse as if born riding. "Your aunt is fierce, but fair. Look what she did for Elinor. If she didn't admire Elinor in some way, she would never have put her name and yours in jeopardy by helping. I would never do anything that was really bad form, therefore I believe I will always remain on the 'cruel countess's good side."

Riders, walkers, and people in carriages out to see if there was any gossip hindered their progress at the gates of the park.

Aunt Daphne said her goodbyes, leaving three footmen and two maids to follow an appropriate distance behind Sophia and Dory.

They finally got away from the larger crowd. Sophia kept her eyes forward in spite of the fact that everyone seemed to be watching her. "Will Elinor's reputation make a full recovery?"

A loud sigh accompanied Dory's shrug. "Not unless Michael Rollins returns and offers for her. If someone else offered and she accepted, that would do as well. However, I don't think she will accept another this season. Elinor can seem like a muttonhead, but she is smarter than she lets on. She is also very loyal. She fancies herself in love with Sir Michael and, until she is certain he will not make good on his advances, she will have no other."

"How can you be so sure?" Loyalty to a man who left in her time of need made no sense.

"I have known Elinor since the cradle. Our families' country estates are next to each other. When we were ten, she stood outside my house all day waiting for me to apologize for calling her a name. She was so sure I would apologize, that she would not leave. Eventually, the guilt got to me and I ran outside and begged her forgiveness."

Sophia pictured the two little girls working out their argument. She loved the idea of a lifelong friend even if she had none to compare. "What did Elinor say?"

"She hugged me and said she had already forgiven me. We are the closest of friends. When I tell you she will wait for Sir Michael until all hope is lost, you may believe it."

"Ladies," The Earl of Marlton's deeply familiar voice, cut into their conversation. "You are the most stunning pair I have ever seen."

He rode atop a black stallion. His black hat and coat were impeccable, and he grinned down at them from his enormous horse. Even his cravat remained tied to perfection.

The great beast threw his head back and stomped his foot while blowing out his great nostrils.

"I think your horse would prefer if you did not stop to chat, my lord." Sophia kept a cautious eye on both man and beast.

Daniel jumped down and handed the reins to his footman. "I'm sorry if Mangus frightened you. He is a bit high-spirited and much prefers the country to London."

"What brings you to the park this morning, my lord?" Dory asked, smiling her most wicked smile.

"I decided a bit of air and exercise was in order. You had

mentioned you would be taking a morning ride. I confess, I had hoped to meet you, since Miss Braighton and I were engaged in an interesting conversation last evening, before the countess's desire to cut the evening short."

No. She must have misunderstood. He couldn't have come to the park expressly to see her. "Oh, I'm sure your evening continued unhindered, my lord. Don't all men go to their clubs and drink until dawn after the ballrooms empty out?"

His smile was bright, and his eyes lit up with mirth. His full laugh rumbled out.

She was drunk from the sound.

"We do, of course, but I felt quite unsatisfied."

The word unsatisfied triggered Sophia's temper. Men always looked to their own satisfaction with little care about others. She gripped her reins too tight and her horse pranced. "In that case, I'm sure there were those who might have taken care of that, as well."

Something about him made her speak when she should be quiet. She wished the words back immediately. She had said too much the night before and now she felt exposed. If only he hadn't come to the park. Tears pressed behind her eyes and her throat tightened. She pressed her finger to the corner of her eye and commanded herself not to cry.

He took a step back. "Is it an American custom to insult new acquaintances, or is this just an inclination of yours, Miss Braighton?"

She turned her head to avoid his gaze, dismounted and allowed a footman to take the reins. She walked a short distance away. She cursed her loose lips. Now she would have to apologize, and she was not even sorry. She had only stated the truth.

He took up space in a way no one else did. Standing behind her, his warmth surrounded her.

"You're angry with me?" She rubbed her arms. "I admit to being confused by your obvious anger."

"I suppose I should apologize." Once she banished her unshed tears, she turned to face him.

"Only if you are sorry and I can see from your eyes you are not." His smile made her stomach do a pleasant flip.

"I do apologize for my outburst, my lord." She used the practiced tone of her days at Mrs. Mirabelle's School for Young Ladies.

He frowned. "I accept, even though you do not mean it. I believe it was very hard for you to make the attempt, and I'll be the bigger man and not challenge your sincerity."

"Thank you." She felt her mouth turning up in a smile in spite of her embarrassment.

"Would you like to tell me why you have such a low opinion of my sex?"

"No."

He smiled brightly. "Just, no? No further explanation?"

She felt her cheeks warm. "I believe 'no' is a complete sentence and needs no other qualification, my lord."

Dory interrupted. "The two of you are causing quite a stir."

Carriages and riders alike slowed to get a good look at whomever his lordship was speaking to so intimately.

Dory took Sophia's arm. "Perhaps this conversation might continue in a few days at Lady Cecelia's ball. I do believe both Miss Braighton and I will be there. I'm sure you will not miss your own sister's debut, my lord."

"I'll be there." He never took his eyes from Sophia. He bowed to them both, launched himself into the saddle of the beast he called Mangus, and trotted away without another word.

Sophia stood for a long time, staring out over the lush trees of the park. Dory was like a long-lost sister, but she wished she were alone. She could not face him at his sister's ball. She had allowed him to kiss her and lost her temper. He must think her a fool. She must learn to keep her feelings to herself, especially in the face of a man she barely knew.

Dory cleared her throat and a wide grin spread across her face. "I believe you have taken the Earl of Marlton off the marriage market, Sophia. You two will make quite a stir."

Sophia spun around so fiercely that her dark hair came loose from the pins holding it. "I don't want to make a stir. I don't care what he does, and I will absolutely never marry him." Tears sprang into her eyes and soaked her face. She dashed them away, mounted her mare, and road toward Collington house at a clip.

Dory called her name. Horses clomped behind her.

As soon as she reached the steps to Collington House, Sophia dropped down from her mare without assistance and ran up the front stoop. Once Wells opened the door, she rushed through and up the curved stairway. She didn't want company, but Dory trudged behind her.

She longed for time to brood and perhaps have a good cry.

Once in Sophia's chambers, Dory turned to speak to Marie, who had rushed up the steps as well. "Marie, your lady will not need you for now. We will ring if there is a need."

Marie curtsied and stepped out of the room. Dory closed the door behind her.

"What on earth is wrong, Sophia?" Dory demanded.

"Nothing. Oh, Dory, go home. I'll be fine by the next time we meet." She loathed the begging quality in her voice.

Dory sat on the edge of the bed and watched while Sophia paced back and forth across the fine rug.

"I will not go, so you may as well tell me why you dislike the Earl of Marlton so intensely."

"I don't dislike him." Tears were running freely down her

face now. She tried to dash them away, but more followed and she gave up her efforts.

"But you will never marry him?"

"I won't marry at all. Never." She plopped herself down in a chair near the empty hearth.

Dory got up, crossed the room, and knelt in front of her. "Why not, Sophia? What happened to make you so set against it? Not to mention how rude you were to the earl who you just told me you do not dislike. No one has said you must marry him. Did he do something on the veranda last night that upset you?"

"He kissed me." Her voice shook.

"Was it terrible? John Allendale kissed me last week, and I found it quite pleasant. I was not rude, though I did stop him rather quickly."

"No. It was very nice. Lovely, actually." She whispered and wiped the tears from her cheeks.

"I don't understand," Dory said.

Sophia's chest was so tight, she gripped the front of her riding habit and tore open the jacket. In her haste, several buttons skittered across the floor. Telling one person the truth even if it was a mistake would let off the pressure building inside her. She took a breath and met Dory's gaze. "I'm not a virgin. I know you will hate me now that you know and that's why I didn't want to tell you." The words tumbled out of her mouth in a rush. Now that Sophia had said it out loud, she felt stronger. "I did, so much, enjoy having you as a friend, and I would appreciate it if you kept my secret. I would so hate to embarrass her ladyship."

Dory sat back on her heels and looked up at Sophia. Shock registered in her clear green eyes. Pity or maybe sorrow created deep creases around her downturned mouth. "I'm still your friend, Sophia. Would the blackguard not marry you?"

Chills ran up Sophia's spine at the mention of the life she might have had. "He offered, but my father tossed him from the house, and I thanked God he did. I cannot imagine a worse hell than being married to that horrible man." She shuddered with another violent chill.

Dory stood and turned away.

Sophia's heart sank. She had ruined one of only two friendships she had in London.

Dory's back was rigid, and her hands fisted. She turned and stared at Sophia with narrowed eyes. Maybe she would strike her. "He forced himself on you."

Sophia only nodded. The night in her father's study rushed back to her memory pushing more tears to the surface.

"How old were you?" Dory knelt before her again.

Sophia was surprised at how angry Dory seemed. Angry at a man she didn't even know. "Sixteen. It was my first season out." Her heart slowed its pace. Dory hadn't rushed from the house the minute she heard of Sophia's shame. She didn't call her the terrible names that rolled through Sophia's own mind. Dory had knelt before her with sympathy.

"He should have been shot for what he did to you. How did your father not kill him?"

For the first time since that horrible night, she had told someone outside her mother and father the truth. Her imagination had painted a picture of the result that included shame and remorse.

Dory stared at her eyes wide and hands shaking as she gripped hers.

Sophia's heart lightened, and the pain long in her chest eased. "I think father would have enjoyed exceedingly to have killed him on the spot."

"I thought you Americans went around shooting each other

willy-nilly." A small giggle escaped. She put her hand over her mouth.

"Not generally."

Dory paced with clenched hands. "All right, then. If you do not want to marry, then we shall devise a plan so you will not have to. Will your father not allow you a small income?"

"He would, but mother insisted I come to London and try to find a husband. She said I must put the incident behind me. But really, I can't. I can't stand the thought of a man touching me." The night before rushed to her memory and her skin tingled. "Though, when the earl kissed me, it was quite soft and enjoyable."

"I wish I knew more about such matters. My mother has been very closed-mouthed on the subject. However, I must believe that rape is not the same as whatever one would have with a husband. I'll give the matter of your remaining unmarried some thought. In the meantime, don't worry so much. No one has offered for you, so there is no reason you should not enjoy your season. If someone does offer, then we shall think of reasons why each and every one is unsuitable. I can be clever when I need to. I'll send your maid in and order you a bath. I shall call on you tomorrow with Elinor."

Sophia jumped up. "Oh, don't tell Elinor. Please."

"Of course not." Dory hugged her. "We shall just come for a visit and discuss gowns for the Fallon ball."

Sophia wanted to hug her new friend and never let go. She couldn't have dreamed anyone would take her part, let alone fight on her behalf. "I'm glad you're my friend, Dorothea Flammel."

Dory smiled. "I am as well."

Once Dory left, Sophia called for a bath and Marie helped her undress. She closed her eyes and sank deeper into the warm water. Perhaps everything would be all right. The idea of a small house, either here or in Philadelphia, crept into the back of her mind. She would like to be in the country, where she might grow a garden and no one would gossip about her lack of a husband. That would be perfect.

No husband meant, no children to ever call her mother and in turn, none of the grandchildren her mother coveted so desperately.

Perhaps not perfect.

∼

The dress glimmered in the color of rich butter and gave her skin a golden glow. Marie had outdone herself styling Sophia's hair, entwining crimson ribbons and crystals through her dark tresses. The same color ribbons flowed down from just below her breasts, which mounded above the scooped neckline. But the cleverly made dress would keep her safe from embarrassment.

The Fallon's London home was larger than Collington house. Upon entering, there were two grand staircases that curved around an oval foyer. The wood gleamed and a tasteful chandelier hung in the center. Its crystals polished to a miraculous shine illuminated the entry. To the right, the ballroom took Sophia's breath away.

Aunt Daphne joined the dowagers where they clustered together like hens.

Sophia found herself standing alone watching the dancers and staring in wonder at the beauty of the house.

His presence warmed her even before he spoke and her spine stiffened. Her stomach did a little flip in spite of her resolve to be unaffected by him.

"Do you like it?" He spoke softly just behind her left ear.

The ceiling had to be forty feet tall, with golden arches and a fresco of kings and queens enjoying a picnic in the park. Tall glass doors lined one entire wall and silk curtains gleamed in the candlelight.

The sound of his voice gave her a quiver inside. It took her several beats before she found her voice. "It's a lovely house. Do you live here?"

"No. I have a home not far from here. My stepmother and sister live here."

Her interest was piqued. "Was that part of your father's wishes?"

He shrugged and his broad shoulders creased the crisp lines of his black jacket before everything settled into place as if ordered to do so. It was as if he commanded his clothing to obey and the cloth wouldn't dare defy. "I really have no idea. My mother enjoys living here when she is in town, and I like for her to be happy."

"You get along well with your stepmother, then?"

His smile warmed his face and sent a quiver through her belly. "My own mother died giving birth to me and my father remarried when I was five. Janette is the only mother I have ever known. She raised me as her own and gave me a wonderful little sister, whom I adore. Why should we not get along?"

She constantly said the wrong thing. "I did not mean to imply anything, my lord. It is only that you have no legal obligation to keep them housed and many men in your position would not bother to care for a stepmother and half-sister."

With a shrug, he met her gaze. "I suppose that is true of many."

"But not you." She wished she could find a cruel streak in him, walk away and not think of him again. It would be much easier to ignore a man who would put the women who depended on him out in the street. But he obviously loved his family and that made him even more endearing. She forbade herself to like him.

"Would you like to meet my mother and sister?" he asked.

Before she could stop herself, she nodded. For some reason, she wanted to meet his family. Though, for the life of her, she couldn't imagine why. He was nothing to her.

He walked only a few steps before stopping suddenly.

She stumbled and gripped his arm tighter to keep her feet. Looking up, she found him staring down at her.

His eyes shone with intensity making her heart pound.

The music changed to a waltz and he bent his head an inch from hers. "Perhaps a dance first, Miss Braighton? I hate to let an opportunity to hold you in my arms slip away."

"I wish you would not say such things."

"Is that a yes, or a no, to the dance?" His eyes filled with mirth.

She nodded, and they circled the dance floor. In his arms, it was difficult to think of anything she decided before the ball. She planned to avoid him and, if she did run into him, she would be cool and polite. However, now that his hands were on her and his heat radiated through the flimsy material of her gown, she longed to be close to him. There was safety in Daniel's embrace. A word she never thought to apply to any man besides her father.

"Why do you wish I would not say such things to you, Sophia?" He whispered closer to her ear than was appropriate.

Running was her best option, but she stood her ground. "You should not call me Sophia. It is not right and I have not given you permission to do so."

"It seems impossible for me to behave correctly with you, Sophia. I promised myself I would avoid you, but as soon as you entered the ballroom, I was aware of your presence, and I could not keep away. I do not know what draws me to you and believe me, I would prefer to be indifferent to your allure. I felt this way once before, and it ended quite badly." He shook his head, and his posture stiffened, not at all like his flirtatious manner of a moment before.

Her heart raced and she was certain he could hear her heart pounding, but she couldn't think of a thing to say in response to his personal admission.

He smiled. "You must think me a fool."

"No."

He laughed. "There is that word again. If you were English, you would elaborate."

"Yes, you are a long-winded bunch. However, my father is English, my Mother Italian, and I'm American, so, 'no' will often do." She missed her family and the wonderful differences that made them unique.

"I suppose it shall have to." He whirled her around one last time before the music ended. He bowed.

She curtsied.

The crowd watched with avid interest.

He escorted her back across the crowded ballroom.

One fact about his admission nagged at her. "Why did it end?" "I beg your pardon?"

"You said you felt this way once before and it ended badly. I wondered why it ended."

"Would it be rude of me to say that I would rather not say?" He towered over her and stared into her eyes. His closeness filled her head with vanilla, spice and another scent uniquely his.

She breathed deeply to commit the scent of him to memory. "Not if it is to protect the lady."

Without a word, he led her across the ballroom.

Elegant and petite, with chestnut hair, and bright eyes, Janette Fallon beamed luminously at her stepson. She didn't look old enough to have been Daniel's mother for over twenty years.

He bowed and kissed her cheek. Adoration shone in his eyes.

If she never married, she would never have a son who would look at her that way. Her blood chilled, and she closed her eyes against the wave of sorrow. She swallowed, took a breath, and pushed those thoughts aside. "Mother, I would like you to meet Miss Sophia Braighton. Miss Braighton, this is my mother, Lady Janette Fallon." His smile warmed and his gaze softened as he made the introductions.

Lady Marlton stared so long that Sophia braced herself against the urge to fidget. Her gaze was not unkind and a small smile remained on her lips as she assessed Sophia from head to toe. "It is a pleasure to meet you, Miss Braighton."

"Thank you, Lady Marlton. It's an honor to be here."

Janette's eyes widened. "You are American. Have you just arrived in London?"

It was Daniel who answered. "Miss Braighton is Lady Collington's great niece, Mother."

"I see." Janette's smile brightened. "I seem to remember that your aunt had a nephew who left for America the year I made my debut. He was married to a lovely Italian girl. I also recall that Charles Braighton made quite a good deal of money in shipping. Is that your father, Miss Braighton?"

She loved that someone knew of her parents. It was almost like they were there. "Yes, my lady. My parents and my brother are still in Philadelphia."

"You have a brother? How marvelous." Now her eyes were bright, the marriage market mamma coming to the surface. "Is he older or younger than you, my dear?"

"Mother, Cissy is only making her debut tonight. Don't go sending her off to America just yet."

Sophia giggled. "Anthony is older but only by one year. I'm afraid he's not quite ready for marriage."

Still grinning Janette shrugged. "Perhaps a bit too young for Cissy, but one never knows."

"Mother, you are incorrigible."

She frowned, but her eyes were still twinkling with humor. "I'm a mother with two unmarried children. It is completely normal to try to find them suitable mates. In fact, it would be remiss of me if I did not."

He beamed at her. "Perhaps, but it is the unabashed way you go about it that is tiresome, dear mother."

"Why should I not be shameless? If I'm not, then what will become of my daughter?" The lament was met with a chuckle from Daniel.

He tipped his head to one side. "Here is the wastrel now. I'm sure Miss Braighton can see why you are so worried. How will we ever get her married off?"

The girl who approached was as petite as Janette with the same hair and eyes. Her skin was fair and unmarred, and she had a pert little nose and a strong chin. For a girl of perhaps sixteen, she walked with decided confidence. She saw Daniel, and her eyes lit up. Her joy made her even more stunning as she hugged and kissed him. "You came. I'm so glad."

"I would not miss your debut, sweetheart."

Sophia thought about her own brother's expression when he learned of her plans never to marry. He'd been upset with her and disappointed that she refused to do her duty. She couldn't tell him the reasons. She was too afraid of what he would think of her, or worse, he might decide to do something rash and get himself in trouble. No, it was better he didn't know, even if it meant he thought she was disobedient and willful.

The Fallon's affection made her long to see her own brother and beg his forgiveness.

Daniel made introductions, but Sophia was miles away in her own thoughts and snapped out of it when she heard her name repeated. "I'm so sorry. It is a pleasure to meet you, Miss Fallon."

Lady Marlton stared her head tipped to the side. "You must miss your own family very much, Miss Braighton."

Daniel's mother's intuitiveness surprised her. It was either that or everyone could read her thoughts as Thomas had said. "I do, but my aunt has been wonderful, and I'm enjoying London immensely."

"I wonder if you and your aunt would come to tea tomorrow?" Lady Marlton asked.

Sophia tried to hide her shock at the invitation, taking deep even breaths and relaxing her face. "I'll have to check with Lady Collington, but I don't think we are otherwise engaged. We would be delighted. Thank you."

"Until tomorrow then, Miss Braighton. Cecilia, I would like to introduce you to Lord Hadlington." With that, Daniel's mother turned to walk away with Cecilia in tow.

"Yes, mother." Cissy followed, rolling her eyes, but her smile never wavered.

"They are very nice," Sophia said.

"I agree. Shall I return you to your aunt, Miss Braighton, or would you be willing to walk in the gardens with me?"

His voice was so soft and imploring, she nearly said yes to his invitation.

Dory and Elinor ran across the ballroom skirts fully flowing like two ship's sails in pale pink and sky blue.

"What a marvelous ball. Your mother has outdone herself, my lord." Elinor bubbled with enthusiasm.

He bowed to the two young ladies. "I shall tell her you said so, Miss Burkenstock. If you ladies will excuse me? Perhaps another time, Miss Braighton." He bowed again, took her hand, and kissed it.

Her heart thundered so violently, that she might need to take a seat.

Then he was gone.

"What was that about?" Dory demanded.

Sophia shook her head. "Nothing. He just introduced me to his mother and sister. They are lovely. Miss Fallon is so pretty she took my breath away."

Dory's eyes narrowed. "Indeed."

"Have you seen Sir Michael? I thought perhaps he would be here, since he and Lord Fallon are such good friends." Elinor's words came in a rush.

"I have never seen him, so I would not know him if he was here in this crowd," Sophia said.

Elinor perked up and her blond curls bounced. "Yes, that is true. He could be here and I just have not seen him yet. Perhaps I'll take a turn around the room and see if I can spot him. Will the two of you join me?" With no way out of it, both girls agreed to walk the perimeter of the ballroom in search of Sir Michael. They were not successful in their quest, but they did manage to fill up their dance cards.

An hour later, Sophia danced with Thomas Wheel. "What happened to Lord Fallon's fiancée?"

Thomas's brows drew together. "Perhaps that is a question for his lordship."

"He didn't wish to tell me," she admitted.

"Then I shall not tell you either."

Sophia knew she should drop the subject. Yet it nagged at her. "How long were they engaged?"

He sighed. "Nearly six months. The wedding was only two weeks away."

"That's awful. Who broke it off?" She stopped dancing.

Thomas pulled her along. "Do not lose your step, Miss Braighton."

She liked Thomas. He was real and honest when most people pretended. "Mr. Wheel, would it be terribly inappropriate for us to call each other by our given names? I do so like you, and I think we shall really be good friends."

"But nothing more." His voice was sad but he kept the crooked smile in place.

"I'm afraid, while I'm fond of you, I shall never have those kinds of feelings for you, Mr. Wheel."

"A shame to be sure. Addressing each other by our Christian names is completely inappropriate and therefore, I insist you call me Thomas or Tom and I shall always call you Sophia when we are out of earshot of the ton."

"Excellent!"

The dance ended and they walked to the side of the room, where he obtained two glasses of lemonade.

"It was him, wasn't it? He broke off the engagement, didn't he, Tom?"

He nodded.

"Why?" Her voice was soft, so as not to have anyone overhear their conversation. The noise level of the party was such, that it was unlikely anyone over a foot away could hear a word. Hundreds of people talked, argued, and laughed. The band played and the pounding of dancers' feet made it quite difficult to have a private conversation.

Thomas shrugged. "The lady's honor came in question."

Sophia stiffened. "I see."

"Do you?" His crooked smile had returned.

She looked him in the eye. "Of course. Someone claimed the young lady did something and everyone believed it. Thus,

her reputation was ruined and his lordship ended the engagement to save his own reputation. It is very clear to me."

His eyes widened and he took a step forward. "Sophia, you
are mistaken. I cannot go into the details, but your friend, Dory,
was out at the time. I think if you ask her, she can tell you
more."

She'd heard enough about Daniel Fallon to last a lifetime.
She stood straight. It was a relief to find his flaw, yet her heart
sank. "I'm sure that won't be necessary."

The next dance started, and she was swept away by
another gentleman.

Chapter Five

The garden was cool and quiet. Sophia had talked Elinor into joining her for a walk. She needed to get away from the crowds and noise to think. The idea that Daniel had ended the engagement because he questioned his fiancée's honor continued to roll through her mind. How could Daniel not stand beside her when she'd needed him most? He was no better than every other man. It was almost a relief to know his true character, so she would no longer have trouble dispelling her feelings for him.

"I was not out yet when the earl was engaged. I only know the rumors," Elinor said.

"And, what was the rumor?" Sophia's anger burned higher.

Elinor cringed.

Sophia sympathized. "Never mind, Elinor, you need not tell me."

"I hate rumors." Elinor's weepy tone sounded much more a little girl's than a young lady's. "They often get exaggerated and none of us really know the truth. Well, except those involved."

"Yes, of course you're right."

The bushes rustled to their right. A young man watched them.

Her heart skipped a beat and she grab Elinor's arm ready to pull her into a run toward the house.

He stepped into view as soon as their gazes met. He bowed and the firelight shone in his dark hair and bright blue eyes. His fine clothing was rumpled and a leaf stuck to the shoulder of his jacket. "Forgive me, ladies."

"Michael," Elinor said.

Sophia's nerves settled down. At least this was not some kind of attack.

"I was trying to wait until I could speak to Miss Burkenstock alone. I hope I did not startle you." His fingers clutched and released while he moved from one foot to the other.

Elinor blushed and tears already filled her eyes. "Shall I leave, Elinor?" Sophia asked.

Elinor looked at her as if just remembering she was there. "Thank you, Sophia."

"Are you certain you will be safe?" Sophia gave Sir Michael a stern look. He smiled. "You have my word I shall not harm her in any way."

"Elinor?"

"I will be fine."

Sophia nodded and walked away only looking back once to see the two gazing longingly at each other.

Sophia walked away from the lovers hoping she was doing the right thing. It would be a disaster if they were discovered. Elinor would never recover from two indiscretions.

She walked and admired the torch-lit garden. It was grand and elegant. The full moon and the fine weather made for a particularly bright night. Not at all the dreary, rainy place her mother had described.

A beautiful fountain displayed several cherubs. Planted all

around were the most stunning yellow roses. She knelt and breathed in the sweet fragrance when she heard footsteps. She looked up and Daniel appeared as if out of the ether as he always seemed to do.

"You will ruin your dress." He walked over and offered her a hand up. She hesitated before taking it then she pulled away. "Thank you."

"You are angry with me again." It was not a question.

"I barely know you, my lord. Why should I be angry with you? I can have no reason." The echo of Thomas's words rippled through her mind.

"I do not know, Miss Braighton but since you are incapable of keeping your feelings from your face, I can see clearly you are angry."

She stepped away aggravated with herself for not being able to hide her feelings.

He followed and put his hands on her shoulders. His fingers gently rubbed the skin of her neck as he spoke. "I do not recall doing anything to upset you this evening. We did not argue, and my mother liked you very much. Whatever it is that I have done? You can tell me, and I shall make every effort to make it right."

As gentle as his touch, his calluses surprised her. Why was an earl doing the kind of labor that would create rough hands? It wasn't gentlemanly. "I don't wish for you to make anything right with me. You haven't done anything to me and I have no claims on you. You may do as you wish."

Her heart pounded. Why did he have such an effect on her? She took a step away and touched a yellow rose climbing up a nearby trellis.

Once again, he was behind her and his scent flooded her senses. Then his lips touched her neck.

Her heart pounded and she struggled to catch her breath. "What are you doing?"

He kissed further up her neck and put his hands on her hips to pull her back against him. "I do not know. Whenever I see you, I lose all rational thought."

"Then perhaps we should avoid each other." Her feet were rooted in place.

He caressed her from her hip to just under her breast. The sensation of his touch reached every inch of her body and culminated between her legs. She'd never felt anything so wondrous and frightening in her life. She was afraid, but she didn't stop him. In fact, she wanted more, more of Daniel and more of his kisses.

"You are right of course. That's my other problem. I cannot seem to stay away." He traced the edge of her dress with his lips spreading kisses along the line where it met her shoulder, and he pushed the light fabric aside. His hand crept around her waist until his palm was flat against her stomach.

She couldn't breathe or think. In three years, she'd never allowed herself to be alone with a man. This was a mistake. She should leave. He was so warm, safe and it felt so right to be in his arms. Safe? A crazy thought to have about a man.

He pressed her more firmly to him. Through the fabric of his trousers and her gown, he was hard against her backside. Her breath caught in her throat. A weight constrained her chest. Nothing about the garden scene was warm and safe. Reality crashed down around her, she shuddered and backed down the path. "No."

"Sophia, there is no reason to be afraid. I would never harm you." He stepped forward.

"Stay away from me." She put her hands out as if that might ward him off. She had to escape, had to get away from him.

He stopped. "I will not harm you. I will not touch you if you do not wish it."

"Just stay away, Daniel."

"I will not advance, Sophia, but if you do not watch where you are going, you will tumble into the fountain and then we will really be in dire straits."

She looked back, and he was telling the truth.

"Do you want to tell me why you are afraid of me?"

She shook her head. Telling him the truth wasn't an option and her throat was tight with emotion.

"How about telling me why you were so angry with me a little while ago?"

Nothing she could say would make any sense. She repeated her head shake.

"I'm sorry to hear that. I hope you will change your mind at some point but until then, perhaps you had better return to the ballroom." His voice was kind and soft as if he were talking to a lost child.

Yes, the ballroom would be safe. She sidestepped around him and ran toward the noise of the house. She went several yards before turning.

He sat on a bench near the fountain with his head in his hand. She wanted to comfort him. He was no different from every other man. None of them were trustworthy. She ran.

At the veranda, she sat on a low wall and took deep breaths. It was unfathomable that she had allowed a man to take such liberties. She smoothed her hair, stood, adjusted her dress, and stepped into the Fallon Ballroom. She searched for Elinor, Dory or Aunt Daphne, a friendly face in the sea of strangers.

Someone bumped her then grabbed her arms. She turned about to apologize.

Alistair Pundington, the one person she truly hated, stared

at her with angry eyes and a twisted smirk. "Sophia, what a surprise to see you here in London."

A shiver ran down her spine. Vomiting in the middle of a ball would ruin her. "Mr. Pundington, I'm equally surprised. If you'll excuse me, I must find my aunt."

Tall and lean, his musky cologne filled her head with horror. He might be older, but his grip bit into her skin enough he would leave a mark. "Don't rush away, Miss Braighton. I'm happy to see you. Perhaps we can rekindle our friendship. I'm only in London for a short while but I would make it worth your while."

She swallowed down the bile rising in her throat. "I'm not a whore, you pig of a man. You will stay away from me, or I will make you sorry you ever lived."

His beady eyes narrowed under bushy gray brows, but he sniggered at her. The sound haunted her nightmares. Whisky soured his breath as he leaned in. "What can you do to me, little girl? And I assure you, that you are no better than a common whore, just better dressed." He tore the cap sleeve of her dress.

She gasped and clutched the fabric closed. Panic started deep in her stomach rising fast. She searched for an escape route.

"Oh dear, I am so sorry. What a brute I am." His smirk was thin and made her stomach turn. The devil who stole her innocence gave the appearance of a perfect gentleman. No one else took notice of his evil.

"Miss Braighton, are you quite all right?" Thomas's voice was so welcome she sank against him before managing to upright herself.

"I have been clumsy and torn my dress. Can you show me to the ladies retiring room?" She spoke loud enough so people nearby would hear her excuse. She hoped her tone was even and the gossips wouldn't make more of the incident.

"Of course." Thomas offered his arm. He nodded in greeting. "Mr. Pundington."

"Mr. Wheel."

Once they were out of sight of Pundington, Thomas spoke in low tones. "Sophia, what was that all about?"

"Oh, Tom, please don't ask me that. Just bring me somewhere where I can have a few minutes alone to gather myself. Will you be my friend and do that for me?" She was close to tears, and she didn't want to have to explain anything. How could she? She couldn't.

"Of course." He took her to a large double door off the central corridor and pushed through. It was the library, an enormous cavern filled from floor to ceiling with books. An arrangement of chairs and a couch filled the center of the room, while a large desk was set off in the back corner.

Thomas led her to the couch, and she sat. He sat across from her in one of the chairs.

She stared at the floor. Pundington was in London. It was a nightmare.

Her nightmare, come to life.

He broke the silence. "Should I stay or leave you? Would you like me to find your aunt? Really, Sophia, I'm not sure what to do for you, but I do want to help. Are you sure you will not tell me what happened out there with Pundington?"

She shook her head. "Tom, would you mind finding Dory for me?"

He nodded, jumped up from the chair and rushed out to search for Lady Dorothea.

She didn't know how long she sat staring at a spot on the ornate rug. She was lost in the horrible past when the door opened. She didn't bother to look up. "Oh Dory, I'm in trouble. He's here."

"Who is here?" Daniel asked.

Her head snapped up.

His face was a mixture of surprise and concern.

"My...my...lord. I...I'm...sorry. Of course, this is your library. I did not mean to intrude. I was...just...resting a moment." She stood and backed away.

"Sophia, are you truly so afraid of me, or has something happened since the garden? What happened to your gown? What did you mean when I walked in? Who is here and what kind of trouble are you in?" He advanced on her.

"Don't." She held up a hand as if to stop his blow from hitting her face.

He stopped. It was as if all the air had rushed out of the room. "You think I would strike you? You think so little of me?"

The door opened again and Dory entered. She shut the door behind her. "My lord, what is going on here?"

He turned toward Dory. "I am not certain what has happened, but clearly Miss Braighton is upset. I shall leave you ladies. Please take as long as you need. You will not be disturbed. I shall see to it."

He bowed and left the library.

Sophia couldn't breathe. Her heart was in her throat and her stomach churned as it had on the open sea.

Dory came close and spoke softly. "Sophia, what happened?"

It was all too much. Sophia's knees gave way and she collapsed in a heap on the floor.

"Oh, damn." Dory rushed forward and knelt beside her. "What on earth is going on? Did Marlton do something to upset you?"

"No, he...and then...in the garden...I came in...and he was there... and...tore my dress..." She didn't get further.

Dorothea's eyes grew narrow. "The Earl of Marlton tore your dress?"

"No, not Daniel," Sophia cried.

Dory's eyebrows rose. "Who then, dearest?"

"Alistair Pundington." More tears followed.

"Let's sit down on the couch for a few minutes. You can catch your breath, start from the beginning and tell me exactly what has happened."

Her legs shook, but she got up with Dory's help. They moved to the dark red couch and sat quietly until Sophia's breathing steadied, and she forced herself to stop crying.

"Alistair Pundington is the man I told you about. He is the one who raped me." She spoke in a whisper but her voice was steady. She was determined to be brave.

Dory nodded her eyes wide. "Start from the beginning, Sophia. Why were you afraid of the earl?"

Sophia told Dory about the meeting in the garden. She didn't mention Elinor and Sir Michael. That was Elinor's story to tell and she wouldn't betray her trust. She also left out a good bit of detail regarding how far the touching had gone with Daniel. She told her she had not initially been afraid. The fear had come later and as soon as she asked him to, he had stopped and not gotten the least bit angry. She explained about the terrible encounter with Pundington in the ballroom and how the monster had intentionally torn her dress. Finally, she told her about Daniel finding her in the library.

"But his lordship did not intend to strike you. You were just frightened because of what happened in the ballroom and you reacted falsely."

"Yes." The word came out in an exhausted rush of air.

Dory wrapped her in a warm hug. "Do not worry, dearest,

everything will be fine. I'll go and find your aunt and tell her you tore your dress on the door latch and would like to go home. It's late and everyone is growing tired. No one will suspect a thing. Now, let's have a look at you." She brushed out the lace on the skirt so it looked less wrinkled. There was no help for the torn sleeve, so she tucked the lace under and nodded in approval.

"Your hair has held up quite well considering the events of the evening." Dory grinned.

Sophia actually giggled at that. "Thank you, Dory."

"This is what friends do. You must let me use your maid for my hair. I swear she is a wonder. I'm sure all of my curls have fallen."

Dory was trying to distract her and doing an excellent job. "You are as beautiful as ever."

"Now, you wait near the door and I will find your aunt and order your carriage brought around."

Sophia nodded and opened the door.

The butler, a short thin man of perhaps sixty, stood just outside the door. He bowed deeply at the sight of the ladies. "I'm Fenton, my ladies. His lordship asked that I wait to see if there is anything you need." He then stood stock-still waiting for a reply. He was stylish for his age. It was thoughtful of Daniel to have the library guarded.

"Would you have Lady Collington's carriage brought around, Fenton?" Dorothea said.

He bowed stiffly. "Of course."

He walked off but a second later, a footman appeared by Sophia's side.

Dory raised an eyebrow and went in search of Lady Collington.

Chapter Six

Tea was served in the finest china Sophia had ever seen. Sunny roses hand-painted on every cup and saucer with not a chip or scratch. She was uneasy in the house Daniel owned, but he was not in residence, so she calmed her nerves. The countess poured tea while Sophia kept her hands clasped in her lap, making every attempt not to fidget.

Sophia rested most of the morning. She arrived to break her fast, and Daphne had declared her unpresentable and told her to return to her room. When she joined her for luncheon there was no mention of what had happened the night before or her state that morning.

"Are you enjoying London, Miss Braighton?" Daniel's sister, Cecelia sat on the white and gold overstuffed chair, completely relaxed as if she were one of the tea roses in the garden.

In comparison, Sophia was a great gangly oaf. "I have only been here a week but it has been quite distracting so far."

"How long will you stay?" Cecelia asked.

"I suppose until my aunt tires of my taking up so much space in her home."

"Nonsense." Daphne grumbled.

Lady Marlton chuckled and sipped her tea. "Cecelia, take Miss Braighton for a walk in the garden. It's another glorious day and Miss Braighton has not seen the gardens in the daylight. They are quite lovely."

Sophia's heartbeat tripled and her stomach knotted. How did Lady Marlton know she was in the gardens at night? What else did she know? The other women all wore calm expressions. Perhaps the countess assumed everyone at the ball had seen her magnificent gardens lit by torches and lanterns.

"Would you like to see them, Miss Braighton?" Cecilia asked.

"I can think of nothing I would adore more." Even as she said it, she dreaded any reminder of the night before.

In spite of her hesitation, the garden overwhelmed her with its beauty. However, the intimate embrace shared with Daniel flooded back to her. She struggled against blushing when they arrived at the large fountain at the center of the garden. She breathed in the sweet fragrance of roses and the moment Daniel first kissed her warmed her from the inside out.

She may have become frightened in the garden, but he'd been kind and thoughtful in his library. He'd even gone to the trouble of having her guarded until her carriage arrived.

The yellow roses glowed in the daylight. They surrounded the fountain and their bushes climbed taller than a man. Each one trimmed to leave a wide path around the fountain and four equally spaced paths leading toward or away from the focus of the garden. The water gently spilled over the three-tiered fountain and since her companion was easily silent, they sat and enjoy the twittering of birds and the cascade of water.

"I'm being rude." Cecelia broke the silence.

"Not at all."

"Mother always scolds me for keeping too quiet."

"It has been very peaceful and nice to just sit and think. Most people cannot keep quiet for a moment. I have enjoyed your company, Lady Cecilia."

"Do call me Cissy."

"Then you must call me Sophia. Do you sit out here often? It's a wonderful garden."

"I love it here, but our home in the country is even more beautiful. I love to walk, and I can do so without accompaniment when we are in the country. Daniel's property is enormous and no one ever bothers me. I love to take a book and find a quiet tree to sit under. London is fine, but I prefer the quiet solitude of the country." Cissy's gaze drifted away. She stared off into the garden with the hint of a smile and soft eyes.

"Will you stay in London for the entire season?" Sophia felt a bit sorry for Cissy who obviously longed for her country home. She understood wishing to be somewhere else and not being able to change one's situation. Even in a large city, the circumstances were similar to a prison.

She beamed brightly. "I thought we would. Those were our plans for my first season, but now it looks as if we shall return home for a short while."

"Oh?" The idea of Daniel leaving London sent an ache to her heart. She pushed away the feeling, but it gnawed in the pit of her stomach as if she'd eaten bad mutton. But just because his mother and sister left, didn't necessarily mean he would follow.

Cissy whispered, "Mother is planning a house party at our estate in the country."

"Why are you whispering?" Sophia asked, also whispering.

They looked at each other and both giggled. "I have no idea. But, mother was whispering when she discussed it with me. Usually, that means she wants to keep it from my brother for a little while. She probably wants to trick him into joining us."

"His Lordship does not enjoy the country?" Sophia managed the mild inquiry, and she was pleased with herself for showing so little interest.

"He does. In fact, I think he much prefers that house. It is the house we grew up in. Father hated London and only came to town for political or diplomatic reasons. Daniel enjoys riding and hunting, but he does not like to be manipulated by our mother."

"I see." It was funny to think of Daniel, so big and strong, being ordered about by his petite mother.

"Does your mother usually get her way?" Sophia asked.

"Always. Daniel can deny her nothing or me for that matter."

"I'm sure you ask very little of your brother. Why should he ever say no?"

"Indeed." Daniel appeared in the east entry to the fountain.

Cissy jumped up and rushed over to hug Daniel. "I'm so glad you came this morning."

He smiled and kissed the top of Cissy's head but kept his gaze on Sophia. "I wanted to congratulate you on your spectacular debut last evening. You made me very proud, Cissy."

"Thank you. It was a lovely ball."

He leaned closer to her ear. "What is mother trying to get me to do?"

Cissy hit him playfully. "Do not get me in trouble. You will just have to wait and see. She has a plan, and I'll not be the one to topple it."

He grinned at Cissy before turning his full attention to Sophia. Her heart ached wondering what her brother was doing and how he got on in Philadelphia.

Sophia stood and curtsied. "My lord."

He bowed. "Miss Braighton."

"Your mother asked us to come for tea." Sophia explained her reason for being there a bit too quickly. She didn't want him to think she was there to see him.

"Yes, I remember. You look very lovely this morning, Miss Braighton.

I assume you have recovered from whatever ailed you last night."

Sophia glanced at Cissy who watched them with wide eyes.

She wore a white day dress embroidered with small blue flowers. The dress was voluminous and none of her figure showed the way it had in the gown of the night before. "I'm well, my lord. Thank you."

Cissy asked, "Does mother know you are here, Daniel?"

He cleared his throat and looked away from Sophia. "I stopped in the parlor before I came to find you. I chatted briefly with mother and Lady Collington."

"Miss Braighton and I were talking about the country and how much I prefer the solitude and quiet to the bustle of London."

Daniel nodded. "Miss Braighton, do you also enjoy the country?"

He didn't move closer or say anything untoward, yet she flushed. "I have never been to the countryside of England, but I do like quiet. I prefer a long peaceful walk to the business required by city life. My mother can never understand this tendency toward solitude. She loves the parties, theatre, and house calls."

Cissy practically bounced with agreement. "Oh, I agree with you, Miss Braighton. In the country I can walk for miles. I love it. I cannot wait to get back to it. Though, I must get to

Bond Street and buy some books before we return. I have read everything in the library at Marlton, and the books here in the London house are mostly a bore."

Daniel asked, "Will you go in search of Miss Radcliffe's latest atrocity then, Cissy?"

"I may. And do not call them that. They are vastly entertaining, and I read other books as well. I have read all of Shakespeare." She huffed just a bit.

"Have you? All of it?" Sophia was impressed.

"Oh yes. I spent one entire year reading nothing but Shakespeare. Even some lesser-known plays and sonnets." Cissy smiled with delight. "Have you read much Shakespeare, Miss Braighton?"

Sophia shook her head. "Only the more common plays: Hamlet, King Lear, Romeo and Juliet and a few others."

"Cissy, did you know that Miss Braighton is a talented mimic? I, myself have never heard her perform, but I have it on good authority she is quite amusing."

Cecilia bounced up and down clapping her hands. Her curls bounced with her, and she looked much younger than her sixteen years. "Oh please, Miss Braighton, do an impersonation. Who can you do?"

Daniel crossed his arms over his chest and raised his brows. "Will you be offended, my lord?"

He bowed, his expression mild.

Her stomach flipped and knotted, but he'd asked for it. In a voice remarkably similar to the Earl of Marlton's, she said, "Miss Radcliffe's novels are an abomination, Cecilia. I forbid you to read such rubbish. I shall lock you in the bell tower for a month if I so much as see one of those horrid books in my house."

Cissy laughed so hard she held her stomach. "Oh, that was wonderful. If my brother had ever forbid me from doing anything, I'm sure he would have sounded just like that. Do me. Oh please, can you mimic me?"

Sophia obliged her. "I do so love the country and to read in peace and solitude. London is a bore, but I did look rather marvelous at my debut."

Cissy was as good a sport as Daniel and giggled helplessly. "However did you learn to do such a thing?"

"I could always do it, but I suppose I perfected it by trying to vex my brother, Anthony. He hated it when I mimicked him when we were young. As we got older, his friends were amused by my trick so he found it more tolerable." The more she thought of her brother the more she missed him and her parents. It took a large effort on her part not to become solemn in front of her new friend and Daniel.

"I think it is a marvelous trick. I wonder if cook brought out any sandwiches. I'm rather hungry." Cissy started walking back toward the house then turned. "You will show Miss Braighton back to the parlor, Daniel, won't you?"

He nodded. "We shall be right behind you."

Once they were alone, shyness folded over her. She twisted her hands together then clenched her fists to stop the nervous habit. "I like your sister. She is genuine."

"She is the best thing that ever happened to me. I quite adore her." His voice was low and rang with emotion.

"Are you sad she has grown up?" She stepped closer.

"She has grown up well, and she will marry well, I expect. I just wish things did not happen so fast. It seems like yesterday I was eleven and had a brand new baby sister. I remember coming home from school that first time after she was born and just staring into her cradle. I was completely in love with her at first sight. Now when I look at her, I cannot see that infant at all."

"Yes, time goes very quickly." She agreed.

"How old are you, Miss Braighton. Or am I not allowed to ask?"

She giggled. "You are most certainly not supposed to ask and I'm nineteen."

"When did you make your debut?"

She frowned. "Why do you ask?"

He shrugged. "Just curious. You do not seem to enjoy the marriage market process. I saw you at the ball dancing, but I do not think your heart is in it."

"My heart?" Her voice was just above a whisper.

"Is there someone in America whom you are hoping to return to?"

More than anything, she wanted to lie. She could lie and say she was madly in love with a man in Philadelphia and then he would leave her alone. Perhaps a rumor would circulate and all the men of London would leave her alone. However, when she looked into his eyes and they were so sincere and so blue, deceiving him was impossible. He truly looked concerned. Why should he be? "No. There is no one. I have been out in society for three years, my lord."

"Last night you called me Daniel."

Heat spread throughout her entire body. "That was last night. Today I have regained my good sense." She walked to the edge of the fountain and dipped her fingers in the cool water.

"I'm sorry to hear that. I rather liked the way it sounded." His breath tickled her ear.

She stood stock-still not sure if she wanted him to touch her or not. Well, that was not the entire truth. Part of her was desperate for his touch. But her good sense told her, she should keep her distance.

In any event, he didn't lay a finger on her. Instead, he backed away. "Would you like to tell me now that you are not so upset what happened last night after you left the garden?"

"I wish you wouldn't ask me that. I don't wish to tell you and I'd rather not lie to you. It would be better if you didn't ask." She looked over her shoulder. She didn't know if he was angry at her, but she didn't like the way his brows came together or the way his lips drew tight.

"But Sophia, your dress was torn, you were clearly distressed and whatever happened occurred in my home. I cannot tolerate anything violent taking place at Fallon House. I could insist you tell me."

"Yet, I don't wish to talk about it. And as a gentleman you should not force the issue." Panic raised the timbre of her voice. She tried to force herself to relax but her shoulders stiffened and she trembled. He might insist, and then what would she do?

His expression softened. "Very well. Will you at least tell me if what happened between you and me in the garden was the cause of your dismay? I do not think I could stand it, but I have to know."

She looked into his pained eyes. "No, Daniel. It was not you."

Neither moved for a long time, they stood staring at each other.

Daniel shook himself. "Shall we see if there are any sandwiches?"

She accepted his arm as they went back to the house for tea. His body heat seeped from his arm through both of their clothing and into hers. It then spread out in every direction. It took all of her strength to avoid stumbling as they strode through the house. He didn't speak, but she desperately wanted to know what he was thinking. She was too cowardly to ask.

"Oh Daniel, there you are," Lady Marlton said. "I have decided on a house party."

"Have you, Mother?" He leaned against the door jam and crossed one foot over the other.

Sophia skirted an inlaid table and the gold-embroidered settee then sat near the other women.

"Yes." She nodded and gave him a look that said, don't you dare condescend to me. "It shall be for a week in the country, and I think we should go Friday next."

"We...Who, exactly, is 'we'?"

Jeannette smiled sweetly. "Well, to start, your sister, you, me, several other friends, Lady Collington and her delightful niece, of course. I think you should invite Thomas Wheel and Sir Michael. I shall invite Lord Flammel and his family. You were quite close with the son, were you not? I think I will invite him and his new wife. They live quite close to Marlton. I have to work out the rest of the invitations, but rest assured, it will be a fine gathering."

"I have no doubt, Mother."

Chapter Seven

Most of the ton was off at this ball or that. Rain turned the roads to mud, but that wouldn't stop the marrying mammas from displaying their babies to the eligible bachelors of the season. Therefore, while the marriage mart continued, Daniel and Thomas found themselves ensconced in a game of cards at White's Gentleman's Club. The heavy drapes, wood paneling, and cigar smoke appealed to their male sensibilities. White's was an excellent escape from the horrors of the marriage market.

In spite of his good intentions, Daniel's thoughts drifted to what color Sophia's dress might be that evening. Would she wear her hair up and leave just a few glistening dark curls tumbling around her shoulders? Or, would her mass of hair gently fall around her exquisite face? He hoped it was down covering those shoulders. He'd kissed her there and didn't want to share them with any other man. He shook his head to clear such insane thoughts away. Perhaps he would make a late arrival and see for himself.

Thoughts of Sophia and the ball reminded him of her

obvious distress in his library the evening of Cissy's ball. His guts tightened. She'd been so pale when he found her. Why had she been so relieved to see her friend? Was it because she was afraid to be alone with him or was something else going on? He was sure she had not been that upset in the garden. Frightened by the intimacy between them, but her terror in the library was something different. She claimed he wasn't the cause of her distress, but wouldn't tell him what happened. It was maddening.

Thomas had just ordered brandy, which was an immediate tell that he had a bad hand. Though only Daniel would notice. After playing cards together since they were twelve years old, Thomas couldn't fool him.

"Room for a fifth here?" Alistair Pundington asked. Twice their age, he still dressed like a young dandy in a yellow waistcoat with a white cravat. Daniel and Thomas both preferred a much simpler look for themselves, but the elaborate neckwear was fashionable that season.

"Just finishing this hand." Lord Frederick Brooks was a portly baron who drank too much and played cards badly. In the red for one hundred pounds already, he rarely used good sense and stopped playing until he lost ten times that amount. Sweat poured profusely from every pore and the little hair left on his head was damp and askew. He looked as if he had been in a brawl, but the unfortunate chap had done it to himself as he often did when playing over his head.

Pundington sat and waited for the hand to be decided.

Daniel swept his winnings out of the center of the table as Miles Hallsmith dealt the next round.

Miles was a good-natured young man who had been at Eton with Daniel and Thomas. He was the third son of a viscount but didn't seem to mind his rather low position. His father gave him a tidy allowance, and he in turn ran the family estates. His oldest brother was not adept at running them so Miles acted as a kind of secretary, which he also didn't seem to mind. He had fiery red hair and freckles. There was a sense of calm about Miles, and Daniel liked him.

"Oh good show, Hallsmith." Brooks puffed up like a pigeon and admired his cards and drank more of his brandy.

Thomas shook his head. "Freddy, you know telling your good fortune in this game is ill-advised, don't you?"

Brooks laughed rather dumbly and continued to chortle at his cards, rearranging them this way and that as if they would make better sense if he moved them just one more time. However, when this didn't help, he moved them yet again, all the while drinking and chortling.

As the betting began, Thomas said, "When did you arrive in London, Pundington? I thought you were on the continent."

Thomas's voice was less than cordial. He was generally an affable gentleman, so for him to border on rudeness caused the hair on the back of Daniel's neck to stand up.

"Just got in yesterday." Pundington twisted his long mustache around his index finger. "Surprised to see Lady Collington's niece last night. That old bag is such a stickler for rules, seems odd she would sponsor that one."

He had Daniel's full attention.

However, it was Thomas who spoke. "I do not know what you are talking about, Pundington, but I consider the lady a friend and you had better proceed cautiously."

Alistair continued to twirl his mustache. His grin looked more like a wolf baring its teeth. "Oh? She does make the rounds. Pretty thing. Quite a disappointment to her family though."

"How so?" Brooks asked around another sip of brandy.

Daniel's fingers were grasping his cards so tightly he crushed the edges. His other hand balled in a fist under the table. He didn't know whether to listen or beat Pundington to a pulp.

"Were you not a partner to her father?" Thomas asked. "I seem to remember hearing that your partnership ended poorly not many years ago."

Pundington waved off the comment. "An amicable split after many years together. We both made a tidy sum, I might add."

There was another round of betting.

"You're not after the chit, are you, Wheel? I would advise against it if you want to be sure your heirs are your own." Pundington smirked and asked for a card.

Daniel was quite adept at keeping his feelings to himself. His gut twisted, and he burned with the desire to unleash his rage on Pundington and everyone else at the table.

"You go too far, Pundington. I suggest you say no more about the lady or I'll take offence." Thomas spoke through clenched teeth.

Alistair looked up as if surprised that anyone should care about the subject. "No need to get out of sorts, boy. I had the girl myself. Not as if I'm telling stories out of school."

All four men stared at Alistair.

It was too much. How had Daniel let this happen again? He tossed his cards on the table, resisted the urge to throw furniture, and strode from the club.

M iles called after, "Marlton, your winnings." But Daniel either didn't hear him or didn't care.

Thomas stood. He looked at the footman standing nearby. "Collect his lordship's winnings."

"Yes, sir."

"Mr. Pundington, I strongly suggest what you have just said is fiction. I have no idea why you would slander a lady's reputation, but I will not have it. If I hear that you have spread this rumor beyond this table, I shall call you out. Do I make myself clear?"

Pundington raised his dark eyebrows. "Perfectly." His voice was even and perhaps slightly amused.

Thomas picked up his own winnings and turned to leave, but then turned back. "If you ever call me 'boy' again, I'll run you through without the delicacy of a proper duel."

His own temper raged but he knew Daniel well enough to know that the Earl of Marlton was dangerously angry. He left the club and had his man drive him to Daniel's home. Entering the small townhouse, he gave the parlor door a push. "You left in a hurry, old friend."

"I'm in no mood for company, Tom." Daniel threw back a glass of whisky.

Thomas poured himself a glass. "Do not believe that old goat. Sophia is a wonderful girl and not capable of what he implied. Besides, she looked terrified of the bastard when she saw him at your house."

"Terrified because she thought he would disclose her secrets." He drank another glass in one swallow.

"It's sour grapes I tell you. There was a falling out between Pundington and her father. They had a long-time partnership that ended. This is all fiction."

Daniel smiled, but there was nothing nice about it. The hate in his eyes filled the room. "You can believe any fairy tale you like, Tom. The lady means nothing to me, and any rumors about her virtue are irrelevant."

"Yes, I can see by the way you are enjoying your fine whisky, that you don't care."

"Take your sarcasm and yourself and go somewhere else. I

have had enough for one night." Daniel's capacity for blindness was beyond good sense. He was blind.

Shaking Daniel would do no good, so Thomas bowed more deeply than was necessary. "As you wish, my lord."

~

D aniel downed another glass of whisky and then threw the fine crystal goblet across the room, where it smashed against the door, sending shards in a spectacular starburst. He then lost his balance and fell to the oriental carpet with a rather loud thud.

That is where his valet found him a few minutes later. And that is where he left his lordship until the next morning when he woke him by throwing open the heavy curtains. "Good morning, my lord. Beautiful day."

Daniel felt as if an elephant had run across his head. He pushed himself from the floor and squinted against the bright sunlight streaming in the tall windows and glaring off all the fine wood paneling of his parlor.

Perhaps he would fire the maid who'd polished the wood. "Close those damned blinds, Sutter."

The valet picked Daniel's coat up off the chair and shook it out. "I have taken the liberty of having your breakfast brought in here. I thought you might need a bit of food after the whisky ran out last night."

"You are an impertinent sod, Sutter."

"Indeed, my lord."

Daniel stumbled then sat on the dark brown sofa. The tray of food made his stomach turn. He picked up the coffee and took a sip. His head cleared and the events of the previous evening came rushing back to him. A maid cleaned the glass from the doorway and another was wiping down the door and polishing the wood where his whisky glass had struck. Daniel silently cursed himself for a fool. *She means nothing. She was nobody, the daughter of an American businessman, nothing more. Not even worth the price of the broken glass.*

Standing a bit too quickly, he held his head until the room stopped spinning. He ambled to the desk, scribbled a note, folded it and handed it to his valet. *What did he care about a cheap little piece of skirt from America?* "Sutter, have this message delivered and have the messenger wait for a response. Then have a bath drawn for me and I would like to wear my green jacket."

"Yes, my lord." The valet's answer was stoic as always.

～

The next morning, Sophia had not yet finished her toilette when Aunt Daphne burst into her room without knocking.

"What is the meaning of this?" Lady Collington narrowed her eyes to fierce points directed at Sophia as she threw down the morning paper. Several hairpins scattered and tinkled to the floor.

Sophia gasped but managed, with shaking hands, to pick up the paper and read the article.

This reporter is astonished to learn, a certain Miss B who is recently in London is not nearly as innocent as she appears. She had us all fooled, even Lord M and Mr. W.

Sophia's heart lodged in her throat. She swallowed and took a shuddering breath. "Marie, would you excuse us?"

The maid left the room quietly, closing the door behind her.

"Well?" Aunt Daphne bit out.

Sophia took a deep breath. "Alistair Pundington."

"What about him? Heinous man. I never understood why your father did business with him."

Sophia stood. "Please sit down, Aunt. It is a long story, and I don't think I'll be able to get through it if you're hovering over me."

Daphne's expression softened marginally, her pursed lips relaxed, and she sat in the vanity chair Sophia had just vacated.

Sophia's hands shook, and she clutched them in front of her. She supposed it was always only a matter of time once Pundington saw her at the Fallon Ball. "Alistair Pundington and my father attended Eton together. He was best man at my parents' wedding. Whenever he was in Philadelphia, he stayed at our house. Anthony and I called him Uncle Alistair. I debuted after I turned sixteen and Uncle Alistair visited shortly thereafter. He was different on this visit, and I couldn't say why. One night, I said goodnight to mamma and papa and made my way through the hallway to go up to my bed when I was grabbed from behind and dragged into my father's study."

Lady Collington gasped and covered her mouth.

Sophia took a deep breath and wiped away the tear rolling down her cheek. She trembled and sat on the edge of the bed. "I tried to scream, but a large hand that smelled of cigar smoke covered my face, cutting off all air. I kicked and struggled, but to no effect. It was a few seconds before I realized it was the man I called uncle, a man I had known my entire life. He hit me and tore my dress. I smelled whisky on his breath." She gasped for air the way she had that night. There was more to tell and Aunt Daphne deserved to know the truth. Her body shook with the memory, but she needed Daphne to understand. Sophia desperately wanted one family member to know what she suffered and not blame her for that terrible night.

She pushed the words from her mouth. "He violated me. I

was bruised, battered, and bloody when my parents came in and found me lying on the floor unable to speak or even cry.

"Father beat Pundington to a pulp and when he dared call the next day to ask for my hand, father beat him again. Mother just held me and cried. I didn't cry then. My heart was dead and no tears would come."

Sophia took another breath and wiped both her cheeks dry. "I didn't want to partake of the Philadelphia season after that and for the first year, my parents understood. The following year they were less understanding and then last year they became quite insistent I look for a suitable husband. I refused. So, they foisted me on you, dear Aunt Daphne, and I still cannot avoid the stain of that night. I'm so sorry to be such an utter disappointment. I did so want to make you proud." Sophia dashed away more tears she wished she could stop from falling.

Daphne stood looking a bit pale. She walked to the bed and sat next to Sophia. "Sophia, I wish your parents had informed me. I did not even know Pundington was in London. I had heard he and your father were no longer in business, and he was on the continent. With all the trouble in France, he has probably just arrived. I did not see him at Lady Marlton's ball."

"He was there," Sophia said.

"This must be vengeance for declining his offer of marriage. At least your father had the good sense not to accept him. Some would have taken the easy way out."

Sophia shuddered. "I would have killed myself."

Daphne patted her knee. "Well, thank goodness it did not come to that."

"I'm sorry, Aunt. I know you planned for me to find a husband and with this report in the paper, it will be impossible." In spite of the stain on her name, relief came with the report. Sophia would not be subject to any offers of marriage now.

"Nonsense," Daphne said. "More difficult perhaps, but definitely not impossible."

Sophia sighed.

Daphne stood with her hands on her hips. "Sophia, you do not have to marry."

"I don't?"

Daphne shook her head. "No. If you choose to remain unmarried, you can be my companion here in England. When I die, I shall leave you a small fortune with which you shall be able to live comfortably for the rest of your life. I have a bit of money left to me from my mother's side and a small cottage, which is not part of the Collington estate. It is not entailed and shall be yours if you wish. I'm also quite certain in spite of your parents' wishes for you to marry, your father would settle an amount on you should you decide a life of solitude suits you."

The breath Sophia had held for three years gushed from her, and she relaxed for the first time. Her muscles ached from the strain. Her heart filled her throat and a new batch of tears threatened. Sophia held them back not wanting to spoil the moment with crying. She stood and hugged her. "Thank you, Aunt."

"I do, however, expect you to finish the season. We will not let that horrible monster ruin us for society. We shall go to the theatre tonight as planned and you will hold your head up and look everyone directly in the eye. We will not let him win. Do you hear me, girl?" Daphne's voice filled with passion. "What that man did to you is a crime. Society may not see it that way and people prefer to brush these things under the rug, but that does not keep him from being a criminal. We shall not let a criminal rule our lives for even one evening."

Some of her elation slipped away. Sophia was not as enthusiastic. "As you wish, Aunt Daphne."

"I'll not be cowed by that devil and neither shall you."

"Yes." Her voice was just audible. Still, all she need do was to get through the season and there would be no more talk of marriage. Euphoria settled over her making her lightheaded.

Daphne sat and took Sophia's hand. "But you know, Sophia, if you do not marry, you will have no children. Are you sure that is what you want?" That weighed heavy on her. Never to know the love of a baby and watch him grow to a young man or woman. Never to have someone call her mother. She pictured a little boy with Daniel's eyes staring up from a cradle. She shook off the idea. "I don't see how I can marry. I cannot bear the idea of any man touching me."

With her lips pursed as if she tasted something sour, Daphne scanned the room before settling her gaze back on Sophia. "It is a difficult subject, what happens between married people."

"I suppose so."

"But this is not the time to be squeamish."

"I didn't think I was so." Sophia almost laughed.

"Not you, dear. Me. My marriage was arranged by my father, but your great uncle was a good man, and we had a fine marriage, I feel confident in telling you that your experience was not normal." She looked out the window then brushed out her skirts. "If you should like to marry and have a family, your husband would be kind to you."

"How do you know?" Sophia didn't know where to look. Not even her mother had broached this subject and now she could see why.

"I certainly would find you a kind and caring husband, perhaps even someone who was affectionate toward you."

Daniel had been affectionate, yet she still ran terrified from him. "I will give it some thought, Aunt Daphne."

"Good." Daphne stood. "You may come down for breakfast,

then I would suggest you rest until it is time to get ready for the evening. I'm sure this has been exhausting for you."

As she left the room, she bumped into Sophia's maid. "Very loyal, Marie."

"Yes, milady." Marie curtsied, and Lady Collington stalked down the hall.

Chapter Eight

At the theatre, there was nowhere to turn without bumping into someone. Sophia had endured being squeezed into a corset and having her hair curled and twisted. The effect was stunning. Her dark hair shone and the gold gown was exquisite. She looked much more assured than she felt. However, she'd promised her aunt and herself to keep her feelings neatly tucked away. As they sauntered toward the Collington box, she smiled and nodded and looked everyone full on. She made a special effort to ignore the people whispering behind their hands.

When Lady Pemberhamble smirked, she walked over to the pinched-mouthed gossip. "How do you do this evening, Lady Pemberhamble? I think this is going to be a singular evening, don't you?"

Lady Pemberhamble tugged at her heavily powdered wig. "I think it should be, Miss Braighton."

Sophia curtsied. "Enjoy the performance, madam."

"Well done," Aunt Daphne said.

They managed to arrive at the box without incident. The

hardest part was when only she and Aunt Daphne waited in the box alone. People watched them and there was nothing to distract her. Elinor and Mrs. Burkenstock's arrival was a welcome addition to the box. Sophia was close to unraveling until support arrived.

"Are you all right?" Elinor asked.

Sophia said, "I have had better days."

Elinor patted her hand. "We shall get through this together."

"Don't you even want to know if it's true?"

She cocked her head. "It is not true, Sophia. I admit to only knowing you a short time, but I know without a doubt you are one of the finest and most honest people I have ever met."

Sophia used one gloved finger to dry the corner of her eye. "Thank you."

Dory arrived with her mother in tow. Lady Flammel didn't stay long, however, and from the puckered expression she wore she was not pleased with Dory's insistence to remain in the Collington box.

"Did you receive an invitation to Lady Marlton's house party next week?" Dory asked.

Elinor bobbed her head excitedly.

"I believe we did. I don't know how I'm going to talk my aunt out of making me go."

"Why would you not want to go? It is the invitation of the season." Elinor gaped at her.

Dory squeezed her hand. "Elinor is right, you know. You must go or you will insult one of the most influential women in London. Besides, we shall have a wonderful time."

The theatre darkened and the first act of the play began. In the dark, it was easy to ignore the people around her.

The play was terrible, but she paid it close attention anyway. It was about a man tricked into marriage by a witch who appeared as a beautiful maiden. After the marriage, he discovered she was an old hag. He ran away, and she put a curse on him. She swore he wouldn't find love unless he honored his marriage vows.

At the end of the act, the lights came up.

Elinor bubbled with excitement. "Michael is here. Dory, will you come with me to see him. I cannot go alone."

Dory looked at Sophia. "It's all right, Dory. Go with her. I'll be fine."

Lady Marlton arrived a moment later. She, Lady Burkenstock and Aunt Daphne spoke in hushed tones about something. Sophia didn't try to hear what they were whispering about. It was rather amazing Aunt Daphne had friends who would stand by them in such desperate times. She might cry and pinched her arm to keep the tears at bay. Loneliness fell over her like a worn blanket.

Thomas arrived in her box and sat next to her.

"Tom." His name came out on a gusty exhale. "I'm so thankful you're here."

"Are you all right? I cannot believe he managed to get that in the paper. I warned him."

"You spoke to Alistair Pundington?" She asked shocked.

"Do not lose your calm now, my dear. You cannot fall to pieces here. So far, you have managed to make a fine appearance. I'm impressed considering how you usually show every bit of emotion. Just keep it up for the rest of your life and you shall be all right."

They both laughed. But then Sophia's anger at Alistair and society burned in her stomach. She sat up straighter and her eyes filled with anger. She nodded toward the crowd watching her to see if she would give a sign that the report in the paper was true. "I'll not give them the satisfaction of winning."

"Good. May I say that you look very beautiful tonight? I have never seen anyone so resplendent."

"Are you flirting with me, Tom?"

"Would you mind it terribly?" He leaned a fraction of an inch closer.

"Of course not. I would never forgive you if you didn't." She giggled in spite of the knot in her stomach.

"You two appear to be having a good time."

Both Sophia and Thomas turned toward Daniel's voice. He stood in the entry to the box with a beautiful woman on his arm. He grinned as if all was right with the world.

"We are," Thomas confirmed. "Will you join us?"

Daniel shook his head. "I just wanted to introduce Miss Braighton to my friend, Charlotte Dubois. Miss Dubois is all the rage this opera season."

Sophia stood and politely curtsied to the stunning blonde attached to Daniel's arm. "A pleasure to meet you, Miss Dubois. I hope to have an opportunity to hear you sing."

"Enchantè, Miss Braighton, this is my wish as well." Charlotte's words were doused with a heavy French accent.

"Well, we must be off. I promised Charlotte we would not miss a moment of the play." Daniel nestled into the opera singer's neck. She giggled.

He didn't introduce his opera singer to the countess or the other ladies who sat watching the exchange. There was a sense the other ladies were too good to meet his opera singer but Sophia was not. She gritted her teeth and kept her expression serene.

"I'm sorry, Sophia," Thomas said, after Daniel had gone.

"Why would he do that?" She had not expected an answer.

"He is extremely taken with you."

Sophia shook her head. "He is no such thing."

"If you say so, but why else would he bring a woman of questionable reputation over here to meet you?"

"Perhaps he believes I have a bit in common with his opera singer." Bitterness laced her words.

"You do not." Thomas's voice was strong and sure.

"No. I don't believe so."

"You should forget about my friend and focus on me. I could easily fall in love with you, Sophia. I'm half in love with you now." His voice had gone to a whisper and his eyes crinkled at the corners.

"Are you serious, Tom?" The knot tightened.

His eyes were bright and stunning and she wished she were in love with him. However, when she looked at Tom, she didn't get the same quiver in her stomach that she felt when Daniel was near. When she looked at Tom, she saw a friend and nothing more.

"I could not be more serious."

She touched his hand. "I have decided to never marry, but if I change my mind, I shall certainly think of you."

"You are teasing me." His voice sounded a bit sad.

"No...I—"

He held up one hand. "It's all right, Sophia. I know you do not love me. In fact, I'm rather certain you are as in love with my good friend as he is with you. All I'm saying is, if you and Daniel cannot be together, then you should consider me. I'm wealthy and I like you tremendously, which I have never said to any woman before. I think we would be good friends in marriage and it would not be such a bad way to get along in life. Spending one's days with a person they consider a good friend is not so terrible, is it?"

"Don't you want to find someone who loves you and whom you love?" She was flattered by his offer and a bit scared because she gave it serious thought. She didn't love him and she never would, but it would make her parents and Aunt Daphne so happy to see her settled.

He chuckled. "I have never considered it. I must marry, but I always thought it would be someone amiable and who might tolerate me. Now I see that perhaps there is an alternative, if you will have me."

She wrung her hands together. The stupid white gloves twisted this way and that. "Must I give you an answer here and now?"

"No. In fact, I think we should wait until the end of the season. If Daniel does not come to his senses, then you should consider my offer. I would not wish to stand in the way of true love." He chuckled, but it was a hollow sound.

She looked up. "If what you say about your friend is true, then don't you risk your friendship by courting me?"

He shrugged. "Daniel is a fool. Besides, our friendship goes back a long way. It can survive a marriage between you and me. Daniel will be angry, but mostly with himself."

"You are serious. You have thought this through quite considerably." She'd assumed he was joking, but Thomas had given the notion of marrying her consideration.

He smiled. "You should close your mouth, Sophia. As charming as you look sitting there gaping at me, I think the crowd is beginning to notice." She did close her mouth and soon after, the lights went dark again.

Thomas stayed for the second act and Dory and Elinor returned. It was nice to have the support of so many friends. All her friends in Philadelphia had abandoned her under the weight of the rumors. Everyone speculated and gossiped about why she declined all invitations. Sophia hadn't helped matters, becoming more and more reclusive as time went on.

In only a few short weeks in London, she'd made three true friends who now stood by her.

In the second act, the husband returned battered and lonely. Under the pressure of the curse, he was unable to find the love he sought so diligently. He climbed mountains and crossed seas searching for his love, but in the end, he found only more loneliness, and he was starving to death. The witch didn't send him away as Sophia had hoped. Instead, she welcomed him home after years of absence. She fed him, bathed him, and gave him clean clothes. She let him sleep for three days to recover from his journey.

Sophia wanted the witch to throw stones at him until he bled.

At the end of three days, the husband was so grateful, he took his wife to bed to thank her for her kindness. He promised to stay with her and be a faithful husband and lover. As soon as the words were out of his mouth, she turned back into the beautiful maiden he'd originally married. She then explained that all she ever wanted was for him to love her not for her beauty but for herself.

Sophia dashed away a tear with disgust. A ridiculous story and not at all how life really was.

Thomas escorted her out of the box. They met up with Daniel and his opera singer in the lobby.

"Did you enjoy the play, Miss Braighton?" Daniel asked.

"Not very much, Lord Marlton." She kept her expression calm. It took quite a bit of effort.

"Really, why not? I should have thought you would love such fanciful ideas. All young women love a happy ending."

"I prefer the truth."

"That surprises me coming from you." He bit out the words and narrowed his eyes on her. His free hand fisted at his side and the beautiful Miss Dubois occupied the other.

"Marlton," Thomas warned.

"Always her champion, Wheel. A pity she is constantly in

need of your services." He paused. "Perhaps, you should marry her."

Sophia didn't give her escort time to respond. "I shall be happy to tell you anything you ask, my lord."

"Really? Just the other day you told me you would prefer if I didn't ask questions."

She nodded. "I would prefer it."

"Your aunt is waiting, Sophia," Thomas said.

"Of course you're right, Tom."

T he use of Thomas's familiar name got Daniel's attention and he bowed deeply to them both when he wanted to wring Tom's neck and pull Sophia into his arms and kiss her until she told him everything. He'd been joking about Tom marrying Sophia, but he saw in Tom's eyes, he was not amused.

"Good evening. Wheel, I shall see you on Monday at the club. Miss Braighton, until we meet again." His words sounded eloquent enough but even he heard the tension.

Daniel watched them cross to Lady Collington, while his companion chatted with everyone she encountered.

Had he seen tears in Sophia's eyes? He would have sworn he had. Why would she cry? Probably just the lighting.

Once he extracted Miss Dubois from the theatre, he drove her home.

She stepped away from the carriage and then turned back when he didn't follow. "Are you coming up?"

He kissed her hand. "Not tonight, my dear."

"You are in love, Danny." It was not a question.

"No. You are mistaken."

She smiled and tipped her lovely face to one side. "I'm

never wrong about such things. The dark-haired girl who did not like the play."

He choked and cleared his throat.

She giggled. "She seems quite nice and very beautiful, Danny. You should marry her before your friend does."

"I'm sorry, Charlotte, but you are incorrect. I do not even know Miss Braighton. Thomas may have her." It came out a bit more sternly than he intended.

She had a way of shrugging that said the matter was of little interest to her. "He will have her if you do not stop him. Good-bye, Danny. I do not expect I will see you again."

He kissed her hand again. "Good night, Charlotte."

As he did every Monday morning at eleven o'clock, Daniel met Thomas at Jaffers Club for a fencing match. Dulled foils were capped at the end and each man wore protective clothing in case of accident.

The clash of steel on steel filled the long hall. The two gentlemen were well matched and to the passing observer nothing looked amiss. However, after thirty minutes Thomas called a halt. He removed his mask and wiped the sweat from his brow. "You are quite vigorous this morning, old friend."

Daniel removed his own mask. "If you cannot keep up, Tom, we can call it a day."

Thomas raised an eyebrow. "I can certainly keep up. That is not the question. The question is, why are you making such an effort to harm your 'dearest friend' during a sparring match?"

"Harm you, I would never dream." His voice dripped with sarcasm.

"Very well." Thomas lowered his mask and took an *en gardè* stance.

Steel clashed again and with more effort than before, Daniel went on the offence and backed Thomas up to the wall. "Why does she call you 'Tom'?"

Thomas pushed off, caught Daniel off guard and backed him up several paces. "We are friends."

"Friends?" Daniel thrust forward.

Thomas turned in time to avoid the blow and swept his foot catching Daniel at the back of the knee.

Daniel was already off balance and the move felled him.

Thomas kicked Daniel's foil away and put a foot on his chest. "Yes, friends. I would offer for her in a second if I did not believe she is already in love with you. I have told her so."

"Offer then. I want nothing to do with her."

"Really, is that why you nearly took my arm off a few minutes ago because you have no interest? She is a marvelous girl, and you are a fool if you do not at least attempt to have her for your wife." Thomas took his foot off Daniel and removed his mask. He sat on the step that led down from the fencing platform and wiped his face.

Daniel stretched the shoulder he'd landed on and sat next to him. He tossed his gloves and mask aside and rested his head in his hand. "I cannot go through this again, Tom."

"Jocelyn and Sophia have nothing in common. However, you obviously have your doubts. I suggest you talk to the lady and see what she says. Do you really believe Lady Collington would sponsor her if what Pundington said is true?"

"She might have lied to her aunt," Daniel said.

"You must be joking. Sophia wears her emotions directly in those unusual golden eyes. She couldn't lie successfully and certainly not to someone as astute as Lady Collington."

"I just do not know, Tom." He shook his head while rubbing his temple. Thomas got up and gave his foil, mask and gloves to his valet. He removed the protective vest and shrugged into a more fashionable morning coat. "Well, my friend, you had better decide what you want. I did not jest when I said I would offer for her. I think she and I might be a good match. Not a love match, but she is beautiful, intelligent, and I'm fond of her, which is more than I can say for most other women of the ton."

"You are serious." Daniel's heart beat wildly and his stomach twisted in a knot that threatened to upheave his breakfast. The idea of spending the rest of his life seeing Sophia as Mrs. Thomas Wheel was untenable.

"I could not be more so. I can see that you love her and that she obviously is in love with you. Because I care about you both, I shall wait. However, I'll not wait indefinitely. I'll see you on Friday in the country." He bowed and left.

Daniel tried thinking without all the hurt and anger that had guided his actions for the past few days. Everything Thomas said was true. He would give the matter more thought. How long would he allow Jocelyn's actions to rule his life?

Chapter Nine

Sophia spent hours begging Aunt Daphne to allow her to stay in London rather than go to Lady Marlton's house party. But all her pleading was to no avail. It was the invitation of the season, they had accepted, and it would take an act of God to keep them from Marlton Hall.

So, she prayed for an act of God.

Pray as she might, on Friday they took the Collington carriage and made the trip to join her friends and Daniel in the country.

Hills and fields spread out before her and gave a bit of distraction from seeing Daniel. She tapped the windowsill until Aunt Daphne commanded her to stop. Once the rain stopped, she tugged at the sleeves of her dress and squirmed as perspiration ran down her back. A bit of blue sky peeked out for a little while.

The drive up to Daniel's estate was canopied by a mile of giant oak. By far the largest house she'd ever seen, Marlton Hall boasted three stories with large windows. The tall glass reflected blue sky and fluffy clouds. Heaven plopped down in the English countryside. Sophia struggled to catch her breath.

"Not a bad piece of property, eh?" Aunt Daphne chuckled.

"My word. How do they find their way around such a palace?" The drive widened and curved around a reflecting pond. Great stairs rose up to the front door and several servants stood waiting.

"I think they manage, Sophia. It is only a house, a rather enormous one, but a house just the same. Try to close your mouth before we alight from the carriage, my dear."

Lady Marlton and Cissy greeted them in front of the house. They were not the first to arrive. Elinor and Virginia Burkenstock were already in residence and were resting above stairs. Dory and her family had not yet arrived but were expected soon.

Mrs. Wade, the housekeeper, a woman of some girth in a serviceable blue dress, showed Sophia and Daphne to rooms on the second floor. They climbed a steep flight of stairs and walked down two long hallways, all the while Mrs. Wade's keys kept a steady cadence.

Aunt Daphne said she would rest before dinner, but Sophia's mind filled with a thousand different horrors that might destroy the week in the country. Every one of them left her more miserable than the last.

Remarkably, she managed to find her way through the house and into the elaborate gardens. Once she found the garden gate, the property stretched out in miles of rolling hills. However, did he keep track of so much land? One knoll looked much like the next. Fresh air and sunshine warmed her face. She stood on the top of a hill, breathed deeply, and closed her eyes. Warm grass and rich earth, just like home.

"What are you thinking about?"

She gasped and opened her eyes, whirling toward Daniel's voice.

He dismounted his chestnut horse and threw the reins over the saddle. He gave the horse a pat and a few words and it eagerly trotted away. He turned back to her holding up both hands as if in surrender. "I apologize. I did not mean to startle you. I saw you from across the field and you were so engrossed you did not hear my approach."

"I thought I was alone." She blurted out the statement unable to think of anything intelligent to say. Why didn't he look angry as he had at the theatre? Her nerves frayed. The least he could do was be consistent. She was always on edge when he was around, and she didn't like it.

He grinned, which lit a spark in his eyes. "Obviously. What were you thinking?"

She turned away and walked a few steps, creating some distance between them. She considered running back to the house, but he would catch her and even if he didn't, she would still have an entire week of embarrassment over her behavior on the first day. "I was just thinking that this reminds me of home."

He stared out over his property. "It's good farmland."

Papa would visit the nearby farmers once a month and see how they were doing. He kept up good relationships with all the local people and often traded with the farmers. The shipping business did well because Charles Braighton was admired by so many people.

"Thomas told me he intends to marry you." His expression was calm and unreadable.

It wouldn't do to run screaming back to the house now. She swallowed and kept her eyes on the land, the trees, a passing bird, anywhere but at him. "He mentioned it to me as well."

"Will you accept his offer?"

"I don't see how that is any of your business, Lord Marlton." He took several steps toward her.

She stiffened and ordered her feet not to move. He was going to touch her and the air simmered between them.

His hands settled on her shoulders. "It is none of my business, Sophia. I have no idea why you draw me in the way you do. I want to stay away from you, but I cannot seem to do it. Tom is a good man. The best man I know. You could do no better and yet the thought of you marrying him fills me with rage, which I find difficult to control. The idea of anyone else having you is repulsive to me."

His speech took some fire out of her. "I don't wish to marry at all."

"You told me that before."

"I meant it."

"But you will accept Tom if he asks." He said knowingly.

She forced a smile. "Mr. Wheel makes a good argument for a marriage between us. I like him very much." It sounded a bit too simple but it was impossible to lie no matter how much she would have preferred it.

Daniel shifted his weight from foot to foot. "Shall we talk of something else?"

She shook her head. "I think I should return to the house and we should try to avoid each other this week, my lord. I seem to have the ability to make you angry. I do not wish to do so, but it's obvious we can't get along. I'll keep my distance and I would appreciate it if you would do the same."

He closed the gap. "Anger is not the only emotion you stir in me, Sophia. I find I can think of little else but you when you are near. If I could stay away from you I would, but I'm drawn to you like moth to flame."

She took a step back. "All the more reason to stay away from me as the moth never fairs well in that situation."

"You do not like me. You like Tom, but not me." He stared up at the clearing sky, his voice far away.

She sighed. "My feelings for you are unclear, my lord. I'm confused in your presence, and I fear you."

He touched her cheek. "Fear me? That, I could never want, Sophia. I would never harm you."

His lips brushed hers so gently that it was more of a whisper than a kiss.

Her stomach fluttered and her breasts ached. She tried, but failed to stop the tear that trickled down her cheek.

"Why are you crying?"

Helpless, she couldn't look away. "I don't know. I want..."

He buried his face in the crook of her neck. "Yes, sweet, what do you want?"

She shook her head and stepped away again. "I don't know. You scare me, my lord. I don't want whatever this is I feel when you are close. I don't understand, I don't like it, and I would much prefer if you would keep your distance."

She turned and ran toward the house. Every possible emotion swirled inside Sophia. The week was already a disaster.

$\sim$

The party gathered in the formal parlor at seven. The congregation consisted of quite a few people Sophia didn't know. She sought Dory, who introduced her father, Lord Castlereagh. Lady Castlereagh spared Sophia half a glance. Evidently, she was not quite ready to banish the rumors. Dory also introduced her to her brother, Markus and his wife, Emma. Dory had a younger brother who was away at school and unable to join them for the week.

Thomas leaned against a wall in the parlor. Sir Michael

had not arrived though he was expected. Lord and Lady Dowder were present with their twin daughters, Serena and Sylvia. It was the first time Sophia had met them, but the skinny brunettes had flitted around the Fallon ballroom. They both appeared to be in love with Thomas. It would be interesting to see how they intended to work that out. Would they fight over him or just wait and see if he picked one of them? They were silly girls, but she greeted them politely.

After meeting Lady Blyth and Mrs. Hatton, who were sisters around Aunt Daphne's age and both widowed, Sophia was able to sit down with Dory on a settee in the corner of the room. She ran one finger over the blue embroidery of the cushion.

"Where were you today? This is a big house, but I searched everywhere when we arrived and you were nowhere to be found." Dory asked.

"I went for a long walk around the grounds." Sophia bit her bottom lip.

Dory tilted her head to one side. "Did you walk alone, or did one of your admirers join you?"

"I have no admirers."

Both of Dory's curved eyebrows rose up. "Really? Then why is Lord Marlton pretending not to look over here and why is Mr. Wheel striding determinedly in this direction?"

"I have much to tell you, but this is not the time or the place." Sophia turned her head to see Tom walking over and smiling his most charming smile.

"Indeed," Dory said.

"May I join you ladies?" Thomas asked.

Dory said, "I have been ill-mannered and ignored my good friend Elinor since we began the evening. Will you both excuse me?"

Thomas bowed to her as she rushed off on her fictitious mission. "How are you?"

"I'm fine, Tom. How are you?" It was nice to sit with Tom. He was easy to be with.

"Have you thought about my proposal?"

"I have been able to think of little else."

"I wish the thought of marrying me did not create such an unhappy expression on your otherwise lovely face. Is it such a terrible prospect?" His scowl transformed into a congenial smile.

"Oh, Tom, I'm sorry. Not at all. It's a wonderful offer. I just don't know if I want to marry at all. I worry, should I have to decline, you will never forgive me, and I'll lose a valuable friend."

"I shall always be your friend, Sophia. You may count on that regardless of your answer."

"Thank you, Tom."

He grinned and changed the subject. "Daniel and I are going hunting in the morning. Hopefully, we'll have some pheasant for supper if all goes well."

"I wish you good luck." She was glad to have something else to speak about.

His expression turned. "Unfortunately, the Dowder twins have caught wind of our plans and insist on accompanying us."

Sophia giggled. "I think they are both in love with you. It worries me that they'll come to blows over you. I've never seen so many eyelashes fluttering as when those girls look at you."

"Do not joke. They are a nuisance. I would have thought twice of accepting the invitation if I had known those two would be here. They follow me relentlessly if I dare to attend a ball. I cannot imagine how an entire week with them will be. Torture, I tell you."

She laughed heartily at his distress. "They are lovely girls. You should pay them some attention. Besides, once Lord Michael and the other gentlemen arrive, I'm sure Sylvia and Serena will be distracted and leave you alone. Though, you are quite irresistible."

He joined her mirth. "You seem quite able to resist me."

"Oh, but I'm not like the other girls, Mr. Wheel. You would do well to remember that."

"A truer statement was never made."

She didn't get the chance to question his response. The butler called for dinner.

"May I escort you in, Miss Braighton?" He stood and offered his arm. She took it and smiled up at him.

Daniel escorted his mother in to dinner, though he continued watching her. He frowned and a deep crease formed between his brows. Perhaps he would rush over and beat Thomas to a pulp at any moment. She kept her gaze away from Daniel.

Daniel sat at the head of the table with Lady Marlton at the other end. Sophia was near the middle, with Dory's Brother on the left and Lady Blyth on her right. Dory and Elinor were both near the head of the table and Aunt Daphne sat across and several places over.

Lady Blyth made a great effort to ignore her but Dory's brother, Markus was good company. "My sister tells me you two have become good friends. She writes to me weekly and her past few letters, have been all about you, Miss Braighton."

Sophia felt happy for the first time in a long time. Dory's friendship was one of the best things that had ever happened to her. "I don't think I have ever had a better friend than your sister. Dory is very dear to me. I don't know if I could survive London without her."

Lady Blyth made a huffing sound. "Friendships are fleeting. A good marriage is what you need. That will keep you out of trouble and put your poor aunt at ease." Since Lady Blyth was a bit hard of hearing, the comment rang against the wood paneling. The entire table had heard and stared in her direction.

Sophia didn't know what to say. Her cheeks burned and she gulped down the lump in her throat.

Markus recovered first. "I must say, Lady Blyth, I disagree. I have had the same friends since Eton, and I would be lost without them. For that matter, I cannot imagine my marriage would be half so wonderful if I did not consider my wife among my closest friends."

She huffed again. "That's fine for a man, but hardly good advice for a woman. Young women need to find husbands, preferably rich ones."

"I shall not argue, my lady. I shall just disagree and leave it at that." Markus said, diplomatically.

Lady Blyth's blue hair bobbed up and down. Far from finished with the topic, she chewed her dove. "I was married at seventeen. This girl is approaching twenty. It's appalling that she has not married. I have it on good authority she had a fine offer from Alistair Pundington years ago."

Sophia stopped breathing. She was going to faint. Heat infused her face and sweat beaded above her lips. All the noise in the room was drowned out by the muffled roaring in her head. In her lap, her hands turned pale as parchment. She was actually going to faint dead away in the middle of dinner as if she was some character from a novel. She forced a deep breath, but it ended up only a gulp.

Then Thomas stood over her. "Miss Braighton, I think the heat must be too much for you. I wonder if you would spare me a few minutes in the garden?"

She gasped for enough breath to speak and took his offered hand. "Yes, thank you, Mr. Wheel."

Sophia looked down the table at Daniel. He stood as did all the men when she did. Daniel scowled and his face colored dark red as if he might fly across the table and strike her down. She curtsied briefly and Thomas rushed her out of the dining room.

The cool air helped tremendously. As soon as they entered the garden, Sophia began feeling better. "Thank you, Tom."

"It was nothing." He waved off her thanks.

"It was much more than nothing."

"Well, nothing any good friend would not have done for another."

"Yes. I suppose." She doubted many of her friends would have been able to extricate her from that dinner, but didn't mention that. "May we sit a minute?"

He directed her to a bench a few feet from the door. The large veranda, surrounded by a rather wild garden looked nothing like the orderly garden at Fallon house in London.

Her face cooled and she breathed normally again.

"Sophia?"

Her eyes were closed and she concentrated on her breathing. "Hmm?"

"May I ask you a question?"

She opened her eyes and focused on Thomas. She'd been engrossed in not fainting, remembering to breathe, not thinking about what Lady Blyth said and not remembering how furious Daniel had looked. "You may."

He watched her. "Is it true?"

"Yes," she whispered.

"You rejected Pundington's offer?"

"My father did."

D aniel stood just inside the door. Worried about Sophia, he couldn't sit at the table any longer. When he heard what they were talking about, he stopped. He should have made his presence known or backed away when he heard the nature of the conversation. However, he stood just out of their sight, watched and listened.

"Were you in love with him?" Thomas asked.

"Good God, no!"

"Your father found him unsuitable?"

"He is unsuitable. Nearly three times my age at the time and he's a horrible tyrant."

A tyrant, what did she mean by that? He tried to will Tom to ask her what she meant.

"I see," Tom said.

"No. You don't. You can't possibly know what my life in Philadelphia has been these last three years."

"You can tell me. I'll not betray you."

"I would rather we talk about something else, Tom. Please."

"All right, Sophia."

Daniel waited for more information, but the conversation turned to the weather, and he backed away from the door to rejoin his guests in the sitting room.

Sophia and Thomas arrived in time for tea and cake. Dory rushed to her and whispered something in her ear. Daniel assumed by the relief evident on Sophia's face, Dory told her Lady Blyth had gone to bed early. He didn't know what to make of the conversation he'd overheard or horrible things Pundington had said about Sophia, but when she was near, his thoughts riveted on her. Her face and form distracted him as no other.

If he was going to stay sane, he'd have to keep his distance.

Chapter Ten

"I'm telling you, Daniel, sssomething is not right."

It was after one in the morning and the two men had enjoyed several glasses of whisky together. Daniel pulled a book off the shelf. He had no intention of reading the tome. He just needed something to do with his hands so he pushed it back in its place forcefully causing a loud thump. "What do you want me to do, force the girl to tell us why she refused Pundington? Besides, she did not say she refused him only that her father had."

"I sh...should be angry at you for standing in the door...eavesdropping."

"So, be angry." Daniel stomped across the room for no particular reason. "I already told you, I was coming out to make sure she was all right after that hag Blyth's boorish behavior and overheard the conversation. What did you expect me to do?"

"I 'spect you would act like a gentleman and not skulk in dark corners."

Daniel turned back and stumbled. "I take offence to that remark."

"I take offence to Pundington asking that girl for her hand. What was he thinking? He's much too old for her, but at least it explains why he would wish to ruin her."

"Does it?"

Thomas rolled his eyes and stood on wobbly legs. "Yes. He is ob... obviously still harboring ill will over being tossed oer...over."

"Maybe." Daniel wanted it to be true, but Jocelyn had acted the part of a good girl too and left him looking the fool.

Thomas laughed, stopped and then he laughed heartily.

Daniel watched him unable to keep from smiling at his unexplained mirth. "I have to go to bed, my friend." Thomas stumbled toward the door still chuckling.

"Wait, what is so funny?"

When Thomas turned back into the room, he gripped the door-jam to keep from tumbling to the carpet. "I was just thinking the last girl we both courted was Viviana Winkle. Do you remember? We were all of thirteen."

Daniel rang for a servant. "I remember. She was a fetching little thing with the most charming freckles."

Thomas grinned with half-lidded eyes and a bright red nose. A footman opened the door.

"Please make sure Mr. Wheel gets to his room and his valet is present, Brady."

"Yes, my lord."

Thomas continued to laugh as he strode out of the library. The footman followed him closely.

"Viviana Winkle." Daniel grinned watching Thomas disappear up the steps. He went back inside and lounged on the sofa, satisfied he was not as drunk as Thomas.

He closed his eyes.

∾

A fter twisting in her sheets for hours, Sophia got up and put on her wrap. She tiptoed downstairs to find something to read in hopes a few minutes of reading might tire her. The entire evening continued to roll through her head, and she couldn't seem to close her eyes for more than a moment.

Shadows lurked in every corner. A few of the hall tapers remained lit and she wished she'd brought a candle from her room. She was already halfway down the steps when she realized, not only was it dark, but her slippers remained in her room. Her feet chilled on the cold marble. Her thin wrap was not at all effective against the drafty hall. She walked faster and then stood at the bottom of the steps trying to remember which door led to the library. Certain it was on the left, she didn't remember if it was the first door or the second. The second, with determination she pushed opened the door.

The candles burned down to nubs, but left the room lighted enough to see walls of books.

One step onto the thick carpet and she sighed with relief, though other than her feet, she was still freezing cold. Before traipsing through the drafty house, it might have been wise to grab a blanket for warmth.

She crossed to the shelves and looked for something suitable to read. Perhaps some Shakespeare, only not a romance. A tragedy would be better, or something terribly boring would be the perfect remedy to her insomnia.

"Are you real, or a dream?" A sleepy voice said from behind her.

She spun around clutching her wrap, which was inadequate against both the cold and Daniel's gaze. Her heart leaped into her throat. It had never occurred to her anyone else would be up at this hour. "My lord."

"You must be real. If this were a dream, you would not look

so shocked and afraid. If this were my dream, you would not be clutching that thin white wrap as if you needed protection against the horrible Lord Marlton. If this were my dream, you would come to me with your arms outstretched pleading with me to make love to you. If this were my dream..."

"All right. Enough. I think it is quite clear I'm real and this isn't a dream." His ridiculous monologue had eased her fears.

He chuckled and sat up. His eyes traveled down to her bare feet. He stared at them and smiled stupidly. "Are you cold?"

"What are you looking at?"

"You have the prettiest feet, Sophia."

"Are you drunk?"

"A bit."

"I must go." She ran for the door, but stumbled. Remaining alone with the drunken Earl of Marlton was not an option. A drunken man was the worst kind, dangerous and unreasonable. Besides, if someone found them, she'd really be ruined.

Even drunk, he was swift and grabbed her arm stopping her escape. "Do not run away. I only want to look at your feet." Then he looked at her eyes. He reminded her of a lost puppy. "Why does no one call you Sophie?"

Her heart pounded, and she pulled her arm. Firm but gentle, he held fast. "My brother does, but he is the only one."

"That is strange. You seem more like a Sophie to me. Sophia is so formal."

"I shall allow you to call me Sophie if you will let me go."

"Will you promise not to run away immediately?"

"As long as you keep your distance, my lord." Why had she made that promise? She should have demanded he allow her to leave. What if a footman walked in? She and her aunt would have to leave the house. Daphne would likely send her back to Philadelphia.

He let her go and backed away several steps. His legs

wobbled and he struggled to keep his balance. "If I ask you a question, will you answer me honestly?"

Still, there was something lovely and intimate about being in his company. In spite of his having drunk too much, he drew her in, and she loved the look of him. "Either honestly or not at all."

"Why did you refuse Pundington?"

"Tom told you?" How could Tom call himself her friend and then go running to Marlton with her secrets?

He shook his head. "I overheard."

"You were eavesdropping."

He shook his head emphatically and gripped the back of the couch when he lost his balance. "I came to check on you and overheard. I apologize. If I were a better man, I suppose I would have immediately moved off when I heard the nature of the conversation, but I'm only human, Sophie. I wanted to know why Lady Blyth's words had upset you to the point of nearly fainting into your plate."

"And did you learn anything?"

He shrugged. Then he moved a step closer. "Not enough."

She backed up a step, but he pursued her until he backed her up against the door and hovered over her. His hands caged her in on either side of her head.

His breath was sweet with spirits, and her heart pounded.

She was afraid, but also curious about her desire to be near him. Never had she wanted to be this close to a man and certainly not one who'd been drinking. She whimpered as his head came down and he kissed her neck. She turned her head away. "Please don't, my lord."

"My name is Daniel." He traced a path, with his tongue, up her neck to the soft skin behind her ear.

His mouth sent a jolt down her body. Her legs felt weak as if she too was drunk. She gasped. "Daniel, please."

"Please what, Sophie?" He kissed her jaw and neck pushing away her wrap and grabbing her by the shoulders, he pulled her against him.

She froze. Any curiosity she may have had turned to terror when she felt his shaft hard against her center. Caged and helpless she waited for the pain to come. Tears streamed down her face. "Please, stop, Daniel. Please."

He pulled away and took her face in his hands. Staring into her eyes, her fear seemed to sober him. "Shh, sweetheart. No one is going to hurt you." He picked her up as if she was a child and placed her gently on the couch, then backed away continuing to study her.

She sat up clutching her flimsy white wrap at her neck. "Don't look at me like that."

His eyes were like hawk waiting to pounce on its prey. Once again, a victim in a melodrama, she loathed herself.

His voice was soft. "Sophie, I look at you as a man looks at a woman he wants to make love to. I can look at you no other way."

Wiping away her tears, she sat up straight. Deep breaths steadied her nerves as did the fact he wasn't going to rape her. It was only her fear creating the drama. "I'm sorry for making a scene. I have been quite a bit of trouble for you, and I apologize. Generally, I never cry or faint, and I don't usually traipse around in the middle of the night. I couldn't sleep and I thought a book might help."

"Sophie?"

She looked up at him, but not into his eyes. His intense eyes would only make her cry. Something needed saying, but she was not at all sure what it was. "Thank you for not ravaging me, my lord."

"Go back to your room, Sophie. It might be for the best."

She practically leaped up from the couch and ran to the

door. She didn't even say goodnight before leaving the library and running up the steps to her room.

The hunting expedition was not as much fun as either Thomas or Daniel anticipated. For one thing, they both had a terrible head the next morning. The second problem was there were two nitwits following them around giggling and asking stupid questions.

Serena asked, "Mr. Wheel, why is your gun so much bigger than his lordship's?"

Thomas said, "They are both exactly the same size."

Then, both girls bounded into gales of laughter.

Sylvia asked, "You have shot so much more pheasant than his lordship, Mr. Wheel. Are you not the much better shot?"

Thomas said, "His lordship is by far the better shot."

Serena said, "You seem a much finer walker than his lordship, Mr.Wheel."

Daniel tried to hold back his grin, but failed miserably. He looked down at Thomas's feet. "Definitely a much finer walker, Tom."

"Oh, shut up." Thomas rubbed the side of his head.

It was a shame the silly girls had followed them and because of them, the hunt was cut short. Daniel had wanted to speak to Thomas about the preceding evening with Sophia. Of course, the account would have to be abridged. He would never disclose some of what had occurred, but why had she been afraid of him? Why had her eyes turned from the lioness to a kitten about to be drowned? Something had happened to this girl and he was determined to know what it was.

However, the presence of the twins forced them back to the

house early, and he didn't speak to Thomas about Sophia or anything of importance.

After luncheon, everyone went out to enjoy the stunning weather. A game of ninepin began. Each team had two people and for fairness, each team was a man and a woman. Sophia was not at all sure who had designed the teams, but she suspected it was Aunt Daphne because Daniel Fallon and she were partners. Thomas was Dory's teammate. Sir Michael had arrived and with him two other young men, Walter Gautier, the future Viscount of March and his brother, Hunter. They each partnered one of the Dowder twins. Markus and Emma rounded out the teams.

Sophia had never seen the game before so Daniel explained. "The idea is to toss the ball and knock down as many pins as you can. The team that knocks all the pins down in the least number of throws wins."

He stepped closer to explain the rules, but she stepped away keeping her distance. He might have forgotten the events of the night before, but she hadn't been drinking and her memory was clear. "I'm not very good at sports, my lord, so I'll apologize now for the aggravation I'm about to cause you."

Amusement spread across his handsome face. "We shall manage."

Dory and Thomas took their turn.

The ball was made of some kind of wood. It was half again as big as Dory's elegant hand and she had quite a bit of trouble tossing it. She did manage to knock down three pins and everyone clapped encouragingly. Thomas only knocked down two, but Dory missed her mark on her next throw. Then Thomas took out three more and left only one standing. Dory came close, but she missed on her third try, leaving Thomas to finish the play.

"Six balls," Markus announced. "Dorothea, you really have always had the most abominable aim."

Dory shrugged prettily. "You try it then, if you think it's so easy."

Nodding, Markus and Emma stepped up and waited for the footmen to set the pins back in place. Emma threw the first ball, knocking down two pins. Markus followed, managing to fell four and everyone cheered the feat. Then, with remarkable aim, Emma hit two more pins. Markus missed, and he cried out in anguish.

Sophia laughed at how seriously he was taking the game.

"My brother is very competitive," Dory explained.

"So I see," Sophia said.

Markus patted his wife on the back. "It is up to you then, Em."

"Really, Markus. It is only a game." Emma rolled her eyes and took the ball. With a show of excellent skill, she knocked down the last pin and Markus whirled her around in celebration.

Then it was Daniel's and Sophia's turn.

Daniel asked, "Shall I go first?"

She nodded, and he leaned over and tossed the ball toward the pins knocking down four.

Nervously, Sophia took the ball. She concentrated on the pins and tried to imitate Daniel's moves. She looked down at her positioning to see if she had it correct and was horrified to see how much of her breast was showing. She looked up at Daniel hoping he hadn't noticed. However, his eyes were unabashedly staring at the flesh swelling above her dress.

When he raised his eyes to her face, she tried to give him a scathing look.

He just shrugged.

Heat bloomed in her cheeks, and she turned back to the pins. She swung her arm and the ball came out, sailing off to the right, so far past the pins, one might think Sophia was playing an entirely different game.

Gales of laughter followed.

Sophia covered her face and laughed.

Daniel looked at her and then in the direction of the lost ball. "Her aim is a bit off, but I think that is the farthest I have ever seen a woman throw a ball."

"I think it was headed toward the lake, my lord," Dory said.

"I'll find it," Sophia offered. "After all, it was my throw." She was still laughing, as she headed off in the direction of the lost ball.

Daniel followed, after having to forfeit their turn.

He walked up next to her. "Have you always been so disabled, Sophie?"

"I'm afraid so, my lord."

He frowned. "Daniel. My name is Daniel. You called me that just last night and yet this morning we are back to a formal address."

"I'm surprised you can remember last night, my lord." She exaggerated the formality.

"I remember, Sophie. I'll never forget how you looked in your nightdress or how sweet your toes were as they curled into the carpet." He touched her arm, but she jerked away.

"What are you afraid of?" His voice was so soft, so compelling that she stopped and turned toward him.

She struggled for the words. "I'm not afraid so much as I'm being smart about things."

"Smart about things," he repeated. "What things?"

"You. I'm trying to be smart about you. I don't want..."

Frustrated that the words escaped her, she shook her head and walked on to search for the ball.

He followed.

She looked under a bush and behind a tree. It must have rolled down the steep hill leading down to the lake. She started down slowly, but took off faster and faster until crashing into the lake was inevitable. She could throw herself to the ground, but getting wet was better than risking injury by hitting the ground.

Daniel reached out and pulled her back from the edge of the lake. She slammed soundly into his chest.

His breath was rough with exertion.

"Thank you, my lord." She panted and stared into his eyes. She had no time to think before his lips were on hers. Inside her head screamed for her to push away, but the sensation was so wondrous. His lips were so soft and his arms felt warm and safe. She sighed and relaxed into the kiss. His tongue gently demanded she open for him. When she did, he sighed. His tongue swirled in and out of her mouth in an irresistible rhythm that muddled her mind.

She tentatively touched her tongue to his, and he moaned deepening the kiss.

His breath was warm, and he tasted of coffee and a taste uniquely Daniel. She loved his arms around her. He was a wall to retreat behind and nothing would hurt her. He whispered something in her ear as he spread kisses across her cheek.

His kisses distracted her so much that she didn't understand his words. The tingle, which had begun in her belly, now settled between her legs, and she was certain she should push him away. Unique in beauty and tenderness, she'd never known anything like it.

His hands roamed up and down her back, and his kisses became more ardent and forceful.

Delight turned to fear, her heart beat harder, and her mind filled with the horrors about to happen. She remembered the searing pain of the night in her father's study and the shame that had followed. Sophia pushed him away. When he didn't immediately release her, she pounded on his shoulders.

He stopped kissing her, but he didn't let her go. He crushed her to him. "Sophia, stop this. I'll not harm you. I'll not do anything you do not wish. You are hysterical and must stop this now."

In spite of the force of his words, his voice was soft and calm and it was that steady calmness that made her listen. He was not forcing himself on her. He wouldn't throw her to the ground. He wasn't raping her.

She was safe. She stopped struggling and cried softly into his chest.

"It's all right, sweetheart. No one will hurt you again." He stroked her hair. "I promise I'll always protect you."

When she thought she could, without bursting into a fresh bout of tears, she looked up at him. His eyes were so blue and so filled with warmth and something else she dared not even think.

"Shall we sit?" He didn't take his gaze from hers.

She nodded and swallowed down another bout of tears. It wasn't easy, but she managed to sit down on the grass and look out over the lake while maintaining her composure. Hundreds of thoughts ran through her mind. What made this different than what had happened with Alistair Pundington? Why had Daniel stopped when she asked? He was a man. Her mother had told her, as an explanation for her uncle's behavior, that men couldn't help themselves. Yet Daniel had stopped on more than one occasion as soon as Sophia panicked.

"I know you do not wish to talk about this, but I'm going to ask you a few questions I hope will only require yes or no answers. I would like for you to answer them honestly." She focused now on her slippers, which the run down the hill and the wet ground near the edge of the lake, left ruined.

"Can you do that for me, sweetheart?"

"I'll try," she whispered.

His voice remained soft and kind. "Alistair Pundington claims to have had you in the way a husband takes his wife. Is this true?"

Oh good, she was ruined. When would this nightmare ever end? She tried to answer but a whimper was all that escaped her lips.

"Sophia, please answer." He touched her cheek, brushing a tear away.

"Yes." Tears ran down her face unchecked and unstoppable.

He dropped his fingers away from her face and his hand fisted in the grass. "He took you to his bed and had his way with you?"

"No." A mouse squeaked louder.

"No?" His voice was louder now, not as sweet as a moment before.

She lifted her arm to cover her face and head.

There was no strike.

Silence fell between them. "I'll not harm you, Sophie." His voice was soft again. "What do you mean? You said he had you."

She cried harder. The world crumbled around her. How had this happened? Why couldn't she have had one nice season in London and then retired to the country for the rest of her life? Why did Daniel Fallon have to have come into her life and ruin everything? "There was no bed."

"What happened?" No kindness remained in his biting

remarks. "Were you in such a hurry he took you on a floor, in the garden? Where did this lovemaking take place?"

"Not love," she wailed as her breath came in short gasps. She hadn't realized how much she wanted Daniel to understand until that moment, but she saw now, it was never going to happen. She no longer saw love in his eyes, only hatred and disgust.

"Not love? Lust? Where did this lusty encounter take place?" His eyes were so bright with anger.

Caught between fear for her safety and the desire for him to understand, she gasped for breath. She would likely never see him again after this week, but she wanted him to think well of her. At the very least, he should know she wasn't a whore. "My lord, I shall say this only once and really it is none of your business. I'm nothing to you. We barely know each other." She filled her lungs. "When I was sixteen, a man whom I had known all my life, dragged me into an empty room in my own home where he raped and beat me. You may call it anything you like, but you may not call it love. What I know of men is violent and hateful and has nothing to do with love."

His eyes flashed ferociously and his hands balled tearing grass from the lawn.

Running wasn't out of the question, but she was tired of being a scared mouse. She didn't even know why she'd told him. It wasn't his business. Somehow, she just wanted him not to hate her.

His eyes softened as he seemed to recover from his shock. When he spoke, he said the last thing she'd ever expected to hear. "Marry me."

She must have lost her mind. Had the Earl of Marlton just proposed marriage after learning she was not a virgin? The entire world had gone mad. She stared at him, sure she looked a proper fool.

He watched her and his expression softened even more. He touched her damp cheek. "Marry me."

"I cannot."

He took her hands in his and kissed the back of each while staring into her eyes. "Sophie, I want you to be my wife. Marry me."

Sophia turned her head and looked out at the lake. "I shall never marry."

"Because you are afraid of your wedding bed?"

Even the mention of a bed sent a chill of fear through her. Her body stiffened and all her muscles ached with the effort it took her to keep herself from running.

"What happened to you was an act of violence, Sophie. I swear to you that could never be the way with us. I would never harm you. You may trust me."

She laughed at that. "Really? A moment ago, I would have sworn you were ready to strike me. Go back to your opera singer, Daniel, or find yourself a proper English bride. I'm not for you. I'm not for anyone."

His eyes widened, and his neck pinked. "First, I would never strike you or any woman, but let's put that incorrect assumption of yours aside. I would like to know what you intend to do with the rest of your life. Die an old, impoverished spinster?"

She wiped her face, expecting to see a smirk or a look of superiority but his frown was sincere. Sorrow lived in the depths of his eyes. How adorable those eyes would be in the faces of their children. A vise wrapped around her heart. She would never have children or grow old with someone. "My aunt has generously offered to make me her companion and leave me a cottage and sum upon her death."

"And that is what you want, to be an old maid with no life beyond some cottage in the country?"

Somehow, he'd made something quite pleasant sound lonely and dark. "Don't worry, my lord, I shall manage."

He ran his hand through his hair felling the wavy locks from their queue. "But I shall not."

If she hadn't known better, she would have thought he was truly injured by her rejection. She stood and brushed out her dress. "Oh, I think you'll be just fine. You are the type of man who always survives. You are the type of man who will never lack for the company of women."

"I want you."

"Yes, so you said. I have also made it clear I do not wish to marry. You will have to look elsewhere. I'm sorry." She said all of this graciously and in what she hoped was a slightly haughty tone. Whenever Lady Collington used an air of superiority in her voice, people tended to listen to her and not argue.

"Sophie." It was a whisper. He still sat on the ground, but he looked up at her in such an imploring way she wanted to kneel down and take him in her arms. She wanted to protect him, to cradle him and in turn, to be comforted by him. Impossible.

"You want me, too," he said.

Snapping her head around, she looked out toward the lake. She needed answers, but she had none. She didn't understand the feelings she experienced when she was with Daniel, but she knew fear and whenever his desire for her grew or their kisses went too far, terror filled her and she wanted to scream. She wouldn't make a good wife. That much was certain. If she couldn't perform her wifely duties, he would go to his opera singer or some other woman and that would be unbearable. "It makes no difference. I cannot be a wife. You have seen what happens."

He stood and faced her. "Then the only reason you will not

marry me is because you think you will never make me a proper wife in bed. Is that right?"

She nodded and in spite of the fact she wanted to appear worldly, her cheeks were on fire, and she trembled.

"What if I said I would not demand that of you?"

"Really, Daniel, you must think me a fool. You will not do without your husbandly rights. No man would tolerate that. Besides, you must have an heir."

"True." He put his hand on his chin and stared at the ground. "I have an idea, but it will require you to be quite a bit forward thinking."

"I'm an American."

"You don't trust men because of what Pundington did, and I understand that. What you know is violence and pain. I want to prove to you that what happens between two people who are in love bears no resemblance to what you have experienced. I suggest I come to you tonight after the others have gone to sleep. You will have to trust me, my love, but if I can prove we will satisfy each other in every way, will you marry me?"

The sound of her own heart beating was so loud in her ears it drowned out all the other sounds of the country. The idea didn't repulse her. If she was honest with herself, she found the notion rather exciting. A clandestine meeting with Daniel in her bedroom while the rest of the house slept.

"I think I must sit down." She plopped herself back down on the ground. He sat too but fidgeted and plucked at the grass. His eyes remained downcast and nothing about him was the Earl of Marlton. This was just Daniel.

"I agree to your terms, but I would ask one thing."

"Anything." His smile was so bright she almost forgot her demands.

"I would prefer to wait until tomorrow night. It has been an exhausting day and I don't think I can take much more drama."

He examined her. "Promise me you will not run."

She thought her best curse word. "I promise."

He reached out and helped her to her feet. "Very well then."

She took his hand, and he pulled her forward until he kissed her nose. "It shall be tomorrow. I'll come to you one hour after everyone has retired. Send your maid away and leave your door unlocked."

Chapter Eleven

They didn't find the ball. When they returned from the search, Daniel laughed and joked with the others while Sophia prayed she didn't become ill.

"Oh, Sophia, your slippers are ruined," Elinor said. "No wonder you look so unhappy. Your feet must be freezing. You should go back to your room and put on a new pair."

Sophia looked down at her feet. The light pink satin slippers were now dark where the water had soaked them and mud had caked all around the bottom edge. It was rather uncomfortable now her attention was on it. "I'll go directly."

Elinor smiled. "I'll go with you. The game is over, and I would like to rest a while before dinner. I think Lady Marlton intends for there to be dancing later tonight. Wouldn't that be lovely?"

Elinor didn't require an answer. She talked all the way back to the house. She talked about her dress and the dress she would wear later that evening. She talked about Sir Michael and how wonderful he was and how attentive. Her monologue was so thorough, Sophia was now in possession of the knowledge that Sir Michael and his friends would be staying the entire week. And wasn't that exciting?

Sophia nodded when it was necessary, which wasn't often. She was glad for the company and the constant chatter as it kept her from dwelling too long on the events of the day or the promise she had made.

"Tomorrow we have planned a nature walk. Lord Gautier, it turns out, is an amateur botanist and has agreed to take us all out and explain the local flowers and plants for us." Elinor never lost her enthusiasm for whatever subject she flitted to.

Sophia forced a smile when it became obvious Elinor wanted some reaction. "Really? Won't that be nice?"

"Sophia, really, they are only slippers. You should not get so upset about your clothing. I'll admit they were a lovely pair, but you have others and I'm sure Lady Collington will replace those as well."

Sophia giggled. Daniel and the following night bounced around her head and were so incongruous with the chatter from Elinor. It was funny. "You are right, Elinor. I'm just being silly. Everything will be all right."

"Of course it will." Elinor patted Sophia's arm.

Once she was alone in her room, she considered her agreement with Daniel. All she had agreed to was to allow him to try to make love to her. He would stop if she asked him to. He'd proven that. She also knew she would never be able to go through with it. The deed was too horrible. She cringed at the idea of ever letting anyone do to her what Pundington had done. She would allow him into her room and a few kisses, which she would enjoy tremendously. There was nothing at all to worry about. Pleased with herself, she lay back on her pillow. She had not slept the night before and it had been a difficult day.

Daniel left the playing field and went to his study where he planned to get some work done before dinner. It was almost half an hour later, and he still sat aimlessly staring out the window and wondering how he would ever manage to wait a full day and a half to touch Sophia again. The fact he was begging a woman to marry him when few days ago, he would have bet a thousand pieces sterling he wouldn't marry until Janette forced him to do so, amused him. Now, he worried he wouldn't be able to convince her that he was the one for her.

One thing was certain, Sophia was afraid and with good reason. Another big problem, Alistair Pundington, and how to deal with him. Destroying that evil bastard topped Daniel's to-do list. His hands balled into fists on his desk.

"You look about to have a pugilistic endeavor, Dan." Thomas stood in the doorway. "I hope I am not the object of your rage."

Daniel relaxed and waved Thomas into the room. "Close the door. I'm glad you're here, I need to discuss something with you."

Thomas's brow rose, and he sat stretching his legs out in front of him. "Oh?"

Daniel stood and paced. He clasped his hands behind his back and walked from one end of the room to the other. His friends from Eton found amusement in his pacing. It was some-thing he did whenever he had a lot on his mind and needed to sort through it. Thomas had dubbed it "the earl walk" years ago.

"What is it, Dan. Has someone died? Blyth, perhaps? You do not have to protect me. If Lady Blyth has turned toes up, I can take the news."

He stopped pacing, not minding that his old habit gave

Thomas an opportunity to poke fun at him. "I have decided to marry Miss Braighton."

Thomas's smile faded. "I see. Has the lady agreed?"

"Not yet."

"Are you telling me this because you would like me to withdraw my proposal?" Thomas sat as if he hadn't a care in the world, but his eyes showed he was not entirely happy with this development.

Daniel sat across from Thomas. "Are you in love with her?" It annoyed him how much he was worried about how he might answer. The fact was he would be Sophia's husband and if that meant Thomas would be hurt, he would regret that, but it would change nothing.

"Of course not. Though, I'm fond of her and I would not like to see her hurt."

"And you think I will hurt her." Daniel did his best to hide his relief.

Thomas leaned forward and put his elbows on his knees. "I think she is the perfect woman for you, Dan. I'm sure if you allow her to, she will heal all your wounds. I'm also aware you have never recovered from your last engagement, harbor deep issues about women and fidelity, and you will make Sophia suffer for those issues. Are you in love with her?"

"Maybe." He ran his hand through his curls. "I cannot seem to do without her. She is all I think about. Is that love?"

"More likely lust, but it's a start." Thomas's good humor returned. "I'll withdraw my proposal, but I warn you if you do not marry her, I will."

"I'm going to marry her, Tom." His stomach did a little flip when he said the words. It was not at all unpleasant.

"Shall we drink to it?"

"An excellent idea."

Dinner was similar to the evening before, except Sophia sat closer to the head of the table. Tom was on her right and Emma on her left. Lady Blyth sat at the other end of the table speaking loudly to poor Serena who looked ready to cry.

Regardless of how annoying the twins were, Sophia felt a great deal of pity for the poor girl's situation.

"Do not look. You will get drawn into it," Thomas warned.

She turned toward him. "Tom, don't be so cruel. The poor girl is going to need your help in a moment, just as I did last night."

"Let March save her. I have done my part already this week. We have enough men to rescue young women for each day we are forced to dine with Lady Blyth." He spoke softly so only Sophia heard.

Sophia giggled. "I suppose that's true. What if the other men here are not as gallant as you and leave the poor girl to be devoured?"

Thomas sighed dramatically. "I have faith in my sex, Miss Braighton, but should they fail, I shall be forced to swoop in and save all the fair maidens."

She continued to chuckle and the second course was brought to the table.

Just then, Lord March got up and offered the teary girl his arm and the two of them left the dining room.

Sophia would have to ask the cook to send a small plate up to Serena's room later so she wouldn't starve. When she looked down the table at Lady Blyth, she was babbling to Aunt Daphne as if nothing had happened. Sophia shook her head and turned back to her meal.

Daniel trusted Thomas with his life. Still, the exchange between him and Sophia forced a wave of jealously over him. He pushed away the foolishness, praying in time he would be able to watch his wife interact with other men without having the urge to bash someone in the face.

The notion made its way into his mind that this beautiful American would soon be his wife. Joy started as a bud of warmth in his belly then expanded outward until it engulfed him as if it was a wool blanket on a cool night. Now he only needed to convince her that she needed him just as desperately. His train of thought had him pondering the following night's clandestine meeting. His groin tightened and the necessity to think of something else became urgent.

"My lord, do you agree?" Dorothea Flammel broke into his daydream. "I beg your pardon, my lady, I was lost in thought. What am I to agree to?"

"Sir Michael and I were just discussing the conditions of coal mining sites."

Daniel raised an eyebrow. "I did not realize your interests ranged so widely, Lady Dorothea. What position did you take on the matter?"

"I believe it is the responsibility of the government to make certain the people of England are not taken advantage of by greedy landowners." Her voice firmly dared anyone to challenge her.

Sir Michael weighed-in without fear. "It is the obligation of the landowner to keep his own people safe, my lady. When government involves themselves in our everyday existence it can only cause chaos and misery."

"What is your opinion, Lord Marlton?" Dory asked.

Sophia and Thomas had turned away from their private discussion to hear what he said. How much did his little American beauty know about politics? He hoped she was, at least, curious. He couldn't wait for evenings filled with hearty debates with his wife.

Daniel left a pregnant pause to gather his thoughts and focus on the issue. "I think it is best to leave government out of the day-to-day workings of local business. However, if there is a misuse of the citizens of England, then it is the responsibility of the government to investigate, step in when required, and make provisions when necessary."

"Spoken like a true politician." Thomas punctuated his comment with a chuckle.

"I don't know," Sophia said. "As an American, I believe government should stay out of the lives of its citizens. However, greed can often lead people to forget they have those lives in their hands. The landowner must not only think about the men who go down into their mines but also the families of those miners. If the men in charge do not consider such issues, then government must create regulations to make them do so."

"A rather naïve view, Miss Braighton," Sir Michael said.

Her response pleased Daniel more than it should. Perhaps it was the anticipation of political debate being part of his daily life. "Not naïve, Michael, human. Women have a viewpoint we would do well to add to our own. They think beyond the silver crown. It would not hurt you to go and investigate your own mines and see why they are not profitable. Perhaps it is the treatment of those workmen, which curtails the value of a day's work."

"I did not know you had a coal mine." Elinor spoke up for the first time. Michael smiled sweetly and waved a hand in dismissal. "It's nothing. Just a drain on the family finances. Another one of the bad investments my father made and now I must clean up."

Elinor frowned, but said no more.

The staff cleared the grand parlor of most of the furniture and brought in a pianoforte. Serena, fully recovered from her experience with Lady Blyth, was escorted by Lord March to the instrument and played a reel.

Sophia clapped along with the beat of the happy music.

"Sophia, would you walk with me to the garden? I would like a word," Thomas whispered in her ear.

She nodded. They were in the back of the room and quietly slipped out the door.

Warmer than the previous night, the air was heavy. It was going to rain. They walked across the small lawn leading to the little wilderness-like garden.

"Daniel and I have had a talk."

"Have you?"

He nodded. "Yes. He has told me everything, and I have decided it would be best for me to step aside."

Sophia teetered between mortification and rage. She didn't know whether to cry or find Daniel and slap his arrogant face. He betrayed her. She forced her temper down. "He did?"

Thomas stepped back, his eyes widened. "Well, yes. He told me of his desire to marry you and asked that I step aside. I told him I would."

The breath Sophia held rushed out of her lungs. He had not betrayed her. Her relief was so total she fell mute.

"But Sophia, if you do not have any feelings for his lordship, you should tell me now. I assumed your feelings matched his. I do not wish for you to feel thrown over. I'm still very fond of you and would have no qualms about marrying you—"

"Oh, for Pete's sake, Tom, stop talking. You English are far too loquacious by half. It's like that quicksand I read about. You struggle and struggle and wind up even deeper, when if you would just stop it would probably be all right."

Mouth agape, he stared, then crossed his arms and chuckled. "You are right, of course. We do go on. You should hear Daniel when he gets caught up in a passion about the law or some such."

"I should very much like to see that." She'd seen Daniel's passion but not with regard to politics. She had a glimpse of it tonight at dinner, but he had held back.

"Sophia, should I withdraw my offer? Since I have not yet spoken to your aunt, I shall leave it entirely up to you."

Pushing aside thoughts of Daniel's passions, she focused on the man in front of her. Two gentlemen had asked her to marry them in the short time she'd been in England. Who would have thought such a thing was possible when she had resigned herself to never marry? She touched his arm. "I appreciate the offer, Tom. Truly I do. You are a good and kind man, and I like you, but I'll not marry you."

Sorrow filled his eyes but it was gone just as quickly. "I understand. The Earl of Marlton is an excellent choice. He has been my closest friend for most of our lives. You couldn't do better, and it is always good to marry a man with a title rather than a mere mister."

She gave his arm a squeeze so he would look her in the eyes. "I'm an American. I don't give a fig for titles. I wouldn't care if Daniel were the Prince himself. You shall always be my good friend, Tom, and I would hate to ruin that with a marriage where you would eventually come to resent me."

Laughter and music spilled out of the house and into the garden reminding her their absence would soon be noticed.

"Shall we return?" he asked.

The parlor was loud with both the music and the clomping of feet. Dory danced with Hunter Gautier and seemed delighted with the young gentleman's company. Sylvia Dowder danced with Lord March. Michael and Elinor stared blissfully into each other's eyes. Everyone else had formed small groups for conversation.

Daniel stood alone on the far side of the room shifting from foot to foot. As soon as he spotted her in the doorway, he frowned and stormed over. Was he always so moody?

"My lord."

"Miss Braighton. I trust you enjoyed the night air."

"Mmm, very refreshing."

Thomas trotted over to the pianoforte where Miss Dowder played. "I trust you and Mr. Wheel enjoyed a convivial conversation?"

He was jealous. Why should he be jealous of Thomas? He must have known the nature of their conversation. She looked over at Tom whose attention was riveted on every stroke of the keys. "It was pleasant, my lord."

Daniel watched Thomas. "He cannot resist a good musician."

"Really? Well, Miss Dowder seems accomplished. You know, Lady Dorothea plays the harp, the pianoforte and several others I believe." Sophia looked from Thomas to Dory.

"What is going on in that pretty head of yours?"

She looked back at the earl. "I don't know what you mean, my lord. I just mentioned that my good friend is an accomplished musician. It seemed appropriate to the current conversation."

He hid his laugh behind his hand "Absolutely appropriate. And if I find a suitable moment to mention that fact to Mr. Wheel, would that also be appropriate?"

She shrugged innocently. "It would seem a way to make polite conversation and I know how you English adore such things."

"I shall endeavor not to bore you with my chattiness in the future."

"I did not mean you specifically, my lord." She'd offended him. Why couldn't she keep her mouth shut? "I'll admit Americans are not as good at being polite even when we try. Perhaps it is rather, especially when we try."

He laughed. "Do not fret, Sophie." He bent down until his lips almost touched her ear. "I'm certain you will insult me many more times as we barrel through our life together."

A shiver ran up her spine and her breath caught. "I have not agreed to marry you, my lord. Do not presume I will. I'm quite sure you will, unfortunately, be disappointed."

His expression was neutral, but his eyes laughed at her. "I do not think so."

She was about to argue, but the music changed and was too loud to have a conversation.

Chapter Twelve

The Viscount of March's enthusiasm with regard to the natural world was without equal. Sophia stumbled through the wilderness after the group. She'd worn good sturdy shoes, but after an hour and a half of walking and stopping and walking; she was bored, tired, and her feet ached.

"This is hawthorn. There are two sorts of hawthorn. One way to tell them apart is to squish the red berry between your fingers." And his lordship did so. "If it has one seed inside, then it is the normal hawthorn but if there are two or three seeds it is a Midland hawthorn, which we will see growing more often in woods rather than hedgerows."

Sophia had no idea the outcome of the berry squishing experiment as she distanced herself to avoid listening too closely to the lesson. A butterfly flew across the path. The pretty insect was so filled with life and fancy it made her smile in spite of her desire to be anywhere else.

Lord March's delight equaled hers as he grabbed it harshly off of the flower it was investigating. "Sixteen species of butterfly have been recorded here, including Brown Argus and

Marbled White. The butterflies are attracted by nettles, thistles, knapweed, trefoils, and brambles." He then dropped the poor dead creature on the path.

"My lord, what causes these holes in the old trees?" Serena Dowder asked. Miss Dowder's enthusiasm seemed to equal the viscount's.

Sophia groaned inwardly. The death of that beautiful butterfly had decimated the small bit of enjoyment she'd taken in the walk.

Dory pulled at her arm holding her back even farther, though they could still hear the response.

"Green, Great Spotted, and Lesser Spotted Woodpeckers rely on the standing dead wood to make their nests in late winter and early spring so they are ready for egg-laying in late March or early April. They will often occupy the same holes year after year." That garnered a round of oohs and ahs.

He went on to tell about a pretty white starburst of a flower, which he called bladder campion.

Dory tugged on her arm. "I cannot take any more of this drivel. I think we have listened long enough. Let the Dowder twins have their time flirting. Let's you and I go for a walk."

Sophia cringed. "My feet are aching, Dory. Can we find a place to sit down? Is there no place in this wilderness to take a seat for a while?"

"Let's go and look." Arm in arm they walked away from the rest of the group.

It was a long walk, but Sophia was happy to get away from the crowd. "Are you interested in Mr. Gautier?"

Dory sighed, and her shoulder slumped. "No. He is handsome, kind, and of an age, but he has a wild reputation. Where his brother is titled and a bore, he is poor, untitled, and far too rakish for me. I think I shall find myself an intellectual, but one who is not quite as dull as The Viscount of March."

"Are you sure such a man exists?"

"No, but it's just as well. I much prefer to concentrate on my music for a while. At least until my parents force the issue. I should be able to beg off for one more year and perhaps in that time we shall meet such a paragon."

"My aunt has given me leave to never marry," Sophia said. "Really, why? Have you told her about your trouble in America?"

"Yes. I told her everything when the gossip was in the papers. She has promised me a home and an income, should I choose not to marry."

"That is very generous." Her voice was distant and there was a long pause. "Are you certain that is what you want, Sophia?"

"I can't marry." She said it forcefully but her stomach soured at the idea of a solitary life in the country. Would she have friends? Perhaps she would find a cat to keep her company on the lonely nights.

They arrived at a pretty arbor covered with pink roses. She was close to tears at the sight of the bench beneath it.

"I thought you and his lordship were getting along rather well," Dorothea said.

Sophia shrugged. "I like him, but how can I marry him? He will need an heir, and I can't give him one. It would not be fair to marry anyone."

"I would think you will want to have a child, Sophia. To me, it is the only good reason for marriage. I cannot wait to hold my own baby in my arms and know this little person will love me for as long as I cherish him."

Sophia's eyes filled and her heart ached with the children she would never have. She blinked several times to clear them. "Besides, his lordship has a bad habit of tossing aside fiancées as easily as he does a dirty cravat. I shall not be the next to be thwarted before getting to the altar, or worse, after."

Dory's eyes widened. She touched Sophia's arm. "Dearest, you are mistaken. He had every reason to end his engagement with Jocelyn. It was not a whim. Lord Marlton is an honorable man."

Sophia turned to Dory and took her hand. Had she misjudged him? "I'm not a gossip, Dory, but will you tell me what happened and how you know?"

Dory was quiet for a long time. She looked down at their joined hands. "I was closest of friends with Jocelyn. That is how I know what happened." She looked up into Sophia's eyes. "She'd been my friend since we were in finishing school together and while she had always been spoiled and willful, I never dreamed she would do what she did. Our friendship would have ended much sooner had I known how cruel she really was or how selfish."

Sophia was keen to know Daniel's character. "How was she cruel?"

Pushing a loose curl behind her shoulders, Dory took a deep breath and picked up her chin. "It was shortly before their wedding when Jocelyn told me she was in love with a Mr. Swanery. I advised her she must forget this man. She told me she would not. Her parents prevented her from ending her engagement to a future earl to marry an untitled nobody. She intended to have an affair with this man as soon as she had produced an heir for Marlton.

"I was shocked, told her she was a fool, and Daniel would be a good husband to her if she would treat him well. But she was so selfish, that convincing her proved impossible. I had hoped that once she and his lordship were married, she would see how good and honorable he was, and change her mind. I had further hoped, she would learn to love him since it was obvious he had tender feelings toward her.

"My hopes were in vain. Before they were even married, she began an affair with Mr. Swanery. She was found in an unladylike position with her lover. It was Lord Marlton who discovered them."

"My word." Sophia gulped for breath. "What did he do? Did he strike her?"

"No. He ended the engagement without revealing to anyone why. I only know the truth because Jocelyn told me herself the next day. She was unrepentant and did not understand why he had made a fool of her. It was rather amazing that she felt no responsibility for what happened. I was so shocked I didn't know what to say for a long while, and I allowed her to rant for thirty minutes about what a terrible, and mind you her language was far worse, man Marlton was. He had ruined her, she said. When I found my voice and asked her to leave the house, she was shocked that I did not take her part. She called me some hurtful things and then she left. I have not spoken to her since."

Sophia squeezed her hand. "I'm so sorry, Dory. It must have been terrible for you to lose a friend."

"Worse for his lordship I think. He immediately left England and went to America for more than a year. I think he was truly heartbroken. I have often wondered if Jocelyn had been the least bit sorry for her actions, would he have forgiven her?"

"I cannot imagine he would have. He does not seem the forgiving type."

Dory shrugged. "He is not the same man he was then. What happened changed him, made him more cynical. He might not have returned from America had his father not died suddenly. He had to come back to take over the running of the estates, and he even took his seat in the House of Lords. A lot has happened to Daniel Fallon in the last year."

"I see your point." Taking her hand away, Sophia looked down at her shoes.

"I thought you would be happy to know the truth."

Sophia shrugged. "It makes it more difficult to reject his offer."

Dorothea's bright green eyes widened with surprise. "Has he asked you to marry him already?"

She nodded.

"What did you say?" Dory's grin spread wide and her eyes lit up. Dory didn't need to know about the scandalous promise she'd made.

"I have not replied as yet."

"My word, Sophia, you have only been in England for a month and you have had a proposal from an eligible bachelor."

"Two," she corrected.

Dory jumped out of her seat. "Who else has proposed?"

"Mr. Wheel was generous enough to ask as well."

Dory shook her head. "Indeed! I cannot believe it. I never thought Thomas Wheel would marry."

"He thought we would suit since we are good friends and love would not get in the way of our marriage."

"Goodness, he didn't say that, did he?"

"No, but it was nearly that unromantic. He was very kind. It was his intention to save me, I think."

"I'm a bit jealous," Dory admitted.

Sophia doubted that. "How many proposals have you refused?"

"Eight. But none as intriguing as yours. All the men who have offered for me have been completely unacceptable."

"Really? I understood there was a duke in the mix of your ardent admirers."

"He was forty-two years old. What was I going to talk to him about?" Dory threw her hands up and plopped back down on the bench.

"Indeed." Sophia echoed Dory's favorite word.

"Oh, do not look at me like that. You look just like my mother. I would prefer to find someone I can like. It's not as if I'm waiting on some grand idea of love, for goodness sake. It would just be nice to be fond of the man I marry. Is that so much to ask for?"

"Not at all," Sophia said.

Dory took her hand. "But what of your problem? What will you do?"

"I cannot marry him."

"Excuse my interrupting," Emma walked down the path from the house.

"Not at all," Dory said.

"I'm a bit embarrassed. I didn't mean to eavesdrop, but I did hear you say you could not marry someone."

Sophia shrugged. "That's okay. Everyone will probably find out eventually. I am going to refuse the Earl of Marlton."

Emma had a sweet round face and big eyes the color of the sea. Her curly hair bounced around her face as she slumped down onto the bench across from them. "Dan asked you to marry him?"

"Yesterday." Her flesh was on fire and her voice shook. Fighting tears, she sat up straight and bit the inside of her cheek.

"And you refused him?"

"Not yet, but I must."

"Why? He's a good man. Honest, rich, and titled."

Dory took a breath and raised her hands. "Emma is married. Maybe she can help. Unless you want to discuss intimate details with your aunt?"

Sophia shuddered. "It's rather personal."

Emma stood and rounded the arbor to take a seat on the same bench. "We do not know each other well, Sophia, but Dan and Markus have been friends forever. I would do anything for him, and if he loves you, that extends to you as well."

Swallowing down the bile rising in her throat, she told Emma about her problem. She didn't disclose Pundington's name or that she had been banished from Philadelphia.

By the time she finished spilling the tale, Emma's eyes swam, and she gripped her in a motherly hug. "You poor thing. I want to beat that animal to a pulp for putting you through this." She pushed back and looked from Sophia to Dory. "It is unseemly to tell you anything about what transpires between husband and wife, but I can see this is a circumstance when some things must be divulged."

Dory leaned in and Sophia gripped her hand.

Emma smiled and laughed. "You two look like something out of a Greek tragedy." She sobered. "Nothing about making love to one's husband is comparable to your experience. What happened to you was an act of violence, Sophia. Dan will cherish you."

It took three big breaths to ask, "But the act is the same, is it not?"

With a sigh, Emma nodded. "I suppose. I cannot imagine what you have suffered. My only experience is with a man who loves me. I think you must put what happened with Pundington in the category of a beating rather than an act of love or even sex. I know Dan would never hurt you. If he asked you to marry him, he loves you. Frankly, I never thought he would marry after the mess of his last engagement. Do not turn him away because you are afraid, Sophia. These four men who came through Eton together are good. They served their country and care for their families. Markus might have turned out like his father, but he is honest and loyal. Forgive me, Dory."

Dory waved off the cut to her father. "Father is what he is, and his philandering has made Mother a nightmare as well. My brother is a good man, and he is lucky to have you."

Emma blushed. "I am the lucky one."

Partially relieved and even more terrified, Sophia didn't know what to say. "Thank you for trying to help."

"I hope you will reconsider refusing him, but I wish you well either way you decide."

Sophia hugged her.

Standing, Dory stretched. "I supposed we had better find the others. I would not wish to be branded antisocial."

Sophia flexed her sore feet. "I supposed you're right."

"I have to return to the house before I am missed. I only sneaked away to get a few minutes of peace."

"Is my mother badgering you to have a child again?"

"She is relentless." Waving, Emma took the path back toward the house.

Returning the way they had come, Sophia and Dory ambled through the woods by way of the well-trod path.

The large weight pressing on Sophia's chest eased and her step lightened. "You know, Mr. Wheel is a great admirer of music, I'm told."

"Indeed." Dory rolled her eyes.

"I have it on good authority." She looked at Dory and they both laughed at her obvious matchmaking.

Alistair Pundington peered through the trees. He was watching them. She couldn't breathe. They had to escape.

"Heavens, what's wrong? Are you ill?"

She grabbed Dory's hand and ran, pulling her along behind. Her muscles ached and her lungs screamed for air. She would have screamed for help if she could have spared the breath.

Dory called out for her to stop, but she kept running. He was there, in the woods. Alistair had come for her. The forest blurred past. She stepped in a hole and lost hold of Dory's hand. Sticks and leaves flew by as she slid down an embankment and was stopped by a large bush of brambles, which cut into her skin.

"Oh, hell." She heard Dory cry from the top of the hill. "Stay where you are, Sophia. I'll go for help."

"No!" Her heart pounded from panic as well as exertion. Every instinct told her Alistair Pundington meant to have her, and he would stop at nothing to get to her. Struggling for release, she tried to pull away from the thick twisted branches but every move only fixed her more firmly in their grasp. "Don't leave me, Dory. He will find me. Please, don't leave me."

"All right, calm down. I'll stay." She looked this way and that then turned back to Sophia. "I see blood. Are you badly hurt?"

Sophia looked down at her white morning dress and panicked anew. Touching the red splotches, she relaxed. It was only the dark berries causing all the stains. "No. It's the berries. I'm good and stuck though. Every time I move these stickers seem to tie me up tighter."

Dory called for help.

An eternity passed before Daniel and Thomas appeared followed closely by the rest of the party.

"Whatever is wrong, Lady Dorothea?" Thomas asked.

Daniel looked down the embankment. "I think I see the problem."

Thomas looked too. "Seems to be a pigeon caught in your brambles, Marlton."

"Are you hurt, Miss Braighton?" Daniel asked.

"Stop laughing."

"Not hurt." Thomas inspected the area. "How do we get down without falling into the same trap?"

"Marsh, do you have a knife?" Daniel asked.

"Um, yes." The Viscount handed over a small knife.

"Tom, see what you can do from here. I'll go around to the bottom." Daniel's grin was infuriating.

It seemed as if hours passed where they just stood at the top of the hill gawking at her. The women were all being shocked and calling down to see if she was all right, while the men talked incessantly about the best way to climb down and free her. She was so tired of hearing them, she renewed her efforts to free herself. Fabric tore but she was still stuck.

She heard a noise from the other side of the bush. She was just about to scream, when Daniel's face poked through the bush.

"Hello." He sounded jovial, as if they were meeting for tea.

She actually laughed. "Hello, yourself."

"I shall have you out of here in no time. Do not worry."

"I have already done that, my lord."

He continued to cut bits of the brambles away. "How did you get yourself into this, Sophie?"

Her breath came in short gasps. He had been there in the woods, watching her. "Alistair."

Daniel stopped what he was doing and stared at her. "What do you mean?"

"He's here, Daniel, on your property. I saw him. He was watching Dory and me." She struggled again.

He grabbed her leg, and she squealed. "Stop fidgeting. Are you certain?"

"You don't believe me?" Her heart sank.

He cut another branch away. "If you are certain you saw him then I believe you, Sophie. But, what would he have to gain by seeking you out here. He must know he cannot access you on my property."

"He thinks he is above all consequence. He thinks I belong to him. He will come for me." Every word brought her closer to the dread that had gotten her into the brambles in the first place.

She squirmed again and the brambles dug deeper into her dress. "Sophia! Calm down and listen to me carefully. You are not his. He will never harm you again. I'll see to it. Do you believe me?"

She looked at his beautiful face and sincere eyes. Her heart slowed and her breath calmed at his fierce assurance. "I believe you, Daniel."

"Then be still and I'll cut you loose."

He did just as he said and in a few more cuts, she was free. Her dress had not survived. Stickers shredded the delicate fabric as Daniel lifted her out of the bushes. Sophia was similarly scratched in dozens of places, which couldn't be mentioned, but she was free and otherwise unharmed. Though, her embarrassment was considerable. Her face burned with mortification. "Thank you, my lord."

He bowed. "At your service, my lady."

Getting away from him and her total failure to behave like a lady was first priority. "I'll go back to the house."

"I'll walk with you," he said.

She didn't argue. She was more afraid of being alone and having Alistair find her than she was of additional embarrassment.

"Sophie?" he said.

"Hmm." She stared down at her dress. The week was proving disastrous on her wardrobe.

Daniel's voice had taken on an official tone. "Once I have seen you to the house, I'll have to go and look for Pundington. If he is smart, he will have quit the premises, but we must be sure."

"You do believe me then." She relaxed as relief washed over her.

He nodded. "I believe you. I'll take some men with me to look for him, but will tell them you saw a highwayman lurking in the wood. Can you tell a small lie if they ask questions?"

She nodded. "I won't lie to my aunt though. I'll tell her the truth and Dory of course."

He inclined his head. "I'm certain Lady Dorothea and her ladyship will keep your confidence, my love."

She stopped walking, forcing him to turn. "Must you go after him? As you said, he has likely left the area by now. You could be hurt."

He touched her cheek. "I'll be fine. He would never think you would tell anyone whom you saw. He does not know you told me."

"No, I suppose he wouldn't. A proper lady would not have told a soul. A proper lady would have gone to her grave with the knowledge that she'd done right by her family."

"Sophia." His voice was so stern, she snapped her head up. His expression softened when he looked at her. "I'm glad you told me. You are not to blame for violence forced upon you when you were little more than a child. Telling me was the right thing to do. We shall get through this together."

Tears ran freely down her face. His kindness stung as deep as any censure, and she dashed toward the house.

Their delay allowed the rest of the group time to catch up with them. Dorothea and Elinor rushed ahead and hurried Sophia toward the house.

Sophia rushed up to her room where Daphne and Dory joined her. She told them about Alistair Pundington in the woods.

Dory turned white as parchment.

Aunt Daphne's face burned red. Through clenched teeth, she said, "You rest, my dear. I shall have dinner sent up to your room."

It was strange to see her stoic aunt so close to losing control. Sophia's mind raced with what might have happened if she had been alone on her walk or not spotted Pundington when she had. A knot lodged in her stomach, and she brushed away her tears. He might have dragged her away and no one would have known for hours. If he'd left her dead in the woods, it might have been her final resting place. A chill ran up her spine. It was dark when Marie arrived with her dinner. She ate two bites of the delicious fish before pushing the plate aside. She sipped her tea and focused on the warm liquid sliding down her throat to her stomach. "I think I have gone mad."

The empty room did nothing to quiet her worry. She tried to think of something besides his twisted leer peering out from behind a stand of trees. Those pale eyes too big for his face and set too deep in their sockets brimmed with hate and lust. He had smirked when she saw him.

When she attempted to push that thought aside, her mind wandered to Daniel Fallon's intentions to seduce her that very night. Her life was careening out of control.

She placed her palm against her pounding breast and willed her heart to slow its jackrabbit pulse. Whatever the source of her anxiety, the events of the day, or the events to take place in the night, she had to gain control. Bile rose in her throat.

A knock at her door signaled dinner was over. Sophia called for Elinor and Dory to enter.

Elinor bounced and could only sit for a moment at a time before she was up again. "I cannot believe we were so close to a real highwayman. I'm sure he is long gone now that he knows we are such a large group. You have nothing to fear."

"I'm sure you're right."

Elinor clapped her hands and spun around. "The men all went out. Sir Michael told me he saw no one of interest in the area. I really think it is quite safe. Lord Marlton suggests the ladies not walk the grounds of Marlton Hall without a male escort, but I'm sure he is just being overly cautious."

Dory said, "You need not sound so gleeful at the idea of a criminal on the grounds, Elinor. It is not as romantic as it sounds. Sophia might have been injured in that fall."

Elinor frowned. "I'm not gleeful, Dory. I just think the week has been quite exciting so far. Between the highwayman, Michael being here, and how obvious it is Lady Marlton is trying to push his lordship toward Sophia. It is going to be quite a week."

"Nonsense." Sophia's heart pounded faster. If Elinor had noticed, then everyone else had likely noticed as well. "I have detected no such pressure on the earl."

Elinor rolled her eyes. "She invited you here. As well as all of your friends."

"You could say the same about Dory. Plus, Dory is the daughter of an earl. She is a much better match for his lordship."

"I'm not in the scope of her ladyship." Dory's tone left no room for argument.

Sophia waved it off. "I'm just saying it might as easily be

you and have nothing to do with me. Likely it's not about marriage and only about getting away from the city for a week."

"She put you together for the ninepin game." Elinor's tone turned singsong as she dragged out the last few words.

"It was just a coincidence," Sophia said.

Shrugging, Elinor flipped her blond curls behind her shoulder, got up, and smoothed her dress. "Sophia, if you are certain you are feeling well, I'll say good-night. I'm very tired after such a day. I cannot imagine how exhausted you must be."

"I'm fine."

She kissed Sophia's cheek and flounced out of the room.

"Are you really all right?" Dory asked.

Sophia sighed. "I'm bruised and scratched, but otherwise unhurt."

"I'm sure you know that is not what I mean." Dory took a motherly tone.

"I'm a little scared, but I trust his lordship will protect me as he will endeavor to protect all of his guests." Sophia hid a yawn behind her hand.

"I'll let you get some sleep, dearest. I'll report you are in fine spirits when I return to the parlor for dessert."

"Thank you, Dory."

Dory smiled, they hugged for longer than usual, and she left the room.

Sophia slid between the covers. Too tired to worry anymore, she closed her eyes and sank into the soft mattress. The scent of roses filtered through

the open window.

∾

D aniel came to her room and his body simmered when he found the door unlocked. She had left it open for him but fallen asleep. He stood over her bed. She slept like an angel. He had no intention of waking her to follow through with her promise. He feared she would be waiting up for him.

She looked so young and fragile with her hands pressed together under her cheek.

His fingers brushed across her cheek as if of their own accord. She stirred, and he took his hand away. Watching her as her eyes fluttered open, his heart expanded.

"You're here." Her voice was deep and scratchy with sleep.

His body demanded he override his good sense. He wanted to slip beneath those covers and make love to this stunning girl. He'd never yearned for anything more than to prove to her that their lovemaking would be wonderful. Showing her the difference between Alistair's violent act and what they would share was paramount. "I just wanted to check on you."

Her eyes widened. "I promised."

"Not tonight, my love. I'll see you tomorrow."

"I don't want you to think I would break my promise." Her scratchy voice slid away as sleep tried to claim her again.

"You're tired and with good reason. We'll talk tomorrow night." He leaned down and kissed her cheek before turning toward the door. He closed his eyes for an instant to try to quell his raging desire.

"I have made the most superb friends here in England," she muttered.

Was he her friend? Joy warmed him from head to toe. Jocelyn had never thought of him as a friend. She thought only of his money and her social standing. In a way, they had been using each other. Jocelyn had all of the breeding and connections his father had wanted in a daughter-in-law. Daniel had wanted to please his father more than anything. In the end, his own selfish desire to escape scandal cost him the last few months of his father's life.

He'd been in New York when the news arrived of his father's sudden death. By the time he returned to London, the person he most wanted to please had been gone for over a month. He would never receive the approval he craved.

Nothing had gone as planned and Jocelyn was not to blame for all of it.

Much of the fault rested with him.

He loved that nothing about Sophia reminded him of Jocelyn. She was open and honest. Even the guilt he felt with regard to his father bled away in the face of a lifetime with Sophia as his wife. His father would have loved his little American. She was enchanting.

Silently, he left her to her rest and returned to his own room. What was he going to do about Pundington? His crimes couldn't go unpunished as they had for the last three years. Yet he had to protect Sophia from a public ridicule. He would have to find a way to destroy him without involving her. He'd finish Pundington without society at large finding out how or why. Only Alistair need know the reason his world crumbled. He stayed up half the night devising a plan. He was going to need help from his friends.

Chapter Thirteen

Every muscle in Sophia's body screamed for her to stay in bed. If she'd been beaten with a stick, she would hurt less. Of course, that was nearly what happened as she tumbled through the cursed brambles. She groaned and rose slowly from the soft mattress.

Marie helped her into a simple dress of pale peach. Her hair was pulled off her face, but was left loose to fall gently over her shoulders and back. By the time she descended the stairs to the breakfast room, she felt a bit better. Her legs didn't hurt as much and her shoulders hardly ached at all. Her slower pace that morning meant most of the party was already there.

Sophia made a pretty curtsy. "Good morning."

"Are you all right, Miss Braighton?" Lady Marlton asked.

Sophia smiled. "A bit scratched up and bruised, but otherwise I'm fine. Thank you, my lady."

Cissy fussed with her napkin. "We missed you at dinner last night. After dinner we played games in the parlor. I wish you had been there to entertain us with your voice tricks. I want to see if you can do mother."

Embarrassment flooded Sophia's cheeks. She looked at Daniel's stepmother about to apologize for something she hadn't even done yet. The apology died on her lips as Lady Marlton beamed and didn't look at all affronted.

"From what I'm told, I'm sure Miss Braighton is capable of doing a fine impression of me and probably everyone else at the table." Lady Marlton called the footman to refill her coffee.

The heat rushed from her face down to her toes, which were possibly the only part of her not either bruised or scratched. Sophia drank her chocolate and picked at a piece of bread.

"Eat something, girl," Lady Blyth said. "It is no wonder you're naught but skin and bones. You eat like a bird."

She looked back at Lady Blyth and forced what she hoped was a pleasant expression.

Daniel watched her.

She glanced at him but quickly turned away.

After breakfast, she walked in the garden with Aunt Daphne until a light rain forced them inside where they took tea in one of the parlors with the other ladies. She didn't remember the name of the parlor with the red chairs. The house had so many rooms, Sophia had all but given up trying to find her way around without a footman's help.

It seemed she was to be watched like a hawk by both her aunt and Lady Marlton. The two women would not leave her in peace. By afternoon she begged to be allowed to return to her own room for a rest.

On her pillow was a small card and on it written only "Tonight" and signed by Daniel. Her stomach quivered as if she were on another sea voyage.

She tucked the little card into her personal things and tried to rest. She was nervous, excited and maybe a little scared. She didn't know why she was afraid since Daniel had been so kind and thoughtful. She vaguely remembered him hovering over her the night before and, finding her sleeping, only kissed her head. Perhaps the answer was to pretend to sleep when he arrived. It would be late since he had to wait for the party to break up and go to bed. It would be believable if she were asleep. Coward. No, she would keep her word.

She dozed and slept until Marie woke her for supper. The meal and the card games after were a foggy memory. Her mind was so occupied with the night ahead, she lacked capacity to concentrate on either conversation or cards. When she went to her room and told Marie she would undress herself, her voice cracked a little.

"Are you all right, miss?"

She tried to sound calm. "I'm fine. I just slept too long this afternoon and think I'll read for a while before I go to bed. You go to sleep. I'll be fine. I'll ring if I need anything."

Sitting on the edge of her bed, Sophia conjured a hundred different ways to distract Daniel from his quest. She could vomit. She giggled. It would work.

She was still laughing when she turned, and he was there, just inside her door. Her laughter halted as her fear returned.

"Good evening, Sophie." He bowed deeply.

She made a poor effort at a curtsy but any words stuck in her throat.

He lifted a bottle of wine and the two glasses he carried. "Shall we have a glass of wine and talk a while?"

"You want to talk?" she asked.

He chuckled and walked to the small table where he poured the wine and handed her one.

Mesmerized by his gaze, she timidly took hold of the wine. "I don't drink wine." She stared at the candlelight reflected in the deep ruby liquid in the glass.

"Don't you? I thought a glass of wine and a talk might help relax you."

She took a sip and made a face at the sharp flavor. "Conking me on the head with a bludgeon might work better."

His laugh was a deep rounded sound that filled the room and made her stomach do a little dip. "I think my way is better. How are you feeling?"

"I'm fine, my lord." Still, she hadn't moved from her statuesque position near the bed.

He walked to the window perhaps to hide the deep frown.

She assumed his expression was a result of her use of his title.

He opened the window and a warm breeze brought in the scent of grass and wildflowers. "It's a warm night."

She took another sip of wine and found it didn't improve the flavor. "Why me?"

He turned and looked at her.

She still wore her gown from dinner. It was a dark blue, almost black, dress with red beading on the bodice. It made her look quite regal.

"I don't know."

She giggled and took another sip of the wine, but a wave of lightheadedness forced her hand to the bedpost. It had been a few days since she'd eaten much. She put the glass on the table. It wouldn't do to be in her cups with a man already in her room.

He didn't say anymore and the silence drove her curiosity. She moved from her spot and crossed the room to the window.

"You make me feel."

She turned toward him. "Feel what?"

He shook his head. "When I'm with you, I feel everything. I care about things and not only with regard to you. I have sat on my family seat in the House of Lords for a month now, but until the other night's conversation about coal miners, I did not really care about the miners, only the money the coal extraction provides."

"You had no opinion about the workers?"

"Oh, I had an opinion. I have many opinions. But it was your concern that made me think of them as more than a distant issue about how we will heat our homes." He paused a long time and stared out into the darkness. He looked into her eyes. "I think you make me a better man."

"I don't know what to say." Her skin tingled and her heart ached. It was impossible he meant such a thing. Not really.

He touched her arm. "I hope that does not offend you."

"Offend, No. Frighten, yes." She kept her back to him.

"Why does it frighten you to know you make me want to be a man you would be proud of?" His fingers traced a path up and down her arm.

"If what you say is true, you think I'm special, and I'm not. You will be disappointed as my parents were. My brother will not even speak to me because I have let my family down." Tears spilled from her eyes and she dashed them away.

"Sophia, you have not disappointed anyone. It is a marvel you have survived as spectacularly as you have. Most women would have crawled into a cave and let the world go by them or become bitter. You might have married out of duty and made your husband's life hell and your own as well. You did none of those things. You are a remarkable woman."

She laughed, but the sound rang hollow. "That cave sounds rather wonderful to me."

"Yet you did not crawl inside. You became a woman who is a true friend to people she had never met before and for no other reason than you saw they needed you. Miss Burkenstock's reputation might not have recovered had it not been for you. Do you think Dorothea or Thomas would have befriended a person of lesser character? They see in you the same strength I see. It draws people in and makes them want to know you."

Her own parents had banished her from home because she refused to do her duty. Her only sibling had barely spoken to her in years. "I appreciate your words, but I'm no one to be admired."

Daniel turned her around and pulled her close.

Every inch of her body melted into the hard planes of his.

"But you are admired." Smoothly, he removed the pins that held her hair away from her face.

With the removal of each one, her hair came loose and the pins tumbled to the floor.

He threaded his fingers through and traced his thumb over the light scratch just below her eye. "A reminder of yesterday's events?"

"One of many." Her voice sounded distant.

His fingers, as they combed through her hair, sent pleasant shivers down her neck and arms. His eyes were so bright and so blue, he captivated her. "I'm sorry, Sophie. Such a thing should not have happened on my property." He kissed the scratch gently.

She couldn't catch her breath. "It was not your fault, my lord."

"Daniel. My name is Daniel." His fingers traced up her arm and down again. He lifted her hand and kissed a small scratch on her knuckle. Then he turned her palm up and put his lips there for a long second.

She swayed and put her hand on his chest to steady herself. The room grew smaller or perhaps Daniel just took up more of it. His scent filled her head and everywhere his lips touched drew a new sensation, not at all unpleasant.

Emma's words rolled through her head. Could she trust Daniel?

His thumb traced a bruise on the inside of her upper arm. Placing her hand on his shoulder allowed him to bring her closer. His mouth covered the abrasion.

Sophia gasped. His lips on the tender skin sent a tingle in every direction. She should stop him, but what if she didn't want to?

He buried his face in her hair. "This is what heaven would smell like." His breath teased her ear, and he must have found another scratch on her shoulder, because he kissed her there. His fingers undid the ties of her dress as deftly as any lady's maid. With each tie, he pressed his lips to her skin at the ear, neck, arm, shoulder, and the hollow of her throat.

Dizzy with all the new impulses throbbing through her, she gripped his shoulders.

Her dress fell in a pool at her feet and he began on her corset strings. "Are you afraid, Sophie?"

"Yes," she whispered.

His hands stilled. "Should I stop?"

His offer to stop eased her fear. Daniel would not hurt her. She bit the inside of her cheek. "Don't stop yet, Daniel."

Soon her corset followed her dress to the floor and she stood only in her chemise, stockings, and shoes. He lifted her out of the pile of clothes and sat her on the edge of her bed. Kneeling before her, he looked up, eyes filled with passion, and removed her slippers.

When he slid his hand up her leg to her thigh, she gasped for breath as shocks of heat infused her and settled between her legs.

He stopped, met her gaze and waited.

Her heartbeat was fast, but she slowed her breathing. The walls didn't close in. She was anxious, but not terrified. Drunk with the need for more of his attention, Sophia nodded.

Slowly, he rolled her stocking down her leg.

He was so gentle and caring. Still, her breath came too fast as her anxiety built. "Daniel, stop." Gasping for more air, she ordered herself not to allow fear to ruin such an extraordinary night.

He froze in place with her second stocking halfway down her calf. Sitting on the floor, he crossed his legs. "What are you afraid of, Sophie?"

"I cannot do this. I told you I couldn't. I'm sorry, Daniel. I cannot marry you." Tears rolled down her face and she wept into her hands.

"Look at me."

She forced her hands into her lap and did as he asked. Sitting on the floor, he was just Daniel not the imposing Earl of Marlton.

"I'll stop whenever you ask. I'll do nothing that hurts you or scares you. Have I done anything you did not enjoy?"

Actually, everything had been most pleasant. She shook her head.

"Then trust me a while longer, my love. Let me show you this is not about me. Really, it's not even about making love, sweetheart."

"What then?"

"If we are to be married, we will have to trust each other. I almost married a woman who destroyed my faith in women. I was certain I could never trust another with my name or my heart."

"You trust me?" Her chest tightened. He had as much to lose as she did, more maybe. Jocelyn had destroyed his trust and yet he took a leap of faith because he cared for her.

"I trust you with everything I have including my heart, Sophie. I know you will never break my trust."

"I trust you, Daniel."

He kissed her foot where it connected to her ankle.

Returning to his knees again, he kissed a small scrape he found on her calf and then another just a bit higher. Her legs were covered with tiny scratches and bruises and he took his time kissing each and every one.

He slid her chemise up exposing her knee, then trailed kisses along her thigh.

A strange, pleasant tightening in her lower stomach made her close her eyes and she enjoyed the sensation.

Daniel gentled her knees apart and kissed her inner thigh. With his palm on her waist, he caressed to just under her breast.

Her nipples abraded against the fabric of her chemise forcing a moan from her lips.

He touched her nipple, and her eyes flew open. His thumb brushed the bud, and her body quaked anew. "Have I done anything you do not like, Sophie? I'll stop if I have hurt or frightened you."

She shook her head, and her cheeks filled with heat.

Pressing between her knees yet still kneeling on the floor he kissed her nipple and suckled her through the chemise. Wet fabric cooled and excited her. She arched her back and leaned back on her elbows.

He devoured her breast and then the other until her breath came in short pants, which had nothing to do with panic.

Wanting more, she had no idea how to ask.

He lifted her up and slipped the chemise over her head.

So caught up in the sensations and emotions brought on by his touch, she pushed aside her modesty. She should have been ashamed of her nakedness, but it all was too wonderful.

Silky hair grazed her leg, then his tongue tickled the sensitive skin of her inner thigh and then higher until his mouth covered her most intimate spot. She cried out and sat up. "Daniel, you can't do that."

A wicked smile split his handsome face. "You did not enjoy it?"

"I didn't say that. It's not right." She was ashamed of how weak her protest sounded.

"Oh, but everything we do together in private is right, my love. It is only wrong if you do not enjoy it. Trust me a while longer, Sophia. I promise I'll not hurt you. Lay back and trust me."

She did as he asked, and he kissed her again. She gasped and her hips moved up and down. Something was building.

His fingers skirted the rim of her and then one dipped inside. Instead of pain, she felt only pleasure and the thing building rose higher. A second finger stretched her, and his mouth sucked harder. Suddenly, she floated though the bed remained beneath her. Sensations shattered in a million pieces, cascading around and through her. She cried out and arched up.

Daniel lifted her into his lap and held her. Whispering in her ear, "You are so beautiful, Sophie. Relax and enjoy it, I've got you."

She grasped at him while the waves slammed into her and over her. Her body quaked. Slowly, she drifted down to reality. "What was that?"

"That, my love, was an orgasm. Some call it the 'little death' and it is the greatest joy in lovemaking."

When Alistair had taken her on her father's study floor, she'd felt nothing like that. There had been only pain and him grunting like an animal.

She shuddered and pushed the memory away. "Does this happen to you as well?"

He pushed her hair aside and kissed her ear. "It does. Shall I show you?"

If it was possible to give Daniel the same pleasure, then she wanted to know how.

She nodded.

He lifted her off his lap and settled on the bed. Stepping away, he removed his clothes as if they were on fire.

She couldn't take her eyes off him. She hadn't seen a naked man before. Daniel's body was covered in bulging muscle. He was beautiful, and she wanted to touch him, but he removed his britches and a stab of fear shot through her.

He leaned over the bed and kissed her lips. "I'll not hurt you, Sophie."

Beginning to feel as if she was a dimwit, she was unable to put anything to words. The tingling and tightening began again in her chest and stomach when he kissed her. The rush of delight the orgasm brought her earlier was astounding, and she relaxed. She expected him to get on top of her, but he stretched out next to her and kissed her mouth. When his tongue touched hers, she opened and allowed him to deepen the kiss. His mouth found a rhythm and she wanted to become part of it. Soon there was nothing but Daniel, his mouth on hers and his hands caressing her arms and down to her hips.

Sliding his hand over her stomach, he covered her breast, and her breath caught just as it had done the first time he touched her. She arched against his hand and was rewarded by his gentle worrying of her nipple between his thumb and forefinger. She cried out, but he muffled it with kisses.

He slid his knee between hers.

She stiffened, but then relaxed and opened for him. She would do this for him. She squeezed her eyes shut and waited for the pain that was sure to come.

"Sophie, look at me." His voice was a whisper but brimmed with authority.

She opened her eyes. There was strain in his eyes, but tenderness as well. "Do you believe that I'll not hurt you?"

Wanting to believe it was one thing. Actually trusting what she knew wasn't true, something else entirely. She shook her head.

"I promised you I would not harm you. Relax, just a little."

She tried, but when she felt him breach her, she stiffened and waited for the forward surge and the searing pain that would follow. Her nails bit into her palms where she held them at her sides.

He pulled back, and she felt warmth spread between her legs grow as he rubbed himself back and forward against her wetness.

Unable to stop herself, she lifted her hips. In spite of the agony that would follow, she wanted more of him. The pressure she'd felt when he kissed her private parts built again in her lower abdomen and at the juncture of her thighs. It could not possibly happen twice.

He slid the tip of his shaft inside her again, but she didn't feel pain, only a strange stretching then he pulled back. With each advance, he stretched her a little wider and the pleasure built as well.

Unable to voice her own needs, she cried out, "Please."

His face was a mask of tension. He held himself back and then buried himself inside her.

She arched up and he covered her cries with his mouth.

He held still and her body molded around his hard shaft. "Am I hurting you?" His voice had a tight edge to it.

She didn't answer, but her hips rose bringing him deeper.

He groaned and slid out of her before moving in again and again.

Thrusting slowly, he continued to move in and out of her.

The small room filled with her cries and gasps. Waves crashed around bringing her to another crash of rapture.

Daniel cried her name, and she forced her eyes open.

Arched with his head thrown back, he was the most splendid thing she had ever seen. Love bounded around her and through her heightening her pleasure.

He collapsed forward with his weight on his elbows and pressed his forehead to hers.

Warmth spread through her and she was deliciously satisfied. Even if she'd wanted to move, she couldn't.

Daniel took a deep breath, kissed her head and moved to her side wrapping his arms around her.

She shivered and he pulled the covers over them holding her against him. "It was...different," she said. "I had not expected..."

"What?"

"Pleasure." She buried her face in his shoulder.

"There will always be pleasure in our bed, Sophie. You must put what happened to you out of your mind."

"I don't think I can."

"Then, you must try to never think of what we do together in the same light as that violence. Can you do that?"

"Oh yes."

"You are no longer afraid of me?"

She touched his cheek and then let her hand slide down. When her fingers grazed his nipple, he sucked in his breath. Intrigued, she continued to explore his body.

"Sophie?"

"Hmm?"

"I do not think you know what you are doing," he said through his teeth. She smiled at him, feeling bold. "Oh, but I think I do."

He pulled her on top of him and she felt him hard again

and perched at the entrance to her womanhood. Her eyes widened and she looked at him in question.

"It is sometimes nice for you to be in control, my love."

There was power in straddling his lap. He might have wanted to say more, but she slid down onto him stopping his words.

He moaned deep, and she moved, slowly at first but then faster. His hands gripped her hips and helped her find a rhythm.

She wanted to be in command, but the cadence he set started the pressure building inside her once again.

She continued to move and rock and noted how different angles gave her different degrees of pleasure.

A low groan erupted from Daniel, and he arched up sharply. He touched the tight bud between the folds at her core. He rubbed and her pleasure took to new heights while he filled her. She whimpered as the rapture exploded inside her.

Spent, she collapsed on top of him.

He banded his arms around her. "Sophie?"

"Hmm." Sated, her muscles relaxed.

"Will you marry me?"

"I will." She smiled and turned into his chest.

He kissed her forehead. "I do not think I have ever been happier in my life. I wish I could spend the night here, but I must go to my own rooms before the servants start to rise."

He kissed her again, slowly slid out from under her and tucked the covers tenderly around her. "I'll speak to your aunt in the morning."

Warm and completely satiated, she drifted into her dreams.

Chapter Fourteen

"I'm asking for your niece's hand." Daniel's stomach knotted, though he didn't know why. He was an earl, and Sophia held no title. Lady Collington would be foolish to refuse him.

At the conclusion of breakfast, he'd requested an audience with Lady Collington. After a stern look, his request was granted. They went to his study where they wouldn't be disturbed. He stood behind his polished oak desk while the lady sat in an overstuffed chair several feet away.

She raised an eyebrow and watched him. "Why?"

"Why?" he parroted.

"Yes, my lord. Why do you wish to marry her? It is a simple enough question."

Outmatched, he walked over and sat directly across from her. "I'm very fond of her. I think we would suit."

"I see." Her words were emotionless, but her eyebrows rose. "You are fond of her."

"You are not making this easy, Lady Collington. Do you disapprove of me?"

At that, she smiled. "Not at all, Lord Marlton. However, I wish to see my niece happy in her marriage. You telling me you are fond or you would suit does not really bring me the confidence I was hoping for."

"I love her." The admission came on a breath, but he kept his gaze locked with hers.

Daphne beamed. "Have you told her that?"

He had just realized it himself. "Not as yet."

She waved a hand. "That does not signify. Has Sophia agreed to a marriage?"

"She seemed in favor of the idea." He kept any inflection out of his voice, though the passion of the night before filtered through his mind.

"Very well, then I give my consent."

Daniel let out the breath he hadn't realized he held and stood. "I shall obtain a special license."

Daphne stood as well and narrowed her eyes on him. "Why would we need that?"

"I want to be married immediately."

"Out of the question, the gossips would go wild."

"I do not give a fig about gossip."

"Well, I do. She has been through enough since arriving in London. I'll not have her ridiculed further. You may marry in six months."

He wanted to shake Daphne. "Outrageous. Four weeks."

"Four months."

"Two."

"Ten weeks is my final offer. You will not need a special license, and I can possibly get her parents here in that time. She is very close with her father and would be unhappy if he was not at her wedding. It will also allow for a proper engagement where you will be seen out in her company and the banns can be read. Do I make myself clear?"

Sophia would be his. Joy bubbled inside him and he struggled to contain it. "I understand, Lady Collington. You have nothing to worry about. I really am in love with Sophia. I shall not mistreat her or allow anyone to make her the butt of ridicule."

"Very well, then we understand each other. I'll go and speak to Sophia and send a post to Philadelphia. There is much to do. We shall leave for London today, my lord."

Daniel hated the idea that Sophie would leave the house earlier than planned, but he said nothing.

~

True to her word, Lady Collington bundled them into a carriage by the time the midday meal had finished.

Daniel saw the carriage off, having only a moment to say good-bye to his fiancée. He promised the betrothal papers would be drawn up, and he would arrive in London as soon as they were ready for signing.

He kissed her hand and helped her up into the carriage. Her cheeks flushed red. Maybe she too thought of their night together. He wanted to wrap her in his arms, take her back into the house and ravage her while Lady Collington waited in the carriage.

In danger of embarrassing himself, it was with both relief and sadness when he waved them off. Once they were gone from sight, he went to his study. He wrote a note explaining to his man of business what he needed. Then he wrote several to some discreet acquaintances to gain information about Alistair Pundington's business affairs.

His quill snapped.

"Damn!" Daniel sat back in his chair and ran his hand through his hair pulling it free from its queue. His chest tightened to the point of pain at the thought of anyone hurting his Sophie. That Pundington had defiled her, injured her, and tried to use her to gain riches had his fists clenching.

Crossing the room, he poured himself an early glass of brandy and took it down in one swallow. "Damn." He hurled the fine crystal at the fireplace.

~

The rest of the guests were in their beds when Markus, Michael, and Thomas joined Daniel in the study for a brandy. They sat reminiscing about their school days and sipping brandy.

Daniel needed more information and no one was better at gathering evidence than his friends. "I need to ask the three of you a favor, and it would be better if you asked little about my motives."

"Intriguing." Markus smirked.

"What do you need, Dan?" Michael asked.

Daniel looked at his three friends and asked himself once again if this was the right thing to do. These were his true friends. He would die for any one of them, and he trusted them with his life. "I need to know what Alistair Pundington is doing in London, and I need to know what exactly he is shipping and where. If Pundington is involved, I want to know about it."

Michael nodded. "I'll see what I can find out at the docs and gaming hells. My father's reputation makes it easy for me to frequent such places."

"Very good, but be discreet, Michael."

"Naturally."

Markus shrugged. "I know little of the man, but I'll see what my father knows. I'll make up some story about why I need to know."

"Why?" Thomas continued to lounge in the chair as if he didn't have a care in the world. It was his ease of manner that had made him valuable when they were in service of the crown together.

Daniel looked at him a long time. "I'm planning to destroy him."

The two of them looked at each other a long time. Neither one spoke. Thomas didn't know any details. He likely knew enough to surmise it had something to do with Sophia or her family. "I know some people. I'll see what he's been up to. It may take a while and depending on your exact intent, you may need more information than can be gathered in a short time. Building a case may require patience."

Daniel nodded.

Michael poured another brandy. "I'm guessing you have been investigating him yourself."

"I have."

"What can you tell us that might be useful?"

Daniel would have to supply them with some detail. Sophia had already shed enough tears because of Pundington. His throat was tight when he spoke. "Since his business arrangement ended with Braighton Shipping, he has opened his own shipping company, AP Shipping. He has been moderately successful, but in the last year, his coffers have increased substantially. Recently, he obtained some lucrative contracts in London though there is some secrecy over what exactly AP Shipping is importing. Whatever the cargo, it seemed to be in high demand. He just purchased an enormous townhouse and two more ships."

∾

The closer the wedding date, the happier Daniel became. He wished he'd won the battle of wedding dates, but he enjoyed the courting.

Today they had walked in the park, and all of society slowed to watch them.

"Thank you for the walk, Daniel."

Everything about her brought joy to his heart and he likely wore a stupid grin. He took Sophia's elbow to assist her up the steps to Collington House as he'd done almost every day since their engagement two months earlier.

Her warmth touched him even through his gloved hand.

It had been his decision not to repeat their lovemaking. He often cursed himself for that decision. It took every bit of his will to keep physical contact to a stolen kiss or the touch of a hand. Sophia might have been willing to give more, but he took no chances. In fact, he made certain they were never alone together. Even when they walked together, Sophia's maid followed close behind. "It is my pleasure, sweetheart."

On the days when the London rain forbade going to the park they would take tea with her Aunt Daphne. He made sure he showed up at two events per week. He never told Sophia which balls or dinner parties he would be attending. It was a little game they played and he enjoyed surprising her.

The courtship had been wonderful. He genuinely enjoyed being in Sophia's company. They spoke of politics, flowers, the wedding, and their respective childhoods. The only subject that was never again broached was Alistair Pundington. She didn't bring it up, and Daniel was happy not to discuss it since thoughts of Pundington sent him into a rage.

He hadn't disclosed his plans to his future bride. She knew nothing of what Markus, Thomas, and Michael were doing, and Daniel intended to keep it that way.

Wells opened the door before they had made it all the way up the steps of the townhouse. "Miss Braighton, Mr. and Mrs. Braighton, young Mr. Braighton, and Lady Collington await you in the parlor."

Sophia rushed into the house and threw her gloves and hat at Wells. "Papa?"

Wells was unaffected by her behavior and merely caught the outerwear without a word.

Daniel stood in the doorway and watched her curiously. His heart leaped at the sight of her excitement. There was a rift between her and her family, at least that was what he believed, but perhaps he'd been mistaken.

"The family has asked that you also join them, my lord," Wells continued in the same stoic monotone.

Daniel gave over his hat in a much more courteous manner and followed Sophia to the parlor.

Sophia threw open the parlor door and flew into the open arms of a man with blue eyes and brown hair that had gone gray at the temples. She cried, "Papa."

He shushed her and petted her hair.

Staying in the doorway, Daniel waited. He didn't want to intrude. Sadness bubbled up from his gut. She'd been all his until now. After two months of her undivided attention, he would have to share her. He pushed away the childish notion.

Lady Collington sat on the couch with a dark-haired woman with eyes the same color as Sophia's. She was perhaps forty, and except for the fact that Mrs. Braighton's skin was darker, Sophia was the image of her mother.

A young man with dark hair and the same golden eyes focused solely on Daniel.

Daniel entered the room and extended his hand, but said nothing. Sophia's brother was little more than a boy and had every right to look him over.

Their eyes met and for several beats, Daniel thought Anthony Braighton wouldn't take his hand, but then his eyes changed from wariness to acceptance. Anthony extended his hand. "Anthony Braighton."

"Daniel Fallon."

Daphne continued the introductions.

Sophia, now seated with her mother, Angelica, continued to cry. It took about ten minutes for her tears to play out. She looked up from Angelica's shoulder and saw her brother, Anthony for the first time. "Hello."

"Hello, Sophie."

Charles Braighton appeared to be amiable. The Braighton men were extraordinarily tall. Both stood several inches above Daniel's six feet.

Mrs. Braighton spoke with a thick Italian accent, which made English sound romantic and mysterious.

Mr. Braighton said, "Lord Marlton. I want a word with you in private, if you wouldn't mind."

"Father, whatever for?" Sophia asked. He ignored his daughter.

Daniel nodded, and followed Sophia's father across the hall. He didn't look back, but he heard his fiancée's trepidation.

"Mother?"

Angelica's richly accented voice followed. "Eet will be fine, my dear. Just something a father must do."

They entered a masculine study with a small desk and several groups of chairs for easy conversation. Dark wood paneling covered the walls and a chessboard was set up in the corner. Charles Braighton poured a brandy and lifted the decanter toward Daniel.

"No, thank you," Daniel said.

Standing stiffly, Braighton sipped brandy and acted as if he was reading the titles of books on the shelf. "My daughter."

Daniel was unaccustomed to being nervous, but if the butterflies in his stomach were any indication, anxiety had definitely made its way into his life. He fisted his hands. No one would stop him from marrying Sophia, not even Charles Braighton.

"She has been through a lot. I'll expect if I allow this marriage, you will always treat her kindly." He put the glass down on the desk.

Daniel's gut twisted. Every muscle clenched. "Of course, sir."

Braighton turned. "I knew your father. We were in school together. He was a good and fair man. Devastated when your mother passed."

Daniel just watched and waited.

"I want her happy." It was an accusation.

Daniel pulled his shoulders back. "I want the same." Charles Braighton's face grew red. His eyes narrowed.

Daniel thought the man might be ill, but he said nothing. It took all of Daniel's will to remain quiet while Sophia's father made some internal decision.

"She may be afraid on the wedding night. She has good reason to be." He struggled between protecting his daughter and keeping her secrets.

"Your daughter has done me the honor of telling me of her past troubles."

Braighton's eyes widened. He sat behind the desk and leaned forward on his elbows. "Has she?"

"Yes, sir."

"That surprises me. You want to marry her even though you know she's not a virgin?"

Daniel's rage erupted as if he were a volcano. He bit his tongue. "I proposed after Miss Braighton had entrusted me with the information."

Braighton smiled and leaned back. "No need to get offended. It is unusual to find a man who does not mind his bride being tainted."

"She is not tainted. She is perfect and any taint is on that bastard." If any other man had said those words, Daniel would have challenged him at dawn. As it was, he had to grip the back of a chair to keep from rushing at Charles Braighton.

Braighton's face was still ruddy as he moved to the chair next to Daniel. "You need not convince me, Marlton." He rubbed his face, which seemed to have aged since he entered the study. "I didn't do my duty. I failed to protect her. I pray you will do a better job."

Daniel debated what to say next. "I shall do all in my power to keep her safe, Sir. I feel I should tell you Pundington is in London."

Braighton's face reddened even more.

Daniel returned his voice to its usual calm. "I wonder if you would be willing to share information with me, sir?"

"Information about that blackguard?"

"Yes, sir." Here was a man who had all the information to further Daniel's goals. It was too important to let pass regardless of Braighton's obvious distress.

It was over an hour before they left the study.

Chapter Fifteen

D aniel waited on top of the steps at St. George's as
Sophia's carriage rumbled to a stop.

Delight shone in her eyes, and she took his breath away.
Wrapped in white silk and lace she might have been an angel.
His angel, with dark curls situated atop her head and tiny
pearls entwined throughout.

She touched the rich blue stones of the sapphire necklace
he had sent as a wedding gift and smiled up at him.

It was the greatest day of his life. Nothing could compare to
standing at the altar with Sophia and hearing the vicar
pronounce them husband and wife. It took a force of will to
keep his tears of joy at bay.

He longed to pull her into his arms and kiss her breathless,
but settled for a kiss on her knuckles when they exited the
church. "I'm very happy, Sophie."

"Oh, Daniel, I've never been happier in my life."

He handed her into the carriage and climbed in after her.
As the horses pulled away from St. George's, he scooped her up
and settled her on his lap.

"Daniel." His name floated on a gasp.

It was a sound he could listen to forever. He covered her lips with his, and she melted against him. All the weeks of behaving like a gentleman and waiting culminated in this kiss. He ached for her, all of her.

Sophia clung to his neck and back. She opened for him and their tongues danced and swirled together until he was ravenous to have her naked and beneath him. Pressing her chest against him, she wiggled her bottom in the most maddening way.

He broke the kiss. "If we arrive at your aunt's house naked, we will make quite a stir, my love."

Gulping down air, she settled back on the cushioned bench and patted her hair. "I'm sure you're right."

The carriage stopped too soon for Daniel's liking. He closed his eyes, willing the effects of their intimacy to dissipate enough to step down and hand her out of the carriage. Damn his driver for efficiency, the door swung open and the step pulled down far too soon.

Aunt Daphne hosted a wedding breakfast following the service. In the late afternoon, the bride and groom escaped into a carriage and started their journey to Marlton Hall. They didn't stop, as would have been expected at such a late hour and so they arrived in the middle of the night. Sophia was so tired her husband carried her up to the master's rooms.

Daniel sent Marie away, saying he would attend his wife.

Sophia stood in the middle of the room, her eyes half-closed and swayed slightly with exhaustion. Gently, Daniel undid the ties crisscrossing her back. The dress pooled at her feet. The corset followed. Dozens of pins and the pearls spilled from her hair.

He cursed at the quantity of pins, but finally, her hair fell into loose curls around her shoulders.

He lifted her in his arms and carried her to the bed. The bedding had already been pulled back and he positioned her on the soft sheets and covered her before removing his own clothes and climbing in next to her.

"Do you want me to remove my chemise?" She yawned.

He'd scarcely stopped grinning since the pastor declared them man and wife. "Sleep."

"But it's our wedding night." Her protest came on yet another gaping yawn.

"My penance for not staying in London. It was foolish to drag you up here on your wedding day. I'll see you in the morning, my love." He kissed her cheek and watched her.

A protest built behind her eyes, but then they closed. An instant later, she slept. Whatever argument she was about to make would keep until morning.

Amazed the exquisite woman in his bed was his wife, he struggled to close his eyes. He watched her long into the morning hours. He wanted to kiss her pert little nose, adoring the way it tipped slightly up at the end. Her skin was as rich as warm cream, and he longed to stroke her cheek. He let out the breath he'd been holding. Taking one of her luscious dark curls between his fingers, he allowed the silky tresses to slide back to the pillow where her hair fanned out like black flames.

"Mine." He had to push away thoughts of Pundington lest his rage get the better of him. He must keep calm with regard to that bit of business. Nothing must get in the way of avenging Sophia and keeping her happy.

The corners of her lips tipped up while she slept.

"No one will ever harm you again." He made the vow so softly even he didn't really hear the words and yet they vibrated in the air.

Sophia rolled to her side away from him.

Daniel wrapped his arms around her, and she snuggled

back until her bottom was nestled against his manhood. She had no idea what she was doing to him.

He didn't know when he fell asleep, but he woke with the sun streaming into the room and his wife still nestled against him. His reaction was immediate. He pressed forward, rubbing himself against her bottom.

She mumbled something and wiggled her bottom. "Do you know what you are doing, my love?"

She giggled. "I think so. Am I doing it right?"

Taking her hips, he pulled her even harder to him. "You are doing it exactly right."

He reached around and covered her breast with his hand. Her nipple beaded against his palm, and his shaft jerked with anticipation.

Her back arched and a soft sigh escaped her lips. She rolled around to face him. She bit her bottom lip and frowned. "You should tell me if I'm not. I know I wasn't...I'm not..."

He ran his knuckles from her cheek just under her right eye to the tip of her chin. Leaning up, he kissed her little nose as he'd wanted to the night before. His thumb swept across her lips and continued to follow her cheekbone until he buried his fingers in her mass of hair. He cupped the back of her head and brought her lips down to his. He kissed her deeply and then more tenderly. "You are exactly as you should be, Sophie."

She smiled shyly, but the tigress shone in her eyes just before she wrapped her arms around him.

Suddenly, she pulled away with wide eyes staring at his nakedness. Tentatively, she touched him, then more boldly. The palm of her hand skimmed his skin slowly over his nipple and then down his stomach where she stopped.

He covered her hand with his own and helped her until she held him in her hand.

She gasped.

He gasped for entirely different reasons.

She hesitated and faltered, only grazing him with the tips of her fingers.

He hadn't known how erotic it would be to have her investigate his erection with such innocence. He held as still as possible, not easy while his body strained for more of her touch.

Her fingers continued to drive him mad. Her eyes widened as his skin stretched taut, and her strokes became more ardent.

His hips automatically moved counter point. Clasping her hand, he pulled it away from his rod and rolled on top of her. "I can take little more of that."

"You didn't like it?" Even though she asked it in her most innocent voice, the mischief in her eyes told him she knew the effect she was having on him.

He leaned down and pressed his lips to hers.

Her mouth opened on a gasp, and he slipped his tongue inside. His moan mingled with hers.

Her body was warm and pliant beneath him.

"I think you saw that I liked it very much, but much more would end this far too quickly. I want to enjoy you a while longer."

He rubbed against the juncture of her thighs. Then he moved aside and slid his hand down between them. What he found excited him as much as his first encounter. Her folds were soft and wet.

She arched and bucked against his fingers while he worried her bud.

Sophia's breath came in gasps, and she tightened under his touch.

Holding his weight above her, he poised his shaft at her core and slid forward slowly.

Their cries mingled in the air. He tried to hold still while she adjusted to him, but the sensation was so overwhelming.

She moved, and he lost control. He pulled back and thrust forward with more force than he wanted to use.

The way she snugged around him was heaven.

He reached between their bodies and rubbed her sensitive bud.

She rose up to meet every thrust and called out his name. She screamed, and her body pulsed around him. Her contraction took him over the edge as well.

He arched into her and shuddered before collapsing on top of her. Far too heavy for her, he scooped her up and rolled over so she lay on top of him.

She rested her cheek to his chest and sighed.

S he didn't know how long she'd slept that way, but she woke to his maleness hardening, as he slipped back inside her. Why did women not speak of how wonderful this was? If not for Emma's honesty, she might have died without ever knowing.

Hours later, tucked together as if they were born to fit perfectly, she wanted to sleep. Her stomach had other ideas. "I'm starving."

He shook with laughter.

She rolled around to face him. "Are you planning to starve me to death?"

He laughed harder. It was rich, warm and filled the room and her heart. "No, you will need your strength."

She raised an eyebrow. "Why is that, my lord?"

Grabbing her waist, he pulled her against him. "Because I'm planning on us spending a lot of time in this bed over the next few weeks, and I do not want you to wither away."

She slapped him playfully. "We cannot just stay in this room. What will the servants think?"

His smile was mischievous. "You want to make love in other rooms?

Hmm, the library has a lovely rug. We could certainly try that."

There was a new space in her heart and it filled with Daniel. She pushed away from him, but not with any real urgency.

He tightened his embrace keeping her close. "You are incorrigible, even for an Englishman."

He tickled her ribs sending her into fits of giggles. "Let's get dressed and see if there is any food to be had, wife. Shall we?"

Her cheeks ached from smiling. Wife sounded so lovely coming from his lips. Joy bubbled in her stomach and spread outward, filling her. For three years, she'd convinced herself she would never be called such a thing. Now, she was most definitely the wife of Daniel Fallon. Her heart beat with excitement.

Sophia ate ravenously. A short time later, she leaned back in her chair and placed her hands on her stomach. "I cannot eat another thing."

"I'm not sure that, as The Countess of Marlton, you should sit in such an unladylike position," he teased.

She sat up straight and her heart pounded. Dear God, she'd forgotten. "Countess."

"Yes, indeed. You are the sixth countess to date and by far the loveliest."

"Don't say that in front of your stepmother."

"In mother's presence, she is, of course the loveliest of all Ladies Marlton."

"My, but you are a fickle friend."

"Not at all. You shall always know to me, you are the most

beautiful, and my stepmother can remain happy that her son adores her. What can possibly be wrong with that?"

"Nothing. You are the perfect son and the perfect husband."

"You had better wait to make that judgment, love. You have only been married to me for twenty-four hours. I'm sure to disappoint you at any moment."

"Never." She crossed her arms.

"Shall we walk some of this food off in the garden, or return to our bed?" He raised his eyebrows dramatically.

She giggled. "Can't we walk in the garden tomorrow?"

With no further prompting, he grabbed her hand and they rushed up the steps to the bedroom.

Three days later, the butler, interrupted their dinner. Dorn looked as old as the Marlton country estate. He was vertical but only barely as he handed over a note on a small silver platter. "There is a message, my lord."

"Thank you, Dorn."

Dorn waited by the side of Daniel's chair. Daniel looked up.

"The messenger awaits your reply, my lord."

Daniel read the note and frowned. "I'm sorry, my dear. I must answer this immediately."

"Is something wrong?"

"Nothing to concern you. I'll be back directly." He strode from the room clutching the note.

Something was amiss. She finished her quail and poked at the remains. The staff stood around waiting to serve the next course. Sophia tugged on her napkin and smoothed it back in her lap.

Daniel returned, sat and picked up his fork and knife. "What was in the message?"

Posture stiff, he did not look her in the eye. "It was a note from Thomas about some business we are working on together. I have to meet him the day after tomorrow to talk some things over."

"You're leaving?"

"Only for one evening."

"This is our honeymoon, Daniel." She failed to keep her tone even. Daniel nodded at the two footmen standing near the large oak doors,

dismissing them. "I'm sorry, Sophie. I know it is terribly rude of me to leave you even for just a few hours, but this is urgent and cannot wait. Please understand if it were not critical, I should never remove myself from your side."

"I understand." She said it on a sigh.

"Thank you for that."

Biting her tongue against the lashing she wanted to give him wasn't easy. It wouldn't do to become one of those wives who screamed and complained. She didn't want to turn out like Dory's mother.

Daniel left after luncheon on the day of his meeting with Thomas.

Sophia had been so caught up with Daniel, she hadn't met the other people in the house. She trudged down to the kitchen. A shining black kettle bubbled on the fire and filled the lower level with warm spice and rich meat aromas.

Mrs. Grover, the cook, turned from stirring the pot. "Hello, milady."

Sophia stepped closer and breathed in comfort just as she

often had in her family's kitchens in Philadelphia. "I thought you and I could discuss menus and what his lordship likes to eat."

Twice as wide as the pot she covered, Mrs. Grover popped the cover on, pushed it from the main flame and offered Sophia a seat at the gleaming wood table. "I'm sorry to say, his lordship is not a hearty eater. He does like lamb stew, but only eats when called to the table. Though, perhaps that will change now. He was the same as a boy after her ladyship passed and then his appetite improved when the earl remarried."

"Oh? I hadn't realized you were here when his mother died."

Mrs. Grover stood up with a heavy sigh and pulled two loaves of bread from the oven. "I'll never forget that night."

The yeasty aroma filled Sophia with a dozen happy memories and made her stomach rumble in spite of a hearty breakfast. "It was the night his lordship was born?"

Mrs. Grover shook her head and cut a two-inch slice out of one loaf. She slathered it with butter, put it on a plate and passed the sumptuous bite to Sophia. "No, the poor lamb suffered for three days with a fever before the good lord finally took her. The earl was beside himself, he was."

"Terrible." Sophia put the bread down and gulped back a tear.

"He never recovered. Oh, it was better once he remarried, but the light was gone from his eyes. He did adore the little miss though."

"What about the current earl? Did his father adore him as well?"

"Ahhhch." Mrs. Grover shook her head. "That, he never did. He was brokenhearted over his first wife, and he never really got over blaming the boy for her death."

"But, that's ridiculous."

"People do some strange things when they grieve, milady."

"I suppose that must be true."

"Ay, it is." She looked away, lost in thought then smiled. "It was a good day when the old earl married again. We were all so pleased when Lady Marlton fell instantly in love with our boy. She raised him as her own, and she was little more than a child herself. We was all so relieved the poor little boy had a mum to look after him."

Sophia thanked Mrs. Grover and they arranged to meet each morning after the meal to discuss the day's menu.

Wondering what Daniel remembered of the time before Janette had come to Marlton occupied much of her thoughts. He'd been a baby. Did he even want children? After all, they had never spoken of it. Panic roiled in her belly, but she forced herself to stay calm. He had to have an heir and most English gentry liked to have a spare as well. If she were fortunate, perhaps she would have a girl first and then she might have three children. Three is a good number, she told herself. Now that she was married and not afraid of what happens between a man and a woman, she longed to have a large family.

Living in America away from all of her father's and mother's families, she had felt sad during the holidays when their friends would have large family gatherings and they would only have the four of them for company. She would just ask him.

"So, what is it you think he's doing?" Daniel sat in a wooden chair.

Markus's study had few soft surfaces.

Thomas leaned against the large desk, which occupied most of the room. "The thing is, I'm not entirely sure yet."

Renewed aggravation gnawed at his gut. "How hard can it be to find out what a shipping magnate is shipping?"

Markus, having always been the most reserved of the four, reported the facts with little emotion. "It stands to reason that whatever he is doing is illegal, or it would be quite easy to find out."

Daniel nodded. "Braighton told me before they ended their association they were having a difference of opinion as to what type of business they were running. My father-in-law was perfectly happy, and very rich, shipping spices and grains from the east and America."

"This was not satisfying for Pundington? Was he not getting as rich?" Thomas asked.

"He was quite rich, all right, but he'd squandered some money, and he owed someone a favor. Mr. Braighton wouldn't go into detail about to whom the favor was owed. Pundington had to move goods from the East Indies to England, but he declined to divulge to his partner what the shipment was. Under the circumstances, Braighton refused. Shortly after that, they ended their partnership."

"Sugar?" Markus said.

"I cannot imagine Charles Braighton would be offended by the shipping of sugar to his homeland," Thomas said.

"It must be something illegal."

"Absinthe?" Markus suggested.

"Perhaps, but slaves are more likely." Thomas ran his fingers through his hair.

"Slaves, negro slaves, here in England. Who would he sell to?" Markus stood from behind his enormous desk. The out of character outburst turned all their heads toward their host.

Thomas rolled his eyes. "Don't be naïve, Markus. There are people who will buy, even here, on the king's soil. However, if all of this speculation is correct, I have been looking for information in the wrong place. Michael may be having more luck."

Markus said, "Michael is rather bogged down in his own troubles at the moment. His father has left him in a pickle."

"I'll see what I can do. I have some old contacts from the Army who may be of help." Thomas sat in the other chair.

"I would appreciate anything that would make it possible for me to crush Pundington financially. And, if I can get him tossed from England permanently, that would be a great benefit." For the first time in his life, Daniel wished murder were legal. He would thoroughly enjoy killing Alistair Pundington slowly and painfully.

"If he is trafficking in human flesh, I shall be happy to use all of my influence to stop him, Dan."

"I know, Markus and I'll be happy to take you up on that offer as soon as we know for certain what he's up to."

"How is your honeymoon going?" Thomas asked.

"My wife was most displeased when I left today."

"So, it's going well then." Markus grinned stupidly.

Daniel ignored the innuendo. "How about some of that fine brandy you keep in that massive desk of yours, Markus?"

Markus pulled a bottle out of a desk drawer. "What is wrong with my desk?"

Thomas and Daniel exchanged a look.

"Nothing," Daniel said.

"Nothing at all," Thomas agreed.

Markus looked at them both and then smiled. "I know it's a bit large, but Emma purchased it as a gift to me and what was I to do? I couldn't tell her it is far too large for the room. She would have been heartbroken."

"You might consider removing all the other furniture. And we could all sit on the desk." Thomas rapped his knuckles on the desk.

They drank and joked until dusk when Daniel left them to go home to his bride.

~

I t was late when he arrived home, but he found his wife waiting for him in his study.

She wore a blue dress, which was fetching and low cut in the front.

If he took a guess, he would also say his sweet, innocent wife had dampened her undergarment in order to make her gown show every curve to her advantage. He found himself both intrigued and cautious as to why she felt the need to seduce him.

"You are looking lovely tonight, Sophie." He walked in, leaned down and kissed her cheek.

"Thank you. Do you like the dress? Aunt Daphne said it was obscene, but she purchased it for me anyway." She rose and gave a spin so he saw the entire frock.

"Very becoming and perhaps only a bit obscene." He grinned, knowing he must have looked like a smitten idiot. Perhaps there was truth in that.

She looked down at the dress and mumbled something to herself. "Is something on your mind, my dear?"

In spite of the alluring dress and the coy look she'd given him when he arrived, she frowned and plopped down in the large chair opposite his desk. She looked dejected.

He leaned against the desk in front of her. "Something is on your mind." The door opened and a maid carried in a tray with two glasses and a bottle of wine. She looked at the coffee table near the couch and then at the two of them by the desk.

"It's all right, Molly, you may leave it here on the desk."

Molly looked at the earl and then at Sophia's frown. She

rushed over, placed the tray on the desk, curtsied and ran from the room.

Daniel poured the wine. "You have laid an elaborate trap to catch me, Sophie, and you already have me. What happened in the last few hours to make you think you needed to go to such lengths to attract me and why have you given up? I can assure you, your trap would have worked."

She looked up, and he saw the tigress. Then she was gone. "I thought to woo you and then ask you something. But now I'm not sure about the wooing or the question."

He handed her a glass of wine and crouched in front of her. "Ask me."

"I should not."

"Sophia, have I ever been harsh with you? Have I led you to believe you cannot talk to me? You may ask me anything." His heart beat faster. What had changed in so short a time?

"Do you want children?" She blurted it out without looking at him.

A smile pulled at his lips. Relief flooded him. She worried about the most amazing things, his little American. "Look at me."

She did.

"What brought this on?"

"Do you?" she asked.

"I'll tell you when you tell me what brought you to such worry over the subject."

She stood suddenly.

He grabbed the arm of the chair to steady his perch or be knocked over.

She paced. "I was speaking to cook. She told me about your mother passing after you were born, and I realized we had never discussed them. I really don't know you that well, and I do love children. I only have one brother, and he is often reticent. I became worried you would not want children, but I thought if I pleased you it might be possible to talk you into more than just an heir, and so I planned all of this."

He leaned back against the desk. "Do you breathe at all when you ramble like that? I'm very fond of children. I have never given the idea of having them much thought beyond the necessity for an heir. However, I should think as long as your trouble in giving birth to the first was not life threatening, then we could possibly have a few more, if you wish it."

She smiled and jumped around the room until she found him, wrapped her arms around his neck and kissed him soundly on the lips. Her wine was forgotten across the room and his now spilled on the rug. "I'm so glad."

He steadied his breath and controlled his emotions. She bewitched him. "I can see that you are. But I'll not tolerate you taking unnecessary risk, Sophia. One child first and then we shall see."

"Yes, my lord." Her smile remained enthusiastic.

Chapter Sixteen

On the tenth day of their honeymoon, Daniel read a missive and then came to break his fast. "I have to leave you again today, Sophie. I have a meeting."

"Here in the country?"

"It's important. I shall leave after luncheon." She nodded.

An hour later, they were in the garden enjoying one of the last fine days of summer, when Jasper, Sophia's footman, delivered a message to his lady. She opened it, paled, and the paper fell from her hands.

Daniel picked it up from the grass. Lady Collington wrote that Mr. Braighton had been struck down by an episode, and the doctors suspect apoplexy. Heart pounding, Daniel called out to the retreating footman. "Have her ladyship's maid pack her trunks as quickly as possible and call for a carriage to be brought around. You will go with your lady, of course."

Jasper started for the house, but stopped. "My lord, what is amiss?"

Daniel was not accustomed to servants who asked questions, but he accepted that this footman was not English. Besides, the man was concerned for Sophia. "Mr. Braighton is gravely ill."

The footman's eyes widened, and he ran. "Sophia, look at me."

She looked up with vacant eyes.

"I cannot go with you today. I have to attend to some important business. I'll follow in a few days. Do you understand me?"

"Yes, I understand."

Gloom settled over Collington House. Wells opened the door, but said nothing as he took Sophia's hat and coat. She moved passed him into the parlor.

Angelica's eyes were red and swollen. Sophia tried to remember ever seeing her mother cry before and only the night when Pundington had raped her came to mind.

"How is he?" She hugged her.

"The doctor was just here."

"What did he say?"

Angelica's eyes were so sad and lost, Sophia looked at the ceiling or the floor, anywhere but at her mother.

"Your father was asking for you two nights ago. He was a bit confused then he stumbled and fell. He has not woken since then. I talk to him, but he does not hear me."

She hugged her again. "Go lay down, Mamma. You're tired. I'll go and see papa."

The sick room was dark and stuffy. Aunt Daphne sat beside her nephew.

Sophia thought for the first time Daphne looked small and old. "Hello, Aunt."

Daphne stood with the help of the tall bedpost. "How are you, dear?"

"Fine."

Daphne looked toward the door. "Is Marlton here?"

"No, his lordship had business that could not wait." She didn't recognize the cool tone of her voice.

"I see."

"How is my father?"

Daphne shook her head and hugged her. It was the first time Aunt Daphne had initiated affection. "I'll not lie to you, Sophia. The doctor does not hold out much hope. We must pray for a miracle."

Sophia nodded and sat in the chair Daphne vacated. The left side of Charles Braighton's face drooped and his skin was tinged sickly gray. His normally robust presence diminished. The large bed made him look small and insignificant. This man, who had been her whole world for most of her life, reduced to nothing in a sickbed.

"I'll have a light meal sent up. You must eat something." Daphne left. Sophia hadn't realized Daphne was still in the room. Her stomach knotted at the idea of food. When she entered the room the scared little girl of years past pushed past the adult. When she was young, Anthony went away to school, and she was often by herself. She was lonely then and felt the same sense of desertion sitting in the darkened sick room.

She reached beneath the blanket and took his hand. "So cold." She tried to rub the warmth back into him.

"Papa, please wake up now." Holding his hand in both of hers, she leaned her forehead on top of their clasped fingers and prayed. She was still in that position when a maid delivered a tray of food. And hours later when Angelica returned to the room in a fresh dress and looking a bit more rested. Sophia still held papa's hand and prayed while the food had gone untouched.

"Sophia, it is late. Go to bed. I'll sit with him through the night," Angelica said.

"I would like to stay, Mamma."

Angelica walked around the bed and kissed the top of her daughter's head. "Give me a few hours alone with him, cuore mio."

Reluctantly, Sophia left the room and found her bed.

When sleep claimed her, so did her nightmares. She hadn't experienced the terrifying dreams since before her wedding. She'd thought her husband chased her fears away. Not so.

When the terror woke her, the sun was already seeping around the heavily draped bed. She went to the washbowl and splashed cold water on her face.

The dream had always been a recollection of the horrors of the night that changed her life forever, but this time the visions were distorted. The beating was the same, the pain and the realization that someone she trusted would hurt her were still present. When she turned her face up to see his, it was a twisted version of Daniel glowering back at her.

She shook away the ghosts of her nightmare, washed and dressed.

Charles's room was dark and only the man who had comforted her when she was sad and encouraged her throughout her childhood, lay alone in the bed.

She wanted to move the oversized chair to the opposite side of the bed. For some reason, she thought he felt her more if she was on his right. His left side was so limp and lifeless, she hoped to reach him from the other side. She had managed moving it halfway around the bed, when the door opened.

"What are you doing?" Anthony demanded.

She continued to pull the chair. "I want to sit on this side."

Anthony strode over and lifted the chair as if it weighed nothing. "Where do you want it?"

"Just here." She pointed to a spot near the head of the bed. He placed the chair in the spot she requested.

"Thank you."

He nodded, and then looked down at his father. "I never thought to see him like this. I fear I'm ill-equipped to deal with any of this, Sophie."

His admission took her by surprise. They had not spoken in confidence in years. She moved closer, wrapped her arms around him, and put her head on his chest. "We shall all do the best we can, Anthony."

He hugged her briefly. "I should be stronger, but when I see him looking so small, I want to run from this place and never come back."

"I understand."

Anthony walked around the bed, leaned down, and kissed his father on the top of the head. He stood straight again and unshed tears shone in his eyes.

"Why don't you go for a walk? Then you can spend some time with mother. I'll remain with father."

"I think that's a good idea. I would like a walk, or perhaps I'll go for a ride. Some exercise might do me good." He headed for the door, then turned back. "I almost forgot to tell you, I saw Uncle Alistair yesterday."

She balled her fists with rage. "Don't call him that. He's no uncle of ours."

"Why not? We've always called him uncle." He narrowed his eyes at her. "Where did you see him?"

"I arranged to meet with an old school chum from home and we went to one of the gaming clubs. He was there. It was nice to see him. He said he has some opportunities for me. I—"

"No! You are not to have anything to do with him,

Anthony. He is not to be trusted." She gripped him by his jacket. The idea of what Pundington might be up to took her breath from her. His attention on Anthony could only be for malice.

He took her hands and released his clothing. Then he looked her in the eye. His own filled with anger. "Since when do you feel you have the right to tell me what to do? Are you going to tell me why you hate him so?"

He waited for an answer, but she said nothing. Thrusting her hands away, he left the room.

She should go after him and confess everything. If Anthony knew the truth, he wouldn't go into any business with Pundington. Why did everything have to be so complicated? Her life would never be normal. She held her father's hand. It was warm compared to the other side. Perhaps he felt her there and there was hope. "Papa, I'm here. Don't worry, I won't leave you."

She wanted to believe she had felt his fingers tighten around hers, but it was more likely what she wished for rather than reality.

When Daniel arrived three days later, he found Daphne in the foyer gazing up the steps.

"Lady Collington?"

She wore a dark gray dress and looked in mourning already. The wool dress must have been uncomfortable, but maybe that was the point. Her face, which was usually animated, appeared dull and tired. "It is a lost cause now. Only a question of when God decides to take him. Even Angelica has accepted this, but Sophia will not leave him. She has not eaten or slept in two days. We have all tried to convince her that she must take care of herself, but she is stubborn."

How could they have let his Sophie neglect herself? He forced words out through clenched teeth. "Have a tray sent up. Broth and some toast." Daniel took the steps two at a time. He opened Charles Braighton's bedroom door and found his wife thin and slouched over the edge of the bed. Her anguish-filled eyes were red-rimmed and her cheeks sunken. Her hair was in need of brushing and washing and lay straggly down her back. Charles's weak breathing filled the room. Sophia clutched his hand and stared at his face.

"Sophie."

"Hello, Daniel." She didn't turn and sounded as if she'd expected him.

Her voice was bland and cold. "You must eat something."

"Is that all you have to say to me?" She remained with her back to him.

"I understand your anger. I should have come sooner. I could not get away. I'm sorry." He touched her shoulder.

Her spine stiffened. "I needed you."

"I'm here."

"You can go. I don't need you anymore. I can handle this myself. I learned that while you were taking care of your business." The last word bit with disgust. "Frankly, I have nothing left for you, so just go."

"You must eat." The tray arrived.

"Just go." Her voice rose louder than was appropriate for a sick room.

Petting her father's arm, she apologized.

Daniel's anger churned inside, but he remained outwardly calm. "I'll not leave the room until you have eaten, Sophia. If you will take some nourishment, then I shall go."

The look she gave him was hateful. His beautiful, happy bride was gone, and it was at least partially his fault. He should never have left her to deal with this alone.

He watched as Sophia forced herself to drink the broth and eat the toast.

When she finished, Daniel kept his promise and left the room.

He checked on her at regular intervals. Every three hours he had a tray sent up and bullied her into eating. She refused to sleep, so he made sure she was fed.

Daniel stood in the shadows watching his wife pray over Charles Braighton's hand. She'd lost several pounds and her dress gapped along her shoulders, back, and waist.

Angelica arrived in the room late in the evening. She sat on the edge of the bed, facing both her husband and her daughter.

Daniel was an intruder, but he wouldn't leave Sophia again.

Angelica's face was drawn and sorrow filled her eyes. Sophia had told him how close her parents were. Angelica was losing not only her husband, but her closest friend and confidant.

The strength of Angelica's voice surprised him. "Sophia, I think he is holding on for you. You must tell him that it is all right to go. It is cruel to leave him in this state for so long. A man as strong and willful as he has always been is suffering to be left this way. I can barely look at him for my tears blind me to see him. Let him go, cuore mio. I beg of you."

Angelica hugged her daughter and kissed her on both cheeks. She also kissed Charles and whispered something in his ear.

Daniel had never been comfortable with raw emotion. His own father had never shown any signs of sentimentality. As

Angelica passed him, she gave him a sad smile and kissed his cheek before leaving the room.

⁓

After her mother left the room, Sophia sat watching his labored breathing. The weight of the world settled on her shoulders. No amount of prayer would change the outcome. Tears slid down her face.

As the sun tipped over the horizon, she leaned close to him. "I love you, Papa. You have done enough. I'll be all right. It was not your fault and never for one moment did I blame you though I know you blamed yourself. I'm well protected now, and you should forgive yourself. For me, there is nothing to forgive. You have been a perfect father these nineteen years. No girl could ask for more than you have done even putting up with my mimicking you and everyone else at every opportunity.

"I know I should have been a more dutiful daughter and more of a lady like Mamma. I think perhaps you preferred me just as I am and that's why I love you so, Papa. It is time for you to go now. God must need you more than I do. I love you, Papa. I'll think of you always. In every aspect of my life, you will be there." She kissed his cheek.

His breath rattled. He squeezed her hand once more. He left the earth with Sophia's cheek against his and her tears rolling down his face. He was not alone.

⁓

Daniel lifted Sophia away from Braighton's body and carried her to her own room. She slept fitfully, but she slept, and he sat near the bed whenever the business of Pundington didn't call him away.

She called out in her sleep so he moved to the edge of the bed and brushed her hair out of her face. "It's only a dream, my love."

She opened her eyes and screamed. Hands flailing, she cried and fought him as if he were the devil. "No."

"What is it, Sophie?" His gut twisted as if full of live snakes.

"No, Daniel, not again. Why? Why have you done this?"

She made no sense. It had been necessary to remain in the country, but he was still riddled with guilt. Was that the cause of her nightmares? It seemed unlikely. There was no sense in dwelling on it.

"What do you dream, Sophie? Tell me." He held her, but she struggled against him.

After a long struggle, she calmed. "I cannot." Her eyes closed, and her exhaustion claimed her again.

He released her and touched her cheek still wet from tears.

Again, she slept fitfully, but he allowed her to sleep through the dream. He'd only made it worse by waking her. Tortured by the idea that she feared him, he had no idea what caused her agitation. Deciding it was only the shock of losing her father, he let it pass.

They traveled to the country to bury Charles Braighton in the family plot at Grafton Hall. After the funeral, Sophia returned to London. She made it clear she would prefer to travel alone, but Daniel sent his stepmother and sister with her.

Daniel followed a few hours later and his arrival at the townhouse created quite a stir. He hadn't lived there since leaving school.

Janette glided into the foyer. "I thought it would be you, Daniel. Your rooms are ready. I have moved to the rooms at the other end of the hall. They are quite comfortable and the light is good. Sophia is settling in nicely. Cissy and I will remove to the country as soon as it can be arranged. I thought the Dulcet estate would suit us nicely, if you agree."

The Dulcet estate was a small holding on a pretty piece of land about an hour's ride from Marlton Hall. Janette had always admired that house. "Dulcet needs work. I shall commission workers immediately and you can oversee the changes if you wish. Cissy must have her season. You should stay here, Mother."

She shook her head. "You and your new wife will want to be alone. It is not right for me to remain in Fallon House when I'm no longer the countess here. Sophia deserves to reign over her own house."

"You are very thoughtful. I insist you stay until I can find you a suitable house in town. Cissy should not miss the remainder of her first season. Sophia will not mind, I'm sure. Where is my wife?"

Janette frowned. "She is depressed, Daniel. She went to her room, and I had to command her to come down and eat luncheon. I believe she would starve if someone did not demand she eat something."

His jaw tightened. Daniel was used to fixing things, but he didn't know how to make this right. "I believe you are correct, mother. We shall have to continue to remind her until her appetite returns."

Janette nodded.

Taking the steps two at a time, he bounded up to see his wife. It was amazing how much he'd missed her even though she was not herself. He knocked on the door to the master's suite and when there was no answer, pushed the door open.

Empty. Dark wood, a perfect bed dressed in royal blue with gold trim, two stuffed chairs by the fireplace, Daniel's trunk at the edge of a blue on a cream wool rug awaiting his valet's attention, but no sign of Sophia. It appeared his wife had not even stepped into this room.

A surge of anger started in his heart and rose up to his throat. He tried to control the rage, but when he knocked on the adjoining lady's chamber, it sounded as if an intruding army had come.

"Come in." Her voice was calm, but not welcoming.

He opened the door and strode in. "What are you doing in this room?" Her eyes were wide and red from crying. "I was given to understand that this is my room. Janette insisted I take it, and she moved down the hall. If she has changed her mind, I can certainly move."

He took several deep breaths while he tried to get his temper under control. Reminding himself of her loss and her obvious distress, he began slowly, knowing losing his temper was not an option. "Janette is quite content. I had hoped you and I would share a room as we do at Marlton. Why would you think to take this room?"

"My lord, it would be better if you would respect my decision and return to your own rooms." She sounded like a countess.

"Why. What have I done? I have done nothing. I could not come to London at that moment, Sophie. The matter I attended to was equally urgent. It is not as if I left you alone. Your family was with you. You were cared for." His voice rose in spite of his efforts to stay calm.

"What matter was so urgent?"

He struggled for a heartbeat to find a calm tone with which to respond. "I cannot discuss my business with you at this time."

She turned her head, but the weepy tone returned. "Go away, Daniel."

For several seconds he watched her. "I implore you not to do this, Sophie. Do not destroy what is between us."

When she didn't respond, he walked through and closed the door.

Chapter Seventeen

When she didn't come down for meals, Daniel sent trays up to her. He accompanied the tray and watched, refusing to leave the room until he was satisfied that she'd eaten enough.

It grew cold in London and Janette and Cissy prepared to go to the country. The house was in a constant state of motion with all the packing and preparing. Still, Sophia didn't come out of her room.

He never missed a meal and little progress was made with regard to Pundington. If he didn't keep his wife healthy then there was no point in destroying the man. He needed to be present at meal times and soon realized, even if she said little and didn't appear happy to see him, he enjoyed seeing her. He contented himself in the fact she never demanded he leave.

"Janette will move to Dulcet Hall soon." Daniel tried to draw her into conversation with small talk.

"What is that?" Her voice rang with concern.

"A lovely house we own not far from Marlton."

"It will be nice for her to be close, but she need not leave Marlton Hall on my account."

Her good nature filled him with joy. "I told her as much, but she insists that you must have your own time as countess without her interference."

"I'm sure I should not mind her staying." She looked out at the dreary day lost in her sorrow once again.

"I'm buying her a house in London as well. She refuses to come back here next season. I believe I have found something suitable. Would you like to come and see it tomorrow?"

She shook her head before he'd even finished the question. "Another time. I'm tired, my lord. I'll sleep now."

"You sleep too much, Sophie. You need to get out of this room."

"Soon." The word rang empty and false.

At some meals, they wouldn't talk at all. They would eat, then he would leave and return with the next meal. He never asked her to come back to his bed. She would have to make that decision for herself, though he hoped she would return soon.

Often, they would speak of the weather. Mostly, he would tell her it was a fine day, and she should consider walking in the garden or the park, which she always declined.

His worry increased with each day she refused to leave her room. Mrs. Braighton had visited, as had Lady Collington. Neither had managed to get Sophia to rejoin her life.

Daniel sat with Dory and Elinor while they waited in the parlor. "I'm sorry for the wait, ladies."

Elinor sat with her feet crossed and her hands on her knees, perfectly comfortable. "It is no trouble, my lord."

Dory narrowed her eyes. She paced like a warrior about to

enter the battlefield. This was the third day in a row Sophia's friends had come to see her. They had been sent away the last two days as Sophia refused company.

Daniel sent up a prayer that today would be different.

Janette entered the parlor frowning with her hands clenched. "Ladies, I'm sorry, but the countess is not ready to receive company at this time."

Elinor nodded and rose as if to leave.

Dory pursed her lips and put her hands on her hips. "I have called these past three days and been told the same thing. It is enough."

"I'm sorry."

"So am I, Lady Marlton. Please forgive me." Dory walked past the dowager countess, into the hall and strode up the steps.

Both Janette and Elinor stared after her with open mouths.

Daniel laughed. "Have I ever told you how much I admire Dorothea Flammel, Mother?"

S ophia made no response to the incessant knocking on her bedroom door. Maybe they would just go away if she ignored them.

Dory pushed through and hovered over her. "I have called for three days and written you letters."

"Hello, Dory." Her heart ached, and not even the sight of Dory brought any joy. She looked out over the gardens. She was still in her white dressing gown in spite of the noon hour.

"Hello, yourself. What is going on? Why have you refused to see anyone? There are people who care for you, Sophia. Thomas Wheel has also called a number of times. I saw him last evening at the Blessington ball and he asked me how you are. I told him that I have no idea."

Part of her was dead. Everyone should see that and leave her alone. "You could have lied."

Dory gaped. "Lied? What in the world has happened to you?"

Sophia did her best to hold back another bout of tears. "Nothing really. People lose their parents every day."

Dory rushed over and knelt in front of her chair. She clasped Sophia's hands. "I know you are hurting and you miss your father, Sophia, but you cannot stop living. You must go on and this is no way to do it."

Turning her head, she pulled her hands away. She wanted to scream or beat someone until they felt as bad as she did. "You would have me out at balls as if nothing was wrong?"

Dory touched her cheek. "No, dearest, not that, but I would have you washed and dressed each day and perhaps taking a few callers who wish you well. No one expects you to go out dancing, but you should get out of this room."

When she said it like that, it seemed like so little to ask. Sophia hung her head and let out a breath. "I'll get dressed."

"Every day." Dory's voice took on the warning tone, which sounded like her mother's.

"I'll get dressed today and come and have tea with you." Even the thought of it exhausted her.

"If my presence is required then I shall come calling each day and drag you down for tea. If you can do it today, then tomorrow will be easier and the next day even easier. Promise me you will dress and have tea in the parlor every day."

Sophia heaved a deep breath. It was such a small thing. "I promise I shall get washed and dressed every day."

Dory narrowed her eyes and frowned.

"And go down for tea." It came out on a long-resigned sigh.

"Good." Dory paused. "I do not know if I should bring this up, but there have been rumors, Sophia."

"What rumors?"

"They are saying your marriage is failing. It is none of my business, but servants talk to other servants, and they tell their employers. That is how rumors get from household to household and then to the ballrooms and clubs. I do not know what has happened between you and his lordship, and I'll not ask. I would like you to know, that if you need to talk to someone, I'm here for you. You should be careful, dearest. The ton is a cruel lot and they can tear down even a strong marriage."

"Then mine should be an easy effort for them." Daniel would be happy to be rid of her. She might get her quiet home in the country after all.

"Do you want to tell me what has happened?"

"No. Nothing has happened. I'll get dressed and come down for tea if you have time to wait."

Dory stood. "I'll send in your maid and see you downstairs."

As promised, she washed and dressed before joining her guests. She said only what polite conversation demanded.

His lordship excused himself after she entered the room. It was kind of him to sit with her guests while she was above-stairs. Likely, he didn't want to start a new bout of gossip. Sophia's heart pounded watching him go, but she sat and had tea.

~

The crowd at Whites pressed in so Daniel stood near a fireplace rather than try to squeeze into one of the card tables. He sipped his whisky and watched the crowd.

He was in a temper after having just wasted ten minutes fending off regrets about his failing marriage. How the ton always knew when one's throat was exposed, he would never know, but they did. As always, their teeth bared for the kill.

Determined not to allow such things to interfere with his personal life, he sipped his brandy and readied himself for the next wolf. As soon as he figured out what troubled Sophie, they would work out their problems. She had every right to be upset about his delay in getting to London, but he was sure there was something else, something to do with her dreams.

Anthony wound through the crowd and shook his hand.

"You have not come to see your sister." Daniel failed to keep his disappointment from his voice.

"I have my mother to worry about. You can take care of my sister." With a pout, Anthony fisted his hands and crossed his arms over his chest.

"Your mother has come to call almost every day."

Anthony glared as if he might use those fists he still held tight. "Sophia and I had an argument when last we spoke. I'm not in any hurry to renew that disagreement."

"What was it about?" Daniel asked.

"Our uncle."

"Pundington." Daniel fairly shouted the name before realizing the crowd had turned toward them.

Anthony stomped his foot and pointed at Daniel. "Not a word from you about my uncle. He is helping me with my business, and I'm making a good deal of money. I have my mother to take care of now."

With every bit of his strength, Daniel tried to be calm when he next spoke. "I'm not going to interfere in your business, Anthony. I'm only going to tell you two things, and I believe you should listen to me. I'm looking out for your best interest and the safety and security of your mother. First, I think you should be cautious with your dealings with Alistair Pundington. He has a rather loose view on what is lawful."

Daniel held up his hand to stop Anthony from responding with the temper building behind his eyes. "The second is with regard to your sister and why she might wish you to stay away from Pundington. I'm not at liberty to divulge information. However, I strongly suggest that you ask Sophia. I warn you, Anthony, it is a delicate matter, which will require you to control your temper."

Anthony's eyes narrowed. "I don't understand."

"I know. I wish I was at liberty to tell you more, but I cannot break your sister's confidence, no matter how foolish I think her silence is." He wished he was able to resolve at least one issue, but he wouldn't betray Sophia. Not even for her own good.

Anthony nodded and walked away. His eyes were as telling as Sophia's.

Confusion was better than rage. Daniel should take his own advice with regard to secrets he was keeping from his wife.

Thomas's familiar voice broke his reverie. "That boy looked ready to explode."

Daniel shrugged. "He has just lost his father. It is to be expected."

"He might help you in your cause. He's close to Pundington." Thomas said.

"I know, but he loves that bastard. Have you found out anything?"

"I have, but we cannot speak of it here. Can we meet tomorrow at your townhouse?"

"Very well. I'll be out of the house until three, but I can meet you then. I have a lead on the source of the cargo from Pundington's last trip. I believe it came from the colonies and then he was in the West Indies. have a bad feeling about this entire thing."

Thomas looked around at the men crowding the club. "It

would be better to talk in private about such things, Dan. I'll see you tomorrow."

~

As she said she would, Sophia dressed each day and went down for a few hours to accept callers. She was sipping tea when Fenton came to the door. "Mr. Pundington, my lady."

Sophia's heart pounded so loudly in her ears she didn't know if Fenton said more. "Send him away."

Alistair barged in behind Fenton. "I'm afraid I'm already here, Sophia."

Fenton looked from her to Pundington and shifted from foot to foot.

Whatever he had to say, she certainly didn't want to servants to hear it. She stood, squared her shoulders and kept her face calm. "It's all right, Fenton. You may go."

"You look terrible." He smirked and twisted his mustache with one hand.

"Why, thank you, Mr. Pundington. I cannot remember a more gracious caller. You are here to extend your sympathies over the loss of my father, I presume." Her sarcastic tone did nothing to belie the rage and fear just below the surface. Nor did it keep her stomach from churning.

He closed the door and advanced into the room. "Yes, well, old Charles was my dearest friend after all. We worked together for years. He would have had nothing if not for me. I expect to be compensated, niece."

She clenched her teeth. "I'm not your niece, and my family owes you nothing."

"Your family owes me quite a lot." His tone was light but the rage in his eyes turned her stomach.

For the first time, Sophia wished she were a man. She

wanted to call him out. She would have faced prison to see Alistair Pundington lying dead on the parlor floor. "Even if that were true, which it is not, what makes you think I have any power over the money? I was only his daughter. Anthony and Mother will take care of the finances."

"I'm sure you will have ample opportunity to convince your brother how best to invest his new wealth."

"Why would I do that?"

He continued forward until he was only inches from her. "Because, you are mine. I had you first and, therefore, I can claim you anytime I wish. I'll be waiting for you until you return to me. I'll make sure your life is one long horror until I get my way."

His words left her trembling, but fear evolved into fury. "You are crazy, Pundington. Get out of my house."

His laugh was an ugly sound that made her cringe. "Your house. You think because you whored yourself out to an earl, that makes you a countess. You will never be anything more than the whore who gave herself to me thinking to gain my fortune."

"Gave myself, you bastard, you stole what was mine. You are no more than a thief and a criminal regardless of the mask you wear. No matter how you paint yourself, Alistair Pundington, you will never be more than a lowly thief in the night. Even now, you try to steal from my brother."

He slapped her face.

She spun and fell to her knees. Pain shot through her cheek and eye. She ran toward the door.

He grabbed her and tossed her onto the couch.

He pressed his body to hers, tearing at her clothes. Sophia screamed.

Fenton and Jasper rushed in and attacked Pundington, but the maniac was tall and strong for his age.

Fenton took a hard blow, but the effort unbalanced Pundington, and Jasper ran headlong into his gut.

They were wrestling on the floor when Thomas walked in, pulled Alistair to his feet, and punched him in the nose.

There was a satisfying crack, and he went to the floor holding his bleeding nose.

Jasper leaped to his feet and helped Fenton to his. "Shall I throw him to the curb, sir?"

Thomas surveyed the room. "Listen to me carefully. Go call a hack to come around to the back door. Fenton, are you well enough to get a few footmen to put this trash in the hack and see he is taken away?"

"Yes, sir." Fenton straightened his vest and collar.

"Good. See to it then and take him out of here."

Sophia sat on the couch holding her cheek and straightening her dress.

The servants grabbed Alistair under the arms and dragged him from the parlor as if he was a sack of flour.

"He will always come for me," Sophia said. She clutched the shoulder of her torn dress.

Thomas sat next to her. "He's gone. You are all right now, Sophia."

"My lady?" Marie ran into the room. Wide-eyed, she gaped at Sophia.

"I'm fine, Marie," Sophia said softly.

"We should call the constable. You have been injured," Marie said.

Thomas touched her bruise lightly. "She is right, Sophia. We should call the constable and a doctor to have a look at you."

"I don't need a doctor, and I don't want the authorities. There will be a scandal if we call someone."

"You will tell Daniel what happened."

Daniel would be furious. Her past would always follow her and poison everything good in her life. She had done a fine job of that herself. Better for him not to know and maybe they could start again.

"If you do not, then I will."

"I thought you were my friend, Tom."

"That is precisely why I'll tell him. I know you think we are all soft Englishmen, but your husband and I have served this country in many ways. We are not without resources."

Thomas had always been so affable. Why was he so determined when she needed secrets kept?

"I did not know you were in the Army. Was Daniel a soldier?" Daniel had told her little about his past after Eton.

"I was not in the army, and we were both soldiers of a sort. It is a long story and one better told by Daniel. I'm sure he would not appreciate my divulging a past best forgotten."

"What is going on here?" Anthony was so tall he filled the door, but he was only beginning to fill out so he was lanky. His anger was obvious but his youth just made him seem petulant.

"Anthony, what are you doing here?" Sophia asked.

"Your sister has been hurt. Do you know where his lordship is?" Thomas said.

"She was hurt and you just happened by to assist her." Anthony pointed his long finger.

"Tom." Sophia touched his arm to keep Anthony from incurring his wrath. "It might be best if you left. I'll explain things to my brother."

"Explain what to me? I need nothing explained. I have eyes and can see for myself what is going on here. You are—"

Thomas rushed forward and grabbed Anthony's cravat. He pulled him so their noses were an inch apart. "Do not finish that thought, boy. Because of my friendship with your sister, I'm not going to call you out for what you are suggesting, Braighton. I'll warn you, I shall not do you this service again."

Thomas released Anthony, bowed to Sophia, and left Fallon House. Sophia sat on the high-backed chair. "Please, sit down, Anthony."

He turned his back to her. "I would prefer to stand. Who hit you? What was Wheel doing here? Where is your husband?"

He thought she would engage in a dalliance so soon after their father's death and a few weeks after her marriage. Answering might leave him with an even worse impression of her. Her first instinct was to make up a story to tell him. She wanted to protect him from the truth and preserve the innocence that had been ripped away from her. She opened her mouth ready with a plausible lie, but he didn't even look at her. Lies had gotten them to this point. She had to tell him everything.

"It would be easier if you would sit, Tony. You are not going to like what I have to tell you, but I swear to you it is all the truth. Please sit with me for a few minutes if only because I'm your sister."

He sat several feet away from her. He looked ridiculous perched on the little chair as if he might leap up at the slightest provocation.

"What I'm about to tell you is difficult for me, but I should have told you a long time ago. I don't want to tell you, but it is clear the price of keeping my secret is losing my brother. The cost is too high."

She told him everything of the night three years earlier and how she'd never wanted to marry. She explained about Pundington tearing her dress at the ball and finally, she told him what happened earlier that day.

By the time she was finished, she was exhausted and

Anthony was kneeling before her with his head in her lap. She combed her fingers through his soft, dark hair.

"I have been an ass. How can you ever forgive me? Why is that bastard not rotting in a jail cell?"

A smile tugged at her lips. "There is nothing to forgive, though you probably should apologize to Thomas Wheel."

His head snapped up, and he looked like a boy. "My God, yes, I must. I shall try to find him today." He stood and brushed himself off. "The earl knows about all of these past events?"

"He knows. I told him before we were married."

Every emotion and thought shone in Anthony's eyes, his initial surprise at learning Daniel knew the state of her virginity, followed by admiration. She cursed herself for her recent treatment of her husband. Though he'd been late in arriving in London, he'd come, and he'd not railed against her when she refused to share his bed. She had seen his anger, but never feared him. Her night terrors made her send him away, but now it was clear how foolish it was.

The large clock in the corner read half-past four. Daniel should have been home. She hated that he never discussed his business with her.

"Is something else wrong?" Anthony asked.

She shrugged. "No, I was just wondering where his lordship is at this hour."

He sat on the tiny chair again. "I'm sure he will be home shortly. Sophie, forgive me for asking, but why have you not prosecuted Pundington? He belongs in prison for what he did."

"It would have brought a scandal down on the entire family. It would have ruined me and likely made it difficult for you to marry as well. Mother and Father did not want to risk it, and I just wanted to hide from the world."

"And now?"

The idea of letting the world see the true Alistair Pundington was tempting, but she cringed at the public knowing her story. "Now, I would like him to pay, but I don't want to cause scandal and trouble for Daniel. I don't think I could tell my story to a stranger. Look at how long it took for me to tell you."

"Have you discussed prosecution with his lordship?"

His question was so simple, yet so complicated. "I have not."

He smiled at her. "I won't tell you what to do, Sophie, but perhaps you should talk to him. He seems a reasonable fellow."

"I'll think about it."

Anthony stood and straightened his cravat. "Will you be all right if I leave? I want to check and see if I can find Wheel at the club." Anthony had fallen into London fashion with ease. He appeared quite the dandy, and it distracted her from her problems.

"I'm fine. Fenton will not allow anyone else in the house today unless they are family. I'm tired anyway. I think I'll nap until supper."

He kissed her cheek. "Then, I'll see you tomorrow."

Even with her face bruised and sore, Sophia was still lighter somehow. The weight of her secret had suffocated her. Shedding the shame she'd carried around like a turtle's shell, lightened her heart. Now, exposed to all the people who mattered, it amazed her that they all still loved her. The vulnerability she'd expected transmuted into a kind of freedom.

Wherever Daniel was, he would be home soon. She would nap, bathe and then dress for dinner. When he arrived home, she would be irresistible to him. Repairing her marriage was the most important thing.

Chapter Eighteen

Thomas sipped his brandy and thought seriously about going home early. On the way ,he would stop at Fallon House and speak to Daniel then spend a quiet evening at home.

Anthony Braighton cleared his throat and looked sheepishly at him.

Thomas frowned. "What do you want, Braighton. I warn you, I'm in a foul temper."

"I owe you an apology, Wheel. I jumped to a conclusion, and it was the wrong one. I have already apologized to my sister, but felt I should find you and do the same."

"Have a seat, Braighton."

"I'm indebted to you for arriving at such an advantageous moment."

He shrugged. "The footman and the butler were already making good progress. I merely finished the job."

"Still, I owe you." He paused and his inner struggle appeared in every twist of his expression.

Thomas laughed. "Never play poker, Braighton. You and your sister have the easiest faces to read that I have ever seen."

Anthony grinned. "I try to avoid the card table. Unless I'm extremely lucky, I always lose."

"You have something you want to ask me?"

He looked around nervously. "It's about Pundington. I have been foolish and given him some money for a deal. I'm now worried he might be doing something illegal. I'm not sure what to do."

Thomas frowned. "Did you discuss this with Marlton?"

"I will, but he was not home."

"When did you leave Fallon House?" Thomas's heart beat faster. Years of training to serve the crown snapped him to attention.

Anthony sat up straighter. "I just left there thirty minutes ago."

Thomas looked at his watch. "He never showed up for our appointment."

"Perhaps he was delayed."

He narrowed his eyes at Anthony. "I have known Daniel Fallon for over twenty years and in that time he has never missed an appointment. Never."

"You're concerned there has been foul play?"

"I do not know. I'll look for him, and we shall see. Perhaps you are right and he was merely detained by his morning appointment."

"I'll help you look." Anthony bounced and slapped the table. Thomas gave Anthony several places to check, but kept the more delicate locations for himself. He hadn't been to the opera in a while, but it seemed he was going there tonight. Checking his watch again, he had time to check a few other places first.

They parted, saying they would meet at Fallon house at eleven the next morning.

After checking two pubs of questionable reputation, Thomas discovered Daniel had not been in either one in years. He also recalled why they had grown up and stopped frequenting such pitiful places. The stench of the last place lingered on his coat, and he shuddered at the memory of the actual rank odor encountered when he opened the door. He was glad his lost youth was lost, and they had outgrown such folly. They might have ended up like Michael's father and sent their families into ruin over bad drink and crooked gambling.

The opera house was a much more pleasant sight and the air was far better. Thomas strode to the back of the theatre and gained passage to Miss Charlotte Dubois's dressing room.

She wore a red gown with black lace that caressed her figure. He hadn't noticed what opera was being performed, but he would certainly pay to see Charlotte in such a dress for a few hours.

"Hello, Madam." He bowed deeply.

"Monsieur Wheel, how wonderful to see you again. It has been too long. Have you come to hear me sing?" She turned fully toward him showing off the daring cut of her gown.

Thomas gazed at the expanse of full breasts blossoming out of her dress. He smiled and looked back up to her face, which was also lovely even with all the makeup required for the stage. "I'm afraid not, Madam. I'm searching for my friend, Lord Marlton. I was wondering if you have seen him lately. It is of great importance that I find him."

A sad smile crossed her face, but transformed to her normal bubbly façade. "I'm afraid, no. I have not seen him in months. Not since the night we went to the theatre together. It was clear then he was enamored with a lovely girl with dark hair and unusual eyes. I knew then I would never see him again."

Thomas was both sorry she hadn't seen him and glad Daniel hadn't taken up with his mistress after his marriage. He smiled coyly. "Do not tell me that a woman of the world such as yourself was toppled by love."

She didn't laugh as he expected, but sobered. "Love...no, but I did like his lordship quite a lot." She shrugged and beamed before walking closer. "Perhaps you would enjoy taking me to the theatre one evening, Monsieur Wheel?"

Charlotte's luscious curves and bright wit tempted him. She displayed herself like a candy in the store window eager to be gobbled up. "I can think of little I would enjoy more, but I do not think Daniel would like it even if he is blissfully in love."

"Is he? I have heard a rumor that this is not the case."

"London is full of rumors, as you well know. This one will pass when the ton is bored with it."

She shrugged again. "I'm both happy and sad. I thought perhaps his lordship's marriage would not prevent us from being friends, but if you say it is not true then I must look for another friend."

"I'm certain you will have little problem finding an excellent friend, madam." He kissed her hand, bid her good night, and rushed from the opera house.

At one o'clock in the morning, he instructed his driver to take him home. He was exhausted and drunk. He'd gone to every club and pub he remembered, where Daniel might be found. In each one, he had a drink to encourage easy talk from the other patrons. It had all been for nothing. No one had seen the Earl of Marlton.

Knowing he must be missing some clue to Daniel's whereabouts, he couldn't sleep. He tossed and turned. "Damn."

Thomas tossed the covers aside, grabbed his robe and went to his office. It would be a long night. He rang for coffee and went over all the events once again.

The seat at the head of the table was empty, leaving a gaping hole in the conversation as Sophia, Janette and Cissy sat down for supper. Daniel had not come home. It was the first night, since papa's death, that Daniel missed supper. In fact, it was the first meal he'd missed since they'd arrived in London.

Sophia understood while Daniel had been a dutiful husband when she was above stairs, now he probably returned to his own life. His mistress must be well pleased that his inconvenient wife was feeling better. Bitterness and jealousy pierced her heart in a flash, surprising her. She hadn't known how hurt she'd be when he returned to his opera singer. She shouldn't be surprised. She had no one to blame but herself. After neglecting him all this time, what did she expect? Men would always be eager to have their needs met.

He'd been so sweet and patient while she mourned and refused to eat and slept so fitfully. He'd stayed by her side. The least she could do was to allow him his own life. If that included another woman, she would just have to live with it. It was her behavior that had pushed him to it.

Straining against tears, she ate some of the soup and avoided the pitying looks of Janette and Cissy.

Janette broke the silence. "We are to leave tomorrow for the country."

"It will be strange to be here without you." Sophia liked Janette and Cissy. They were both sweet and charming.

"I'm so pleased your mother has decided to go with us."

Sophia nodded. "The fresh air will be good for her. I appreciate you having her with you until Daniel and I can go to Marlton Hall."

"You will go to the country soon as well and then we shall all visit regularly."

"I cannot wait for Christmas. I do so love the country at Christmas." Cissy clapped her hands causing her spoon to clatter against the china.

"I wish to invite my family for the holidays. If that would be all right with you," Sophia said to Janette.

"You are the countess now, Sophia. You need not ask my permission for anything. Anyway, I adore your mother and aunt. I look forward to getting to know your brother as well."

"Thank you." Sophia went back to her soup.

By the time the first course arrived, Sophia had chewed the inside of her cheek raw. "Did his Lordship mention to you, he would be out this evening?"

Janette shook her head. "I would not worry, my dear. I'm sure he has just been detained by some business or another. His father was often late."

"I have not noticed that trait in Daniel." Sophia's voice softened as the observation was made more to herself.

Janette took a small bite of the duck. "No. Daniel is normally prompt. I would guess whatever has delayed him must be of the highest importance."

"Yes. I suppose it must be."

Cissy described Christmas at Marlton Hall in great detail. Sophia didn't listen. Her mind whirled with worry over her husband's whereabouts.

It was close to three in the morning, when Sophia padded down the steps. She had planned to surprise Daniel by joining him, but he hadn't come to his room as yet. She walked to the study and knocked but heard nothing. Opening the door, she found the room dark and empty.

She spun around at the sound of footsteps, but it was Fenton walking across the foyer. "Do you know where my husband is, Fenton?"

"His lordship is not at home, My Lady." Fenton's tone gave no hint about his thoughts on the matter. He gave the facts and nothing more.

"I see. Thank you." She climbed back up the steps.

Fenton called up the steps in a lighter tone than before. "Would your ladyship care for tea or chocolate? I can have the cook bring it up for you."

"No. Thank you, Fenton. I think I'll just go to sleep. Good-night." Exhaustion shrouded her and climbing the steps was an arduous task.

"Goodnight, my lady."

Sophia sipped her chocolate at the breakfast table. She'd spent the night tossing and turning while hoping Daniel would come home. It was annoying the way the sun shone through the front window as if all was right in the world. Nothing was right.

She picked up the morning paper from the corner of the table.

> *Mr. W was seen rushing from the home of the prom-*
> *inent Lord M. This correspondent has it on the best*
> *authority that M was not at home, and it was the*
> *lady of the house called upon. Scandal seems to*
> *follow the new Lady M wherever she goes. Sources*
> *tell me, it was the lady's brother who discovered*

*them and evidence of pugilism was present. Signs
are not good for that house. One can only speculate
what Lord M thought upon arrival at home after a
long day.*

"Fenton!" Sophia rushed out of the dining room.

Gasping, Fenton raced into the foyer brandishing the candlestick from the table in the back hallway. It was no wonder, after the events of the day before, Fenton came armed. He must have expected to find bloodshed.

He found the countess standing with one hand on the banister of the stairs and the other waving the morning paper.

"My lady?" He let down the candlestick.

She lowered her voice. "Fenton, thank god you are here."

Fenton's eyes widened, but his tone was as reserved as usual. "How may I assist, my lady?"

It was the first time she'd seen surprise on his face and it almost made her smile, but she returned to the issue at hand. Several maids and the cook peeked around doors and down the steps. She shouldn't have raised her voice, but she was so shocked by what the paper said, she'd lost her temper. What was Daniel going to think? "I need a word with you in his lordship's study, please."

Fenton followed her and gave the other servants a stern look as he closed the doors.

She still waved the paper around. "We have a snitch in the house, Fenton."

"A snitch, my lady?"

"Yes. Snitch, informant, you may call it what you want, but someone who was in this house yesterday told the newspaper the story I have just read. Though I cannot tell you if they gave only half-truths, or if the reporter took some license with the facts. I do not approve of my personal life being fodder for the gossips, Fenton. I charge you with finding out who did this, and I expect they will be dealt with accordingly."

"I'll see to it, my lady." Fenton sounded even graver than usual.

She leaned over the desk while attempting to work out the details. "Fenton, is his lordship a good employer? I mean to say, is he good to those who work for him? Does he pay well?"

"His lordship is a fair man, as his father was before him."

"Then why would someone do such a thing?"

Fenton spoke evenly. "For some, the lure of easy money is too great to resist."

She stood straight and looked him in the eye. "Find the culprit and deal with this, Fenton. I entrust the task to you. I'll not be afraid to speak in my own home. It is one thing to gossip with the servants in other homes, but this is quite another. This story made the paper in a matter of hours. Someone here, in this house, sold the story to a reporter. I want to know who."

Fenton bowed stiffly and left the room.

Sophia collapsed into the nearest chair and rubbed the side of her head, which was now pounding. Why had Daniel not come home? Where was he? She was determined to handle his having a mistress, but he must not be so indiscreet as to not come home. God only knew what would be in tomorrow's paper.

At one minute before eleven in the morning, Anthony and Thomas arrived at Fallon House. Sophia had expected to see Anthony, but Thomas's presence was a surprise. Janette and Cissy had left for the country only an hour earlier so Sophia was alone.

The two men looked so grave, panic built in the pit of her stomach. "Tom, what's wrong? Has something happened?"

He was about to answer, but she held up a hand. "Let's talk in the study."

"What was that all about, Sophie?" Anthony demanded as soon as the study door closed behind them.

"Have either of you read this morning's paper?"

Thomas frowned. "I have. You suspect one of your staff?"

"I have Fenton looking into the matter."

Anthony looked from one to the other. "What was in the paper? What do you suspect? What is going on?"

"Calm yourself, man," Thomas said.

Sophia retrieved the newspaper from the desk and handed it to Anthony.

Anthony frowned and slapped the paper against his leg. "None of this is true."

"And yet, none of it is false either. I did rush from here, you did arrive just before, and there was a fight. As you can see, the story holds facts but little truth. That is the way of these things."

She took the paper back and threw it on the desk. "What are you two doing here? What has happened to Daniel?"

Thomas's eyes were ringed dark and his shoulders slumped. "The truth is, I'm not sure, Sophia. I cannot find him."

Hating her thoughts, she turned away. "There was that opera singer..." Most women would never admit their husband was having an affair. Such things were known, but never discussed. Sophia was tired of lies. They had only made bad situations worse.

"I already went to see her. She has not seen him since the night of the theatre. That was quite a bit before your marriage."

Relief washed over Sophia, but panic overshadowed it. "Then, where is he, Tom?"

"I do not know, but it is not like him to just disappear. I know him, Sophia. He is prone to run when things are bad, but he would not go without saying so. He would not worry his family."

Thomas looked away rubbing his neck. "I'm worried."

She didn't know what to say or do. She wanted to scream, but it would do no good and it was unlikely to make her feel any better. She preferred thinking he was an unfaithful husband over the possibility he had met with an accident of some kind. "Perhaps there is another woman whom you do not know about."

"I'll look into it. I shall call in some additional help and we will find him." His voice rang with intensity and determination.

Daniel was his friend, and his interest in finding him was personal. It had little to do with her.

Still, she worried. She was not entirely convinced he'd met with some kind of trouble. It was possible, tired of waiting for her, he found a more willing woman. Perhaps once he found her, he saw no reason to return home.

Thomas and Anthony discussed how to proceed.

She lost the thread of the conversation. There was nothing for her to do but wait and worry. The room wavered, and she closed her eyes willing the dizziness away. "I'm going to rest."

"Are you ill?" Anthony took her arm.

She patted his hand. "No, just tired. I didn't sleep well last night. You will contact me if you have any information?"

Thomas bowed, his face a mask of concern and perhaps disappointment. "Of course."

She was used to disappointing those around her. After excusing herself, she went up to her room.

Marie helped her to remove her dress, and she sent the maid away.

She padded across her room and for the first time went through the adjoining door to Daniel's room. She stood in the open doorway and stared at the large bed.

Heavy blue drapes were drawn back across the dark wood canopy revealing the high, down bed. She ran her hand over the bedding, pulled back the covers, and climbed in. Warm familiarity surrounded her in Daniel's bed. She snuggled in deeper. Even with the sunshine streaming into the room, exhaustion overcame her.

Thomas sat behind the desk and penned notes to Michael, Markus, and a third to police detective Hardwig. James Hardwig had been a comrade a few years ago when they were both on the continent working for the king. He'd kept in touch, and Thomas had no doubt he would be of assistance.

Thomas called a footman to dispatch the messages then turned to the young man sitting across from him. "Your sister does not believe anything is amiss. I think she is quite certain Marlton has taken a mistress."

Anthony shrugged. "It's not an unlikely scenario. Many men do take on a paramour."

"Not Marlton, not after his marriage." Thomas was certain he was right.

Anthony cocked his head to one side. "I hope you are wrong. I fear if you're correct then your friend is in serious danger."

"That is my fear as well." He paused to think. He was still calculating several different scenarios.

"I may need your sister's help at some point. I hope her low opinion will not sway her ability to assist."

Anthony screwed up his mouth. Thomas had learned in the last few hours, this meant he was thinking something through. "I think she is in love with her husband. She will help if she believes it will bring him home."

"I hope it will not be necessary to employ her in our endeavor."

Chapter Nineteen

It was Thomas's first visit to James Hardwig's office. It retained the thick odor that comes from years of cigar smoke. The wallpaper peeling and the rug worn, the man himself was in similar condition. His brown, thinning hair looked as if it hadn't been washed in weeks.

James desperately needed a shave, but his brown eyes lit up at the sight of his old friend in the doorway. He came around his desk, hand outstretched, and pumped Thomas's hand vigorously. "Got your note, Wheel. No idea what to make of it. But it is good to see you, old man. How are you? Not married yet, I know. I always check the banns to see who's gone to the gallows."

"Good to see you, Hardwig. I have a problem, and I need your help."

James had put on weight since Thomas had last seen him, and his belly hung unceremoniously over his trousers. He went back around to his chair offering Thomas the small wooden chair in front of the desk. "What's the trouble, then?"

"I'll need this to be kept quiet."

James grinned and rubbed his belly. "Just like old times then, Wheel. Everything on the hush-hush."

"Just like old times, James." Except, this time the outcome was personal. Once he'd explained the entire story of Daniel's disappearance, he waited while James thought it all through. He'd worked with James enough to know, that while he was a clever man, he took his time to process information. When they were in France, the waiting had driven Thomas crazy. However, James's careful thought process had saved them more than once, and he had learned patience. The office was sparse with no furniture besides the desk and chairs.

The detective cleared his throat. "Could have got himself a new mistress."

"No. He is in love with his wife," Thomas said firmly.

Hardwig nodded. "Could be on a drunk and does not want to be found."

"That would be quite out of character for his lordship. He is a man of moderation. He is also quite reliable. I knew something was amiss as soon as he missed our appointment."

James scratched the shadow of a brown beard on his cheek. "This Pundington fellow, you say he attacked the wife and you foiled his plans. Could be he is involved, if he has a grudge against the family."

"Daniel was investigating him. He was sure Pundington's business was illegal, immoral, or both. He told me he was going to meet with someone who had more information."

"Did he say who?"

Thomas shook his head. "No. I wish I had asked."

"No use kicking yourself. Were you also gathering information for Marlton?" James tapped the worn top of his desk. "It is your specialty, old man. What did you expect me to think?"

"It was my specialty. Now, I manage my lands, my businesses, and generally do no information gathering. However, when my friend asked for a favor, I did make a few inquiries." He hated to admit that James was right.

"And what did you learn?"

"Pundington is up to something. His shipping business is legal on paper, but I did not discover what it is he's been shipping. All the loading and unloading logs I found said he is moving coal and spices, but I found no buyers for his deliveries."

"You think the manifests are falsified."

"I'm sure he is not moving coal or spices. I have been on one of his ships. Though it was empty, both coal and spices leave their mark on a vessel."

James leaned forward with interest. "What is your instinct?"

"At first, I suspected he was smuggling absinthe, but the odor of the ship was pungent, though not of spices," Thomas said.

"What was it?" The detective was more enthusiastic by the second.

Thomas suspected his old comrade had pushed more paper than criminals since leaving France. "Human, I think."

James pounded his fists on the desk and shot to his feet. "You think he is trafficking in slaves?"

"I cannot prove it, James. I only suspect it."

"What kind of a man is this Pundington?" His face turned bright red.

"The kind who attacks a young newly-married woman in her own home after her father, his oldest friend, has died," Thomas said bitterly.

James paced fisting his hands. "But, slave trading. Why would he come to England? He cannot sell his cargo here?"

"No, not on this soil, but I would hazard to guess he makes

a few deals here in London. I would not put it past him to pick up a few extra bits of cargo as well."

"You think he's taking his majesty's subjects and selling them as slaves?" Hardwig's face paled, eyes widened and he gripped the edge of his desk. He collapsed back into his chair. "This is big, Wheel."

"If I'm right."

"You are rarely wrong." James took a deep breath and straightened in his chair. He put his elbows on the desk and leaned forward before speaking in a conspiratorial voice. "What do you need?"

"I need to find The Earl of Marlton. I have exhausted most of my own resources. If you can help me locate him without society finding out he is missing, then Marlton and I will help you catch Pundington and no one need know you had any help at all." Thomas sat back and watched James process the information.

He had no qualms about helping Hardwig's career. He was an honest man who was always on the side of right even in the face of temptation. He'd saved Thomas's life on two occasions and his soul on another.

"Give me a few hours, Wheel. I'll see what I can find. I'll have to do most of it myself if it's to be kept on the hush. I have a few men who can be trusted in delicate matters. It will not be too hard to keep Marlton's name out of it as long as we find him quickly."

"I do not have to tell you that any delay might lead to disaster."

James nodded.

They shook hands and agreed to meet at Thomas's house that evening.

∼

Having no idea how long he'd been unconscious, Daniel waited with his face on a hard floor while waves of nausea roiled his stomach. He held his pounding head and sat up allowing the queasiness to fade by degree. Inventorying his limbs, he confirmed them all present and none broken or injured beyond repair. It was also evident, by the large lump on the back of his skull, he'd been knocked unconscious. He must have been hauled around as if he were a sack of flour since every inch of his body was battered and bruised.

When he was able to lift his head from between his knees without everything spinning, he took his first look at his surroundings. The small room was empty save for a rusted chamber pot. There was one window, but it was near the high ceiling and no light shone in, so he surmised it must be night. There was only one door. The room must have been a storage locker of some kind. The window let in the drone of people and carts, but it was far away and he doubted calling out would help him. He smelled the dank filth of the river and knew he must be near the port.

Struggling to his feet, Daniel walked the perimeter of his prison and shoved hard against the door without success. The memories before he lost consciousness remained hazy. A smoke-filled bar and two men were all he conjured. He sat back down on the cold floor and waited for the jumble of thoughts to sort out. Eventually, his meeting with a Frenchman in a red waistcoat came back to him. The meeting was about Pundington's import business.

Daniel had posed as a potential client for white slaves to be delivered to the West Indies. Everything was going well. The Frenchman's name was Jean LeBute. He had two associates who stood nearly a foot taller than Daniel, but the Frenchman was a slight man with large eyes and a hooked nose. They were just about to arrange a meeting with his associate when the hair on the back of Daniel's neck stood on end followed by a sharp excruciating pain and then nothing until waking up on the hard floor.

A wave of dizziness forced him back to the floor. When he heard the door creak open, he kept his head down glancing up only enough to see the fine shoes of the man who entered the cell.

"I'm pleased to see that you are not dead, Marlton," Alistair said.

Daniel looked up. "Why?"

His captor laughed. "You have an amazing ability to keep cool even when your own life hangs in the balance. I like that in a man I'm going into business with."

"What happened to your face?" Daniel asked.

Pundington's eyes had black circles under them, and his nose had swelled and twisted to the left. "A small accident."

"Why would I enter into any agreement with a man who had me abducted?" His voice was still unaffected.

A young, shabbily dressed girl walked around Pundington. Daniel thought he noticed her cringe a little when she passed him. Fear or disgust, he couldn't tell. She carried a tray, which she placed on the floor a few feet away from Daniel.

Daniel noted the food on the tray. "Thank you."

The girl looked up with wide, gray eyes but rushed from the cell.

"There are a number of reasons why you will go into business with me, Lord Marlton. Would you like to hear about them? You may even enjoy the benefits of such an association. I saw the way you admired Susan. I can arrange to have her placed here for your amusement if you cooperate."

Daniel pushed himself up to a standing position and one of the large guards from the previous evening entered. "I'm not accustomed to doing business in this way, Pundington. If you wanted to enter into a contract with me why didn't you just make an appointment to see me?"

Alistair laughed again and smoothed his mustache. The sudden guffaw caused him to touch his nose and cringe. "Don't toy with me, Marlton. You have been investigating my business dealings. I have not been fooled for one moment. I knew each and every time you made a pathetic attempt to ferret out information. What was your plan, to ruin me? All that trouble because your wife is a whore."

It was not easy, but Daniel didn't wish to be killed on the spot and the giant still stood next to Pundington.

He kept his anger in check and only allowed his eyes to narrow in response to the obvious attempt to bate him into losing his temper. "I'll ask you again, why would I help you? I abhor everything you do and stand for. Do not suggest I'm interested in that child you have enslaved. I do not believe you knew about all of my research, or I would never have been able to gather quite so much."

Alistair nodded at the guard. All seven feet of him bounded across the cell and grabbed Daniel.

He struggled, but it was no use. He was too weak from the attack of the evening before and his captor outweighed him by a hundred pounds. Pinning his arms behind him so tight, his shoulders were near to coming out of their sockets.

Pundington smirked and walked forward. "You will do as I say because I require a member of this damned English aristocracy to legitimize my business. Once the ton realizes that you have endorsed me, I shall be able to sell my harvest anywhere."

"Harvest. Is that what you call stealing human beings off the street and selling them as slaves?"

"Exactly so." He spoke about his criminal activities as if

they were normal. "Do not act so self-righteous, Marlton. I never take society women, only peasants."

Daniel's stomach twisted, and he was sure it was not from the knot on his head. Everything about Alistair Pundington repulsed him. "And you think that makes it right?"

He stood so close his sour breath turned Daniel's stomach.

"Do not pretend to care about the masses of poor, my lord. I'll lose respect for you."

"You are planning for me to endorse your cause. Why would I do that?" Daniel wished to be anywhere in the world but near to this horrid excuse for a man. Even the brute tearing his shoulders apart was better than Pundington.

"You will sign papers to show our partnership because, if you do not, I'll kill Miss Braighton."

"You have my wife, Lady Marlton?" He said the last precisely. Daniel's heart lodged in his throat. He had failed. Somehow, Pundington had gotten to his Sophia. He had to find her. He pulled forward, but the guard's grip tightened and pain shot through Daniel's shoulders.

Alistair smirked. "I had her first. She is mine. She never was yours, Marlton. You have stolen my property, but only for a time. Yet, I think her safety is important to you, and you will do as I say."

Daniel's heart clenched painfully. The pain in his head subsided in favor of the wretched ache coursing through his chest. He'd failed her. It was his duty to keep her safe, but this monster had gotten hold of her again. "If you are crazy enough to believe she is yours then why would you kill her?"

"I can have any woman I wish. I just don't like to have my property taken from me by some young upstart. You may have a title, boy, but you are nothing to me."

"You are mad."

Alistair nodded to the guard, who responded by slamming Daniel into the wall.

Agony ricocheted from his neck to his legs. Only his head was spared the abuse of the wall.

"I'll be back with the papers for your signature in the morning. I suggest you sign them, my lord. I'll not be able to keep you alive regardless, but I'll spare Sophia if you do not give me any trouble." Alistair turned and walked out the door.

The guard followed.

～

"What have you found?" Thomas asked without preamble, as James Hardwig walked into his study.

The butler, who had announced the detective's arrival, backed out of the room and closed the door.

James came up short when he saw there were two other men in the room.

Thomas made the introductions.

"Sir Michael Rollins, of course, I have heard quite a lot about you and the sacrifices you have made for our country. It is an honor to meet you." James fawned.

"Um...thank you." Michael shook his head and avoided the amused look on Markus's face. Michael's military past had earned him a few moments of embarrassment. He believed everything he'd done for England was quite normal, but many worshipped him as if he'd performed miracles.

Eventually, James snapped out of his idol worship and turned back to Thomas. "Not a tremendous amount, Wheel, but I think it's a start."

"We do not have time to delay, Hardwig. I can feel the clock ticking. Tell me what you have." Thomas sat behind his desk and motioned for the detective to take the seat in front. The other two men remained at the back of the room.

"I'm relatively certain he is being held near the port and is still alive." Hardwig twisted his hands together.

"How do you know?"

James's face reddened slightly. "I believe we would have a body by now if he was dead, my friend."

Pushing back any emotion, Thomas agreed with the gruesome fact.

"I tracked his whereabouts to a meeting two days ago. He met with some unsavory characters at a pub a few paces off of the doc. Sailors love to talk so it was easy enough to find out that he met with a Frenchman, by the name of LeBute. He has quite a few associates whom my office would like to get their hands on. We suspect him of smuggling Absinthe into England. One of his recent associates is Alistair Pundington. No one could tell me what kind of business they are in together, but after our conversation I had a few of my men ask around and there have been quite a few missing persons of late. Most recently, a young girl of sixteen, who served at the same pub, went missing. Everyone was distraught about it, said she was a good girl. Never had any trouble with her, the owner said and she'd never missed a day's work until a few weeks ago, then she just disappeared."

Thomas shook his head. "That is really very little to go on, James."

"Best I could do. Whatever Pundington is up to, he's keeping it quiet. I don't even know where on the docks to start looking for his lordship." He ran his fingers through his thinning hair.

"We need to set a trap." Michael spoke from the back of the room.

"What do you have in mind?" Thomas asked.

"We will need some help. Do you think Mrs. Braighton and Anthony would be willing to help?" Michael leaned against the bookcase and stared out the window.

One could almost see the plot forming in his mind. "I'm sure Anthony will help, but Mrs. Braighton has gone to the country."

"That's a pity," Michael said.

"My sister tells me Lady Marlton is an excellent mimic. I understand she can imitate her mother to a tee," Markus said.

"Brilliant," Thomas said.

"Will she do it?" Michael asked.

Thomas shrugged his shoulders. "I'll ask her."

"What are the three of you talking about?" Hardwig's head whipped around from one to the other.

Markus slapped the detective on the back and laughed. "Sorry. We've been together so long we sometimes forget that everyone else is not... Well, I'm not sure what you would call it, but we always know what we're talking about."

Michael sat in the chair next to the detective. He leaned forward and looked into his eyes. "Can you arrange to have Pundington followed? I'll do my best to keep an eye on him, but it is always best to have several good trackers, men who know how not to be seen."

James nodded. "Where would they be following him from?"

Michael looked up for confirmation. "Southerton's ball?"

"The ballroom has some huge pillars and a few alcoves and the gardens can be quite concealing." A bubble of excitement started in Thomas's belly.

Michael said, "We could not ask for a better set up. Are you sure she can do it?"

Thomas nodded. "She can. I have heard her imitate people, including Mrs. Braighton. She is quite good."

Markus frowned. "The girl has just lost her father, and she believes Daniel has taken a mistress. Are you sure she will be willing to help?"

"I have not known her ladyship long, but I believe she loves her husband, and she will do what she can to get him back. She will do it." Thomas sounded convinced.

Chapter Twenty

"Absolutely not." Sophia's tone shook the walls.

Thomas gaped at her, a degree of surprise Sophia had not seen before.

If she wasn't so angry with him, she might have found it funny.

After arriving for tea, he explained his suspicions and plans to recover Daniel. He'd already recruited Anthony and brought him along for proprieties sake.

She'd spent the entire night tossing in her sheets. Her mind created every scenario of Daniel in the arms of his opera singer and several other women. She tried to be brave and accept the situation, since it was her own fault. Of course, it hadn't worked. She'd cried herself to sleep only to be awakened by nightmares and wept once more.

"Perhaps you should rest and we will come back later," Thomas said.

The comment aggravated her. "I do not need your advice, Tom. I shall do as I please. I'll not help you with this silly scheme of yours either."

"Why not, Sophie? He's your husband. Don't you want to save him?" There was no mistaking the petulance in Anthony's questions.

"Save him from the arms of some other woman. I'll not be made a fool, Tony.

Fire burned in Anthony's eyes.

She'd seen it a thousand times when they fought over the years.

Thomas put his hand up to stop what she was certain would have been a tirade. "Braighton, would you mind giving me a moment alone with your sister?"

"Won't do any good. Stubborn as an ox, she is. Always has been. From the time she was born, you couldn't convince her of anything."

Thomas gave the younger man a stern look.

Anthony left the room mumbling about wives, stubbornness, and some other unintelligible things.

Sophia got up and paced the room. She didn't like being cornered, and she definitely didn't like being reminded that Daniel had chosen another woman over her. "You will not change my mind, Tom. I do not care whom he is sleeping with, but I'll not have my personal business broadcast all over London. I'm not going to a ball alone while there is speculation of his infidelity."

"But, no one will even know it is you. They will believe it is your mother and then you will go home."

"No." She was being stubborn, but she hated everything about this plan.

When Thomas spoke again, his voice softened though it was tight. It was so different from the easy manner she associated with him. "Sophia, I have known Daniel most of my life. I know him better than anyone else in the world. He has never taken a mistress and disappeared. He is in real trouble, or we would have heard from him by now. I had an appointment with him when I called the other day, and I can tell you it was the first time he has ever missed an appointment in his entire life. He is meticulous, prompt, and at least would have sent a note if he could have. If you will not do this for him, then I must beg you to do it for me. I know I'm right about this. You must trust me."

Thomas remained seated throughout his argument. She turned to look at him and his blue eyes seemed to implore her. He worried about Daniel. Was he right? Was Daniel really in trouble? Sophia walked over and stood in front of him. "Let me see if I understand you correctly, Tom. You want me to go to the Southerton ball, pretend to be my mother and pretend to convince Anthony that it is only fair to give Alistair Pundington part of my father's money."

She put up a hand before he spoke. "First, no one will believe I'm my mother, certainly not Alistair. Second, if he realizes our trickery, he will certainly kill me, or Anthony, or both. I cannot risk my brother's life, Tom."

"You will remain in the shadows. You are excellent at imitating your mother. Pundington will never see you only overhear the conversation. Markus and I will both be watching to make sure you and your brother are perfectly safe."

"You really think Daniel is in danger?" Her voice broke. She walked to the other side of the room to hide the start of more tears.

"I know he is."

"He might have taken a mistress and will turn up in a few days. Then, we will all feel like fools, but I'll be the one who will have to live with him knowing I care more for him than he for me." She kept her gaze lowered, not making eye contact.

"You will not be alone, Sophia. Daniel is very much in love with you."

"He told you that?"

There was a long pause. "No, but it is obvious."

Sophia's head hung, but then she stood straight and looked him in the eye. "I'll do it, Tom. I'm not certain I believe he is in danger, but I'll do it because I have not been a good wife thus far and he deserves better."

"I'm sure that is not true. You are just tired. You should rest now. You are looking very pale."

"I have not been feeling well for the last few days," she admitted.

"Go and rest now." He rose and kissed her hand.

"Thank you, Sophia. I do not know what I would have done if you had refused."

She chuckled. "I did refuse."

He had the good grace to look contrite in spite of his grin. "Sir Michael and I will return later with full details of the plan. He is going to take a look at the ballroom and garden to see what will be best for our little charade."

"How will he do that? Is he close with the Southertons?"

He shrugged. "No, but Michael has his ways of getting in and out of places without being noticed."

"Interesting."

The girl with the gray eyes returned the next morning, removed the old tray, and brought him another. It was only tea and bread, but the tea was warm and the bread was better than nothing. He was grateful to have something to stop the grumbling in his stomach.

She was emaciated and jerked away nervously every time he moved.

Her feet were black with dirt and grime. "What happened to your shoes, Susan?"

She took several steps back at the sound of her name from a stranger. There was intelligence in their depths and she narrowed them at him. "He took 'em to keep me from runnin'."

Daniel looked at her more closely. She was young and frightened, but he had a suspicion. "He took more than just your shoes, didn't he, Susan?"

Tears sprang to her eyes. "I'm not s'posed to talk to you."

"Do they just beat you or is it more than that."

Her expression darkened, and she dashed the tears from her face.

"Where are we, Susan? If you help me, I'll get you away from him. I swear it."

She shrugged helplessly. "On a dock, somewhere. I don't know."

"Can you get word to someone that the Earl of Marlton is being held captive?"

Her eyes widened at his title. "He'll kill me." She picked up the tray and started toward the door.

Daniel rushed forward and grabbed her arm. "I'll get you away from him, I swear it." He repeated his words desperate to get her to comply. She might be his only chance to survive and keep Sophia safe.

She scoffed in a way that was much older than her years. These men had battered and likely raped this young girl. All of it showed in the hard line of her mouth and emptiness in her eyes. "What good will it do me now? I was only a serving girl at a pub before. Now, I'm only good as a whore. I was a good girl." Her tears rolled unchecked.

Daniel pulled the handkerchief from his pocket and wiped her face. She was dirty and the tears created clean spots exaggerating the dirt. "You still are a good girl, Susan. I can help you, if you will help me. If not, he will sell you, have you shipped away to some island somewhere and you will never see your family and friends again. He will kill me as soon as he has what he wants. I think I can stall him for a day, maybe two, but no longer. We can help each other."

"I'll try to get word to someone, but I can't promise you nothin'." She pulled away and looked up at him.

"Where is he keeping you?" Daniel asked.

"There's a rundown building a block from here. He keeps me on the second floor, but Bill guards me, and he's too big to get past."

"This building, is it to the east?"

"Away from the water, one block. You're only feet from the boats."

"Is there another woman with dark hair and golden eyes?"

"Who is this woman?"

"My wife." His heart ached so painfully he had trouble getting the words out.

"There's no other woman inside. He keeps 'em in a boat somewhere."

He shuddered at the idea Sophia might be held somewhere in the dark hull of a boat. "Thank you, Susan."

Daniel backed away as the door lock clicked and Bill's beefy hand grabbed her and pulled her out.

The rest of the day Sophia spent either in bed or waiting near the bedpan placed behind a screen in the corner of the room. She might become ill but so far, she was just nauseous. Cataloging her food for the past day, she remembered her illness went back at least three days.

"Sophia?" Aunt Daphne's voice called from the doorway.

"I'm here." Sophia was behind the screen.

"What are you doing back there? Why are you above stairs again? I thought we had gotten past that. You are eating, aren't you?" Daphne's demand was aggressive, kind and particular to her personality.

"I'm eating, for all the good it does and I'll be out in a moment." Sophia found Daphne's gruffness comforting.

When she emerged, her legs wobbled. She'd put on her favorite lavender day dress hoping to lift her spirits, but her weak stomach left her dragging.

Daphne said, "My word, child, you look terrible. Are you ill?"

"I don't know what it is. I have had an unsettled stomach for days now. I feel sick if I eat and I feel sick if I don't eat."

Daphne sat on the chair near the dressing table and watched her shuffle back to the bed. "Sophia, I do not mean to be indelicate."

"What is it?"

"When was your last cycle?"

Sophia considered the question. "I don't know. I was in the country with Daniel, then Papa was ill, and I didn't think about it. I think it has been quite a while."

Daphne just looked at her and smiled pleasantly.

"Oh, aunt." Sophia rushed forward and knelt before Daphne. "I'm with child. I never thought about it. What a fool I am." She quivered and wanted to dance, sing and jump for joy. Most of all she wanted to run to Daniel and tell him the news. That sobered her.

"Do not look as though it is the end of the world. You are going to be a mother. I would guess in about seven months, perhaps less."

Sophia stood and touched her stomach. Daniel's son grew inside her. "A mother."

"I shall have the cook prepare some ginger root tea and toast. Toast was the only thing I could keep down for the first few months I was with child and the tea settles things a bit. Get yourself cleaned up and come down as soon as you can."

"Yes, Aunt."

"I shall call my physician and have him come to take a look at you, unless Marlton has a particular doctor. Where is Marlton? I should like to see his face when you tell him." Daphne smiled brighter than Sophia had ever seen her smile before.

"He is not at home. I don't expect him for some time." At least it was honest if not the whole truth.

Aunt Daphne shrugged and continued beaming. "Well, wash your face and come to the parlor for tea. I shall arrange everything."

Watching Daphne bound out of the room, Sophia sank slowly down onto the chair by her dressing table. A baby. She might have a son who resembled Daniel, or maybe he would be the image of papa. A tear slid down her cheek. Wiping it away, she wished her father had lived to see his grandchild. Perhaps, it would be a little girl with golden curls, bright blue eyes, and papa's nose. She would dress her in lace and bows and name her after Daniel's mother. She realized she didn't even know his mother's name. Better wait to hear what it was, before committing to that.

What if Daniel was in mortal danger? He might be dead already. Panic started in her belly and lodged in her throat. She sprinted behind the screen before what little was in her stomach expelled itself.

Stumbling to the washbasin, she found a towel, wiped her mouth, and then washed her face as instructed. She actually felt a bit better physically, but now her worry over her husband consumed her.

To keep herself from complete panic, she made a plan to go

down to the parlor and have a nice tea with Aunt Daphne. Then, she would try to rest until it was time to dress for the Southerton ball. Suddenly, the dread of being seen out in society without Daniel didn't matter. He was in danger. He needed her. He wouldn't stay away when she was going to be the mother of his child. He must be in trouble.

She would be a good wife to him. She wouldn't complain about his mistress so long as he was discreet, and she wouldn't refuse him in the bedchamber. She would be a good mother to her son. She was certain it would be a boy and she would, hopefully, have more children to adore. They would keep her so busy she wouldn't have time to worry about mistresses and the like.

She just had to get him home and everything would be all right.

~

Surprisingly, the tea and toast stayed down and she was beginning to feel better. She had cook make her some more while she dressed for the ball. Thomas was to arrive at nine to collect her, but at eight-thirty there was a knock at her bedroom door.

"Tell the gentlemen I'll be down in a few minutes. They are a bit early."

The door opened and Dorothea floated in wearing a stunning gown of blue with intricately stitched gold thread. She looked lovely. Her hair shone in the same golden hue as the thread and her color was high and bright. Her smile indicated she was excited about some mischief.

"I wasn't expecting you." Sophia stood and hugged Dory.

"Markus brought me as a distraction," Dory said.

Sophia didn't like the sound of that. "This is not fun and

games, Dory. It is dangerous, and your brother should not have involved you."

"A moment ago you were happy to see me. Besides, I'm a bit upset with you for not telling me what has been going on."

"I'm still happy to see you. You are my dearest friend, which is why I don't want you put in any danger." She went back to her dressing table and sat allowing Marie to finish her hair.

To give the impression of Angelica she wore a black gown big enough to hide all her curves.

Dory watched quietly as Marie twined rubies through Sophia's hair. "I really must have you do my hair one day, Marie."

Marie smiled. "I would be happy to, miss."

"Don't change the subject. You cannot go to the ball," Sophia said.

"You're not my mother. Though, I would not mind if you were. My own has been beastly lately. She is so adamant that I find a husband, she will drive me mad. We leave for the country next week, and she is already plotting next season."

Sophia had despised this plan from the beginning. It was bad enough she and Anthony were stepping into danger, but she hated the idea Dory would be anywhere near Alistair.

"I'll not be in any danger. I'm only to talk to Mr. Pundington in full view of the garden doors and the entire ballroom, while you and your brother make your way out into the garden. The hope is he will excuse himself to follow the two of you out. Then, I'm to go directly to the carriage and wait for you to join me. There are more than a dozen footmen who will be watching the carriage and escorting us back here, where we are to wait for the gentlemen to join us."

"You sounded just like your brother." Sophia laughed.

Dory rolled her eyes. "He repeated the plan to me about fifty times in the last three hours. He must think I'm daft."

"No. He knows he is putting you in danger. I don't like it."

She shrugged. "You have no other options at this point. I'm going and that is that. You look remarkably similar to your mother with your hair that way and in that gown. I think you shall age very well."

"Do you ever say anything expected?" Sophia asked.

"I certainly hope not."

Chapter Twenty-One

D aniel lay flat on his face in his cell.
Pundington was dressed for the evening, in all black with a canary-yellow waistcoat.

It took a strong will to refrain from poking fun at the ridiculous garment, but he remained silent and still.

Another set of shoes, not as nice and much larger, entered with his captor.

Daniel assumed they belonged to Bill, the guard or one of the other apes working for Alistair.

"Marlton, I have the papers for your signature." Daniel didn't respond or move.

"Get him up."

Beefy hands dragged him off the ground and Daniel relaxed every muscle. He fell limply over Bill's arm. He resisted fighting or making a run for the open door. He did neither. He would never make it past the guards, and he had no real idea of where he was. Better to outsmart his captor than to try to overpower them. He remained lifeless while the guard held him up.

"What is wrong with him?" Pundington demanded.

"Don't know, could be sick or dyin'." The guard shook him. Alistair pulled Daniel's head up by his hair.

Pain seared through his scalp, but he remained limp. He kept his eyes open, but unfocused.

"You had better not die before I get my papers signed, or your wife will not live through the night."

Daniel rolled his eyes.

Pundington released his hair. "Hit him."

It was going to be difficult not to brace himself for the blow. He would just have to take it if he was going to escape and save Sophia.

"Sir?"

"You heard me. Hit him hard, in the gut."

"But, Sir, 'e's barely conscious. Wouldn't be right to 'it 'im now."

"I told you to hit him. If you want to be paid, you will do just that."

Drooling, Daniel was hauled to the back wall. Bill held him up with one hand under his right shoulder.

Daniel allowed his knees to buckle, making the guard hold all of his weight.

Bill's large fist struck Daniel's stomach like a head-butt at a full run. A whoosh of air and a groan issued from Daniel's mouth. He wished he could have vomited for effect, but they had given him so little to eat, his stomach was empty. The grunt and more spittle would have to be enough.

"He must be dyin'."

"Bring him to the house. I'll call a doctor in the morning if he is not better. In the meantime, lock him in the last bedroom and keep a close eye on him." Disgust dripped from his words.

Bill tossed him over his shoulder.

Unable to draw a full breath, he pulled small gasps. His ribs hurt so bad, that he might actually lose consciousness. In all his time in France, he'd never given such a performance as he had tonight. He continued to think about the war and his time in France in an effort to keep himself from passing out.

The ground went by upside down, as he hung over Bill's back. Each step up to his new cell brought a new kind of agony. His ribs burned, and his head ached with the blood rushing through his ears. He counted and knew he was two flights up and then down a long hallway. He didn't hear any other voices in the house, but he assumed Susan was in one of the other rooms.

Bill dropped him on a bed, which smelled of mold, but it was soft and far warmer than the floor of his last cell.

He was thankful for the softer surface. He was so battered he didn't think he'd survive another beating.

The door clicked shut and the lock turned. He waited a full quarter of an hour before he opened one eye and made certain he was alone.

Four walls, a bed and a dresser comprised the small, shabby bedroom. A small window faced the street, but it was barred and even if it had not been, it was a two-story drop. All the drawers were empty and it was a miracle the bed still stood. He could tear a leg off and use it to hit Bill over the head, but he had no idea how many other guards there were. His death wouldn't secure his wife's safety.

～

Sophia clutched Anthony's arm. The waiting was killing her. They'd spent a full twenty minutes skulking in a dark parlor. She prayed no one walked in.

Thomas poked his head in and she jumped. "Relax Sophia. Dory is moving Pundington into position. It won't be long now."

"I don't like her being so close to that fiend, Tom."

Anthony pried her fingers loose of his jacket, already severely wrinkled. "It will be fine, Sophie. It's only for a few moments."

"Listen to your brother. I will not let any harm come to her. As soon as Pundington sees you, or rather, your mother and Anthony, he will leave Lady Dorothea." Thomas stepped out.

"I don't think any of this is a good idea, Tony." If only she could be as calm as Thomas.

Anthony patted her hand. "It's the only way to find your husband. Hold on just a few more minutes."

Thomas opened the door. "It's time. Walk straight out to the garden. Do not stop for anyone or anything. Sophia, keep your head tilted down so no one gets a good look at your face."

It was less than twenty feet from the parlor to the French doors out to the garden. Pundington might not even see them in that time. Still, the urge to run through undetected pulsed through her.

Anthony kept her at a steady pace.

The garden was just as Sir Michael had explained, dark with tall, dense shrubbery. Sophia couldn't see Markus or Thomas, but they were hiding within sight of her. As agreed, she and Anthony walked through the garden talking, but she acted the part imitating Angelica's voice the entire time.

"You are too young to marry," she said.

"But she is the only one for me," Anthony complained.

"There will be others, Tesoro."

"I don't want any others, Mamma. I cannot live without her. I would like your permission, but I have enough of my own money now to do as I wish."

She gasped dramatically. "You will use your father's money against my will?"

"Mamma, please."

They stopped in a small courtyard, which had niches cut out of the shrubs. Sophia backed into one of the niches and Anthony stood in front of her, so no matter where Alistair was listening from, he would only hear her voice and never see it was not Angelica.

"No. This is why I spoke to the barrister as soon as your poor papa died. I have made it impossible for you to control your father's money on your own until you are twenty-five."

"Mamma, what have you done?" He raised his voice.

"I have made arrangements for you to manage the business with the help of Lord Marlton. Your sister's husband is a good businessman, and we agree on many things."

"Such as?"

"Alistair helped your father build the business, and he should be paid for his half. Your father was stubborn on the subject, but it is not right what he did to his partner. Now that Charles is gone, I want to make peace with him. Alistair was a good friend to us for many years." Her thick Italian accent made the words easier to say. It made it theatre, and she kept Daniel in her mind the entire time.

"That is a lot of money." Anthony raised his voice.

"I wanted to turn over the money two days ago, but I need Lord Marlton, and he has not been seen. Not even your sister knows where he is. She believes he has taken a mistress."

"The money is mine, Mamma. It is not right to do this to me."

"There is plenty of money, Anthony. You will be well cared for and when you are twenty-five, you shall take control. You are too young now. I can see by the way you fall all over this girl, you are not yet a man."

They walked deeper into the garden. After only a few yards, Markus stepped in front of them. "He's gone. He listened to every word and then dashed away faster than you would believe a man his age was capable of."

"Do you think he will lead you to Daniel?" Sophia's voice shook.

Markus smiled reassuringly. "Thomas and Michael are already following him. Let's get you into the carriage and back home safe. Then, we shall see."

Markus handed Sophia up into the Marlton carriage. She had not expected to find Elinor there with Dory, but somehow her presence seemed right. The door closed, and they rolled down the street with a dozen footmen, Anthony and Markus surrounding them.

"Are you all right?" Dorothea asked.

"I'm fine."

Elinor's eyes were wide. "Did he take the bait?"

"Wherever did you hear such a term?" Dorothea asked.

"In Mrs. Radcliffe's novels." Elinor twisted her hands in her lap.

Sophia's eyes filled with tears she didn't shed. "It is rather like a dramatic novel. The really funny part is, not long ago I was living a quiet life in Philadelphia and no one knew who I was."

Dorothea put her arm around Sophia. "That man really is awful, Sophia. He looked at me as a snake might a rat about to be devoured. I had no idea."

"I'm sorry you got involved, Dory."

Dory rubbed her arms as if there were a chill in the air. "No matter. As soon as he saw you, he bolted across the room. I turned to introduce Elinor, and he was gone. Elinor said he headed out to the garden."

Sophia asked, "How is it you are here, Elinor? I thought I'd kept at least one of my friends out of harm's way."

Leaning across the carriage, Elinor patted her hand. "My

own fault. I followed Dory into the carriage, forced her to tell me everything, and refused to leave."

It was nice to have friends. "I'm glad you are here. I don't know how I would survive London without the two of you."

Dory hugged her tighter. "You shall never have to. You will be living a quiet life in England very soon. You and Marlton will live in peace as soon as this Pundington business is over."

"If they find him and he's alive. Otherwise, the baby and I will move to the country."

"What baby, Sophia?" Elinor asked.

Her tears won the battle and tumbled over. "I'm going to have a baby."

Elinor shrieked with excitement.

Dory bounced and kissed her cheek. "That is wonderful news."

"Do you think so?"

"Of course, we think so. It is the most exciting thing I have ever heard."

The carriage stopped in front of the townhouse and the ladies moved to the parlor. The footmen and butler were given instruction and Markus left the house.

Anthony stayed with the ladies.

"Why are you upset about the baby, Sophia?" Dory asked.

"What baby?" Anthony demanded.

"I'm not. I'm only worried that Daniel will not return or if he does, he will be so angry with me he will not want the child."

"Of course he will want the child." Elinor said.

Anthony interrupted, "All men want children."

All three women looked at him. He was sitting in a large overstuffed chair with his feet up on another. He looked every bit a young lord.

"What do you know about it?" Sophia used a curt, doubtful tone, one she reserved strictly for Anthony.

"All men want children. Even the men I have heard swear that they don't, really do. I once heard Beauregard Trent vow to never have one of those squealing, red things in his house. Two years later, he had not one, but two and was the most doting father I have ever seen. It was disgusting to see the way he fawned over those twins."

"Why did he swear otherwise only two years earlier?" she asked.

Having their attention, he sat up a bit taller, put his feet down and rubbed his chin. "I think, and I'm no expert mind you, but I think it is the difference between someone else's children and your own. Even I preferred my own young cousins to other children when they were small. I always thought other children were a bother, but I enjoyed our cousins when they came to visit. I was even sorry when they grew up and there were no others to play with. I shall be very happy to see your child, Sophie."

Tears flowed freely. "You will be in Philadelphia and never even see my baby."

"I'll visit. Perhaps, I can find someone to manage the business in America and I can stay in England. I think Mother might prefer to stay here." He waved, dismissing the subject. "It is too soon to talk about this. Tonight, we will remain calm and wait. There is plenty of time for big decisions."

Sophia wiped her face on a lace handkerchief and smiled. "You are getting quite wise, Tony. I don't know if I like this new you. I prefer you erratic and out of control."

"Sorry to disappoint you." He grinned.

Chapter Twenty-Two

D aniel lifted his arms over his head until the ache in his shoulders eased. The old boarding house with scratched and rickety furnishing had not always been so banged up. A large square of floor, where a rug had once been, was not as worn as the rest. The bars on the window shone with newness. Conversion to a prison was a recent event. Pundington must have thought that on the docks, a small holding house would go unnoticed for a long time. Maybe he even thought to make some extra money by making the women prostitutes here before he shipped them out of England.

Had Sophia suffered being beaten or worse? Daniel clenched his fists until his knuckles turned white. He pushed it from his mind. It would be dangerous to be distracted from the task at hand.

The lock was simple enough. He needed a pin or wire, two would be better. Once, he would have had all the tools he needed to get out of this type of situation, but that time had passed.

Perhaps a woman had lost a hairpin long ago when it was

still a boarding house. Searching the floor produced nothing. He eased the mattress off the bed frame and checked both carefully, before restoring the straw-filled bed. He eased the dresser to one side and checked underneath. It was painstakingly slow so as not to alert the guards. Crawling on hands and knees, he inspected every crevice of the floor but still found nothing. He ran his hands up and down the walls looking for an old picture hook, but only small holes remained.

The moon made its way across the sky. It was getting late. The door lock clicked, and he leaped onto the bed. He was not prepared to make a violent escape. He moaned and let his head lull to one side.

At the sound of rustling skirts, he opened one eye enough to see Susan walking toward him. She carried a tray, which she left on the dresser before coming toward him. The door locked as she sat on the bed and put her hand on his forehead.

He opened his eyes.

She gasped.

He put a finger to her lips. "Shh, I'm fine, Susan. Do you know how many men guard this place?"

"Usually four, but one went out with him, for protection. He's always afraid someone's after him."

A guard stomped down the hallway.

"Get the food," Daniel said.

She went to the dresser, lifted the bowl of soup and spoon, then returned to the bed. She sat with her back to the door and the bowl in her hand. If the guard entered, he would only see her feeding the sick man soup. "What are you going to do?"

"We are going to get out of here."

"How?" Her hand shook, and the spoon clanked against the bowl.

Daniel covered her hand with his. "Do not be afraid. Where do they keep you?"

"One floor down, but I'll have to go to the kitchen first. I have to bring the tray down." She motioned to the large wooden tray on the dresser.

"You will act as normally as possible. Go to the kitchen and then go back to your room and wait. Do you have a hairpin?" He asked even though her hair was loose down her back.

She put the spoon in the bowl, reached between her breasts and pulled out a small hairpin, intricately etched with a pretty golden butterfly attached to the end. She looked at it before handing it to him. "It was my mother's. A gift from long ago. Use it how you must." Her voice edged with emotion.

He took the bowl and drank half before handing it back and cringing at the bitterness. "It is a shame, but I preferred the dry bread and tea."

She took the bowl back to the tray. Looking back at him one last time, she gave the door a kick. The guard opened it, and Susan walked into the hallway.

Again, he waited after the door closed before he opened his eyes. He tucked Susan's hairpin into his pocket and got off the bed. It was in such bad condition one good kick would have shattered it. Slowly and silently, he dismantled the bed.

Taking his piece of wood, he went to the door and waited. The guard walked up the hall and back again in about two minutes.

Not much time.

It meant, he would have about half the time to trip the lock. It was a risk. A second guard entered the hall. The two men spoke of women and poor pay. The conversation might cover the noise of picking the lock, but then he would have two giants in the hall to deal with. He had no choice. It was his best chance.

He took out Susan's mother's pin and silently apologized as he bent the heirloom. Carefully, he snapped off the other end and went to work on the lock. The tumblers clicked. His heart pounded. Tucking the wires away, he grabbed his wooden bludgeon and waited.

The guards talking continued at the other end of the hall.

Daniel's muscles ached from lack of movement. It seemed hours before one set of heavy boots trudged down the steps.

He waited until the guard paced the hall again. When he reached a point where Daniel thought he was just outside the door, he pulled the door open.

Bill gaped unmoving.

Daniel whacked the side of Bill's head with all his strength. Bill bobbled and then crumbled.

Daniel caught him and eased him onto the floor. Waiting, he expected to hear boots running up the steps. With no commotion from below, he started down the hall, skirted rotted floorboards, and listened at each door before opening them. Where was Sophia?

Soft footfalls alerted him of someone running up the stairs. With his bludgeon raised, he spun into the face of Sir Michael Rollins.

Michael grabbed his arm before inertia completed the blow.

"What the hell are you doing here?" Daniel lowered his arm.

Michael smiled. "Rescuing you, of course." He looked down the hall at Bill. "Though, it looks as though you were doing a fine job on your own. Did that bloke give you those bruises?"

Daniel touched the side of his face. "Some of them."

Michael smiled again and walked up the last step. "The police are surrounding the house, now. I think it's best if we take the back stairs down and avoid all the mayhem."

Daniel plodded down the steps. "I have to find Sophia." Michael caught up with him. "Lady Marlton is at home, Dan."

Daniel absorbed the information. The air rushed out of him. "You are certain?"

"Positive."

Every moment in custody, he'd ached with the knowledge that he'd failed his wife. Leaning over, he grabbed his knees and caught his breath. "He never had her."

Michael shook his head. "He tried, but between your servants and Thomas he did not have a chance."

"Servants?" Daniel questioned.

"I'll tell you about it later. For now, we have to go."

"I don't think so." Alistair spoke from the landing of the lower stairs. He leveled a pistol at them. "I see you have recovered from your sudden illness, my lord. I'm glad of that, but I would prefer if you stayed." Sweat streamed down his face and his cravat had come undone. He looked as if he'd run from town. The gun shook.

Daniel shrugged. "I'm a quick healer."

"That is good news. It would appear I have a use for you after all. It seems, at least, your mother-in-law has some good sense. She is the only one in the family with any."

Michael scoffed.

"I'm afraid your friend will have to die as he is of no use and can only hinder my plans. Too bad too, I understand he's a hero in England." He took aim.

Gunfire resounded against the walls.

Daniel cringed and spun to help Michael, but Michael remained standing and calm.

Alistair cried out, dropped his gun, and fell to the floor holding his arm. Smoke and the sharp stench of gunpowder filled the hallway.

Michael waved away the smoke and picked up Pundington's gun. "Is that you, Tom?"

Thomas stepped through the cloud of smoke. "Of course. Who else could have made that shot?"

"It was a fine shot, but I would have preferred if you had killed him," Daniel said.

The three of them stood around Pundington.

"I could have, but I thought it better to watch him hang," Thomas said. Heavy footsteps clambered up the same back stairs Thomas had used.

James Hardwig emerged, gasping for air. "Got them all rounded up." He looked down. "Is that Pundington?"

"That's him," Thomas said.

"There is one more in the hallway above," Daniel said.

"Right then. I see we have to get this one to a surgeon. They'll keep overnight. I'd appreciate it if you would come in tomorrow for a chat, my lord." James caught his breath. He was all puffed up with pride.

Daniel started down the hall.

"This way," Thomas said.

"I'll be along in a moment."

His two friends followed, while James stayed to watch Alistair carried down the steps.

Daniel tried a door and it was locked. He put his shoulder to it and it gave way easily.

Susan screamed.

"Are you all right?" he asked.

"Is it over? I heard gun shots."

"It is over, Susan. Come along now. We'll get you home."

They walked down the hall and past the detective. Daniel stopped. "I think it might be in your best interest to check the cargo in his boats. I would do it tonight if I were you. I have a feeling little Susan here is not the only Englishwoman who has been kidnapped."

"I already sent some men down there, but I'll go myself as soon as we have this cleaned up," James said.

Daniel put his hand out and the detective took it. "You have done a fine job here, detective. I'll see your superiors know about it."

"Thank you, my lord."

Thomas gave James a friendly shove then he followed Daniel down the stairs.

James Hardwig's smile was so big he looked a bit daft.

When Daniel arrived home, the candles remained lit in the front parlor. He opened the door slowly and poked his head in. Anthony sprawled in a large chair, his long legs draped over one overstuffed arm, one arm hung over the other, and his head lolled to one side. It looked miserably uncomfortable. Dorothea and Elinor huddled on the couch fast asleep and Lady Burkenstock dosed in the corner on the settee.

Sophia stood near the window and must have seen the carriage arrive. When he opened the door, her head was down, but she gazed at him. Her eyes were half the tigress he loved and half the frightened lamb he was just starting to understand. She looked as if she didn't know whether to run and hide or jump into his arms. Traces of her bruised cheek showed through the powder applied to hide it.

Thomas and Michael had regaled him with all that had happened in his absence.

He smiled, though his own heart was beating so fast he had to gulp down a breath. Believing she was in mortal danger and now seeing her safe, he might lose his wits. He stepped fully into the room and opened his arms in hopes of solving her internal dilemma.

A cry escaped her lips and she flew across the room and into his arms.

Pain shot across his ribs, but he crushed her in a hug. The pain would wait for later.

She kissed his face.

He made an effort not to cringe when her lips touched his bruised cheek. But when she cradled his head and made contact with the lump on his skull, he couldn't contain it anymore. "Ouch."

S he took a step back and really looked at him for the first time. She'd been so thrilled and nervous when he first opened the door, that she hadn't noticed how beaten he was. His discolored cheek and tattered clothes were obvious, but the lump on his head concerned her more. "My goodness, Daniel, what on earth did he do to you? I'll send for a doctor immediately."

He pulled her back into his arms and buried his face in her hair and the crook of her neck. "No doctor. I'm fine, Sophie."

They stayed wrapped in each other's arms until Thomas tapped him on the shoulder. "Um, we are all just going to go now. Glad to see you home safe. I'll come by and collect you in the morning and accompany you to see Hardwig."

Sophia pushed her husband away and looked around at seven pairs of eyes all watching them and looking exceedingly uncomfortable. Her cheeks warmed with a blush, and she didn't know what to say. She'd forgotten all about the people who had graciously spent the evening waiting with her.

He pulled his wife back against him. "It's already morning. Come after two and we shall put this thing behind us. And thank you."

His three friends smiled.

Michael slapped his back. "You will return the favor someday, if necessary. Besides, there are more than just the three of us to thank. Nearly everyone in this room played some part in the scheme to retrieve you."

Daniel narrowed his eyes. "I look forward to hearing the entire story, and I thank you all for waiting here for my safe return. I had not realized how many truly good friends I'm blessed with."

Sophia allowed her tears to flow and even Daniel's eyes misted a bit.

They said farewell to everyone and started up the steps.

Fenton loudly cleared his throat. "Excuse me, my lord."

"What is it, Fenton?"

Fenton gripped a footman by the arm. Jasper clutched the man's other arm.

"My lord, as requested by her ladyship, I have found the snitch. This is Colby." He gave the footman's arm a shake. "He's been selling information to the papers. He was approached first by the man who attacked her ladyship then realized he could make a bit more from the papers."

Daniel returned to the foyer. "Colby, is it? Have you been unfairly treated while you worked here?"

Colby's cheek was smudged with dirt. He looked his employer in the eye. "No, sir."

"Why then, would you jeopardize your position?"

"The money was good." His voice was gruff and unrepentant.

Daniel sighed. "Give him a month's wages and put him out on the street, Fenton."

Fenton stared wide-eyed for a long beat. Straightening, he jerked Colby's arm. "As you wish, my lord."

Daniel returned to Sophia.

"That was generous of you, Daniel."

He shook his head. "Without references, he will be hard pressed to find decent employment. I was not as kind as you might think."

"Still, I'm not sure I would have given him a penny."

"He was lured in by Pundington just as your father and brother were. He will pay dearly for that, but it will not be by my hand." Daniel took her hand and they climbed the steps.

When they reached the top, Sophia let go of his hand and proceeded into her own chamber. Too tired to argue, he watched her go and moved to his own door. A steaming bath stood in the corner. Daniel sighed. He must remember to thank his valet.

He rubbed his face, but a shave would have to wait, so he stripped out of his filthy clothes. They wouldn't be salvageable. When he sank into the tub, his whole body screamed in both pain and pleasure.

As he dozed, a gentle hand caressed his face. He grabbed it and opened his eyes. "You are in my room."

She tried to pull away, but he held her. "I thought it was our room."

"It should be. But when last I saw you, that was not your desire."

"A lot has happened since you were taken from me." She gulped for breath.

His own breathing came in short gasps and his heart thundered. "Tell me." She looked at him and then at the bath. "It's a rather long story. You will wrinkle up and the water will go cold before I can tell you half. Would you like to finish your bath and then I'll explain as much as I can?"

"Will you help me?" He handed her the washcloth.

She took it and her cheeks turned the brightest shade of red. His wife was stunning, and his body teemed with desire for her.

They remained silent throughout the bath, and she blushed but didn't turn her head as she handed him a towel then his dressing robe.

She walked to the bed and sat. In her nightgown and wrapper, with her hair brushed out so it fell around her shoulders, she was irresistibly beautiful. Her voice remained just above a whisper. "If you would prefer me to go to my own room, I will, Daniel."

He came and sat next to her. "Why would I want that?"

"I have not been a good wife to you." Her hands twisted into tight fists in her lap.

He pried her fingers open, cradled her hand, and rubbed the tension out of her palm. "Why do you think you have not been a good wife?"

"I sent you from my bed."

"Why did you do it?"

Her brows drew together. "After my father died, I had dreams that disturbed me."

"Tell me about the dreams." He massaged her hand and wrist.

She explained how he'd somehow replaced Alistair in her recurring nightmares.

Daniel's hand stilled. He'd become the villain in her dreams. The only woman he'd ever loved feared him. His heart was breaking. "You know I would never harm you."

"I believe you will never intentionally hurt me." She tried to pull her hand away.

He held it firmly but gently, not allowing her to run from the conversation. "What is it you're afraid of?"

She pulled away and dashed across the room. She hugged her waist and stomped one foot. "I tried Daniel. I really did. I know it does not seem as though I made an effort, but I have been thinking of little else since you disappeared. And I did not know where you were. So, really, it's not so sudden."

"Sophie, what are you talking about?"

"Your mistress." She rolled her pretty eyes as if it should have been obvious. "I really thought I could be a good wife and tolerate you keeping a mistress, but honestly, I cannot. If you must have her, then I shall go to the country and we shall go out in public when absolutely necessary. It is not exactly the life I had in mind, but I think I can live with it. What I cannot live with is the glaring jeers of London society and the whispering in ballrooms as I walk in. I'll not tolerate their pity. Poor Lady Marlton, whose husband pays her no mind." She mimicked in a high English accent.

"My, you have thought about this a lot." He struggled to stifle a laugh, but at least the pain in his heart eased.

She glared at him.

Still smiling, he held up one hand in a sign of peace. "May I ask you what kind of life you did have in mind?"

She sighed and her shoulders slumped. "I'm a dreamer. I love you, and I had dreamed you would love me. We would live in the country with the baby and come to London for the season. You would adore our children and never think of another woman. I thought I would be a good enough wife to you that you would not want a mistress. Then Papa died and I was so...sad...and I was not a good wife and you were so sweet but then you went away all the time to do...I don't know what..."

"What baby?"

She touched her stomach. "Our baby, Daniel."

His brain turned to mush. He stood open-mouthed staring

at his wife. Joy as great as the day she'd agreed to marry him flooded in. He rushed forward, dropping to his knees before her and wrapping his arms around her. His head rested against her stomach. Their child rested inside this perfect body.

"Our baby," he repeated, through a tight throat.

"You're happy about the child?" She let out a breath.

"I'm happy." He kissed her abdomen. He wished he could feel the child growing within her, and he pressed closer.

"I thought we discussed this already." He stood and lifted her into his arms. With her in his lap, he sat in the chair by the hearth.

"I know, but I was so happy when I learned I was to have a child and when we spoke you seemed only tolerant of the idea. I just wanted you to be as happy as I am and now, I can see that you are, so everything is all right." She babbled on, grinning and frowning with each new thought.

He laughed. "I do love when you do that. Sophie, I'm thrilled the woman I love and married will give me a child."

"You love me?" Her eyes were wide.

"More than anything on earth."

She hugged his neck.

"Do not strangle me now." He laughed.

"I'm sorry. I just never thought you would say those words to me."

His expression sobered. "I think there are a few things we should discuss."

She tried to get off of his lap, but he wrapped his hands around her bottom and pulled her in tighter. "I think we can discuss these things sitting as we are. In fact, I think all of our serious discussions should be had in just this way."

"You are impossible. What do you want to discuss?"

"I do not have a mistress, Sophie. Nor, will I take one."

A smile lit her eyes.

"You have not been a bad wife. You were distraught after your father's death. That was completely understandable. I'll not lie to you. It hurt me when you left our bed, but I never thought you a bad wife and I certainly have never for a moment regretted our marriage. I love you, and I'll endeavor to make you happy for the rest of our lives. I'll care for you and our children, and we shall have a life as close to your dream as possible."

"Do you promise?" she asked.

He traced a path along her cheek to her full lips. "I already did, on that wonderful day when we said our vows. I promised you all of those things and more, my love. You're the most beautiful thing I have ever seen."

He meant every word, even as tears ran down her face and her eyes grew puffy and her nose red.

"Thank you." Sophia was crying and laughing at the same time.

"May I take you to bed, Lady Marlton?"

"You may, my lord." She used the edge of her wrap to wipe her nose. "But, I think I should go and wash my face first."

He roared with laughter.

H is lips were warm and seductive against the nape of her neck, while his hand caressed just under her breast. A smile lifted the corners of her mouth, and her heart soared. She turned into him and kissed him boldly.

Groaning, he deepened the kiss, wrapped his arms around her and pulled her tight against him. "I thought I was lost to you forever."

"I believed you had left me for another." He caressed between her legs.

Tiny gasps escaped her lips as the now familiar joy of making love to Daniel stirred inside her.

"There can be no other for me, Sophie. I want only you every day for the rest of my life."

He rubbed her sensitive bud, and her hips arched off the bed.

She dug her nails into his shoulders holding back the delight, which came too fast. She wanted to enjoy him slowly.

He kissed her mouth, and his tongue demanded entry. Willingly, she opened to him and he made love to her mouth in the same manner he would plunge into her core.

She trembled with need. With the lightest touch, she traced a path along the taut skin of his shaft.

He groaned deep in his chest.

She repeated the gentle tickling then gripped his rod.

He sucked in a sharp breath. "Sophie." His fingers worried her delicate folds and rubbed her sensitive button. Perched at her entrance, he glided in slowly, inch by torturous inch until he filled her.

Her cries mixed with his. She rose higher as she met every plunging thrust with the rise of her hips. Her pleasure intensified and cascaded.

Eyes closed, Daniel cradled her head. "Look at me, Sophie."

She stared up into his passion-filled gaze. Love was so plain in his eyes, it shook her. A scream escaped her lips as an orgasm shattered around her. Daniel pumped once, twice and then emptied himself into her in a series of grunts and moans. His ecstasy increased hers and another wave of pleasure coursed through her.

He collapsed on top of her. His weight was a blanket of safety.

She wrapped her arms around him. "I'm so happy you're

home safe, Daniel."

"I'll never leave you again."

～

D aniel was in his dressing room and Sophia rose from the bed and pulled her nightgown over her head. Sun streamed through the windows, catching something metallic on the table.

She walked over and picked up the small gold butterfly. Intricately etched it was a pretty little thing. Beside it were two pieces of wire. "What is this?"

He moved next to her. "It belongs to a girl named Susan, a child really. Pundington held her captive too. She gave it to me to help initiate our escape. It belonged to her mother. I had hoped to have it repaired and return it to her."

Sophia's throat tightened. What that poor girl must have suffered. She was probably misused. She shivered. To have given up the one reminder of her mother to a stranger, she must be a brave girl. Sophia wished she had just some small token of papa's to hold onto. She handed the treasure to him. "You should have it repaired immediately, Daniel. How will you find her?"

"Thomas told me she worked at a pub near the docks when she was abducted. I plan to start there."

"A pub? Oh, Daniel, that is no place for a girl especially after all she has been through. Can't we do something for her? There must be a position here in the house or in the country. Susan could work as a maid or helping in the kitchen might suit her."

He nodded, tucked the hairpin in the pocket of his waistcoat and kissed her cheek. "I'll see if she is inclined to changed professions."

Epilogue

"I do love a house party." Elinor flounced her skirts as she sat on one of the chairs under a large oak tree.

Sophia took a spot on the picnic blanket. "I'm so glad. I'm planning to have one every year." She picked her squealing son from the blanket. Arms and legs in constant motion, he smiled. Her own eyes and Daniel's chin looked back at her, as he made a bubbling sound and dribbled all over her. She hugged him and patted his back. "It is good to get out of London for a while."

"It is also good to get away from the marriage market." Dory's voice held contempt, normal when she spoke of such things.

"Is your mother being very difficult?" Elinor asked.

"You are my biggest problem." Dory pointed at Elinor. Her hand went to her chest.

"Me, what have I done?"

"Not a single day goes by I do not hear how you have managed to catch Sir Michael and why can I not follow your example and lure in a suitable husband?" She made a poor imitation of her stern mother.

Elinor's bright blue eyes were wide and her mouth hung open. "You make me sound quite mercenary."

"Not me, my mother."

Sophia laughed. "Be careful. They will join us for tea shortly."

They ignored her. "I did not lure, or catch, Sir Michael."

"No, what did you do then?" Dorothea asked.

Elinor smiled and acted as if she were smoothing a wrinkle in her dress. "I did nothing. We fell in love, as you well know. Now stop trying to send me into fits. I have known you long enough to be quite used to this game."

"I do so love it when you go into fits."

"Well, it is too fine a day, and I'll not take the bait." She sat up straighter and looked pleased with herself.

"Good for you, Elinor. And Dory, it was a good try." Sophia made an attempt at diplomacy.

The baby squealed again.

"You are in a fine mood, Charlie." Sophia searched for something to wipe his wet mouth.

"Should I take him now, my lady?" Susan asked.

"I hate to let him go, but it is time for his nap." She handed the baby over. "Thank you, Susan. Why don't you borrow a book from his Lordship's library while Charlie sleeps? He has had a busy morning and should nap a long time."

Susan smiled and curtsied politely. "Thank you, my lady, but I borrowed King Lear yesterday, and I should think it will keep me busy for some time."

"Indeed," Dory said.

With the future Sixth Earl of Marlton in her arms, Susan walked across the expansive lawn back to Marlton Hall.

"She has come a long way, Sophia," Dory commented.

Sophia rose and sat in a chair with her friends. "I don't know what I would do without her. Really. Charles adores her and she him. Once I saw how bright she is, it took little work to educate her and make her a suitable nanny. I'm so glad we took her on after the Pundington business was resolved. Cissy comes by several times a week and they talk endlessly over Shakespeare. I have even started to read more as I was feeling quite ignorant with the two of them going on and on about sonnets and plays, which I have never bothered to read."

"It will do you no harm to read more." Aunt Daphne led the rest of the ladies to join them.

Sophia smiled and sent a maid for some tea. "You are, of course, correct. I find reading relaxing."

"Your husband does not mind?" Elinor asked.

She looked out over the field to the east where Daniel walked toward them with Markus, Michael and Thomas. Her cousins, Frederick and Daisy followed behind. Her husband and their life filled her with immeasurable joy. "His lordship is indulgent."

"Whatever happened to that awful man?" Aunt Adelaide asked. There was no need to clarify whom she was asking about.

"Should have been hanged." Daphne pounded her cane into the ground.

"Oh, my." Virginia Burkenstock clutched her throat.

"Oh, do not get so offended, Virginia. The man was plucking Englishwomen off our streets and selling them into slavery in foreign lands. He should have been hanged." Daphne huffed as she sat and placed her cane against the table.

"I can see your point, Lady Collington. I just hate the thought of it." Lady Burkenstock cringed.

"So, what did happen to him?" Adelaide asked.

Sophia still found the subject of Alistair uncomfortable.

"All of his assets were claimed by the crown, and he was banished. They sent him off on a ship to Australia. If he ever sets foot on English soil again, he will indeed be hung by the neck."

"Well, at least he will never bother us again," Angelica said.

Sophia nodded and watched Daniel come close enough for their gazes to lock.

~

"It was a lovely day, my dear," Daniel said in their room, late that evening.

"We had fine weather," she said.

"Your uncle and Lord Flammel seem to be on opposite sides of politics. They were nearly at blows when we took our brandy."

"I think they managed to work it out. I saw them getting quite drunk together later in the evening. You had better lock your liquor cabinet or by the end of the week we shall be completely dry."

Daniel chuckled. He walked to where she sat at her dressing table, took the brush from her and ran it through her long tresses. "You looked grave when the tea arrived this afternoon. Was the conversation not to your liking?"

"It was nothing. Aunt Adelaide asked about Pundington."

His hand stilled for several beats before he resumed brushing her hair. She turned toward him, took the brush away, and placed it on the table. "I hardly think of him anymore, Daniel. There is no need for you to worry." She stood and wrapped her arms around his waist.

He enveloped her and kissed the crown of her head. "But I do worry. I promised to keep you safe and make you happy. I could not live with myself if I broke that promise."

She kissed his chin. "You have never broken any promises. I have all I have ever wanted and so much more."

"Then, your life lives up to the dream, Lady Marlton?"

She smiled and pulled him toward the bed. "My life surpassed my dreams the moment you began to love me."

He followed her onto the bed and covered her body with his. "In that case, you will have to dream bigger, Sophie. Every day my love for you grows beyond the day before and I feel it shall never level off."

"I'm certain my dreams can keep pace, my lord. I have an excellent imagination." She arched into him, making him groan.

Daniel's mouth covered hers, and her imagination soared once more.

Thank you. I hope you enjoyed Tainted Bride. I love this book and I'm so glad I was able to bring it back.
Ready to read more about Sophia's friends? Keep reading for Foolish Bride and find out how Elinor gets her Happily Ever After.

FOOLISH BRIDE

Sadly ever after... unless some dreams really do come true?

Elinor Burkenstock never believed in fairy tales. Sure, she's always been a fool for love—what woman isn't? But Elinor knows the difference between fiction and truth. Daydreams and
reality. True love and false promises... Until the unthinkable happens, and Elinor's engagement is suddenly terminated and no one, least of all her fiancé, will tell her why.

Sir Michael Rollins's war-hero days seem far behind him when, after one last hurrah before his wedding, he gets shot and his injuries leave him in dire shape. He wants nothing more than to marry Elinor, the woman of his wildest dreams. But Elinor's father forbids it... and soon Michael is faced with a desperate choice: Spare Elinor a life with a broken man or risk everything to win her heart—until death do they part?

PROLOGUE

"I was not out yet when the earl was engaged. I only know the rumors." Elinor wished Sophia would change the subject. She had hoped for a nice quiet walk in the elaborate gardens to get away from the ballroom.

Sophia patted her dark hair into place. "And, what was the rumor?"

Elinor cringed. How she hated gossip.

"Never mind, Elinor. You do not have to tell me."

It wasn't that she didn't trust Sophia, but talking of such things reminded her of the newspaper article that had nearly destroyed her. "I hate rumors. They are often exaggerated, and none of us really knows the truth. Well, except those involved."

"Yes, of course you're right."

The bushes to the right rustled, and Michael stepped out of the shrubbery's shadow.

His dark hair hung over bright blue eyes, and he was rumpled from hiding in the garden. "Forgive me, ladies."

"Michael," Elinor whispered.

"I was trying to wait until I could speak to Miss Burkenstock alone. I hope I didn't startle you." He fidgeted, which was unusual. Michael was always in control.

All the waiting, and now she couldn't stop her tears from falling.

"Shall I leave, Elinor?" Sophia asked.

She'd forgotten Sophia was even there. "Thank you, Sophia."

"Are you certain you will be safe?" Sophia crossed her arms over her chest.

Michael's smile was warm. "You have my word I shall not harm her in any way."

"Elinor?" She narrowed her eyes.

A wave of lightheadedness swamped her. "I will be fine."

Sophia nodded and walked away

"Elinor." He said her name like a prayer.

"Yes, Sir Michael?" Pretending she was unaffected by him, she looked away. She wished she could be more like Dory. Dory was excellent at pretending she didn't care.

"I was watching you dance." Taking a step closer, his gaze locked on her. "You seemed to be enjoying yourself. Especially when you danced with Travinberg."

"Are you jealous, Sir Michael?" She turned away from him and examined a yellow rose. Leaning down, she sniffed for its sweetness, looking for anything that would help her keep her composure.

He closed the gap until he was so close, his warmth spread along her back. "I am beside myself with desire for you. I hate every man who even looks at you and even those who only glance in your general direction. The last week has been torture."

All her torment of the last week bubbled up in her belly. She faced him. "Then why did you leave town, and leave me to deal with the scandal all alone? You left me with only a note to keep me company and not much of a note at that. What was I supposed to do?"

His smile widened. "My God, you are even more beautiful when you're angry."

Damn her fair skin for not concealing her blush. "Do not change the subject. I may not be the smartest girl in London, but I know that what you did was terribly unkind. I might have been ruined if not for my good friends."

His voice remained low and calm. "I did not run from you. I ran to try to make myself into someone you can be proud of."

It was impossible to stay aloof. She wanted answers. If not for the kindness of her friends, she would be ruined now, and it was all his fault. "Where did you go?"

He took her hands. "I am going to be worthy of you, Elinor. I promise that I will, if you will just wait for me."

"Wait? For how long? Mother will not allow me to wait if another offer is made. And what if the gentleman is titled?" Panic tightened her chest until she struggled for breath. She would need to make a list of ways to stall Mother's plans.

He pulled her closer and nuzzled her neck. "A few months is all I ask, my darling. Just give me a few months, and I will have enough money to come to your father and make an offer. Surely you can hold off your mother for a few months."

"I suppose I can, but why? I have my dowry. Certainly that will be enough for us to live comfortably."

Breaking away, he looked down at his feet, which he shuffled from side to side. "I do not want to marry you for your money, Elinor."

Her heart beat wildly. "But is that not why you pursued me?"

He kissed the tip of her nose. "I will not deny I came to London this season because I needed to marry to restore the money that my father squandered." He kissed her cheek. "I had every intention of finding a rich bride to enable that plan." He kissed her other cheek. "Then I met you, and you were the perfect solution to my problems."

She tried to pull away, but he held her close and kissed her lips. It was only a peck, but the thrill of it traveled to her toes and hit everywhere in between.

His body filled all her curves as he hugged her and spread kisses along her cheek and neck. "I knew you were the one, Elinor. So beautiful, charming, and sweet, I could not resist you. I want to be worthy of your love, and in the weeks we courted, I found a way to get enough money to repair my country home and still have enough to make a good start to the marriage. I made the deal on some grain. It will take a bit of time for my plans to pan out, but in a couple of months, I should be able to show your father that I am worthy of you."

It was difficult not to let his lips distract her from his words. She heard him say he loved her well enough, though. She breathed normally again, though her heart still raced. "I would gladly have given you my money."

Stiffening, he frowned. "We can take your money and put it away for our children."

"Children." The notion of raising babies with Michael made her sway with joy.

"You do want children, don't you?"

She looked up at him, holding back tears of joy. "Oh yes. I want a house full."

"I have a very big house." The strain around his eyes eased, and his grin spread wide.

"Good." Tears trickled down her face. Elinor had never been so happy.

With his gloved thumbs, he gently wiped the moisture from her face. "You will wait for me then?"

"I will wait, Michael."

Kissing her deeply, he tightened his arms, leaving no space between them.

Her mouth opened under his, and she melted against him. Visions of Michael and a house full of children with his marvelous blue eyes filled her head. Her heart beat so fast, that when he pulled away, she gasped for air.

"I have to go before I really do ruin you." Out of breath, his eyes flashed with passion.

"Must you?" She didn't want him to go. What she wanted was more of his kisses.

He laughed and placed a chaste kiss on her forehead. "It will not be long, my love. I shall return to London as soon as possible, and we will be married."

Once again, loneliness pressed down on her. "Don't go."

"I must, but I will be back. I promise." He took one step away.

"Michael."

He turned.

Straining against emotion, she pushed herself to ask, "Do you love me, Michael?"

He wrapped her in his arms as if he'd not seen her in years. "I love you more than life, Elinor. I will not betray you. Please trust me."

She tentatively kissed the skin behind his ear. "I do trust you. I just want..."

"Yes, my love, what do you want?"

"I want...I do not know." Her tongue touched his ear.

Grabbing her bottom, he pressed her roughly against his arousal.

Surprised but not afraid, she arched against him.

His lips found hers roughly, and he caressed her everywhere. He pulled her deeper into the thick garden shrubs. His breath came hard. He kissed her ear, her neck, then moved down to her throat. He caressed the top of her bodice, then tugged gently, releasing her nipple.

The cool air was odd and delightful on her sensitive skin.

He grazed it with his thumb, then his mouth covered her. She pulled him closer, wanting something but not knowing what she needed. Everything spun the way it did when she drank too much wine. It was wonderful and terrible all at once. She gripped his arms tighter, never wanting to let go.

He pushed her away. "No."

Longing for more, she clutched at him.

He fixed her dress and pushed a stray curl behind her ear. "I must go. It is too difficult to be here in the dark alone with you. I will not be able to stop myself."

"I did not ask you to stop." She surprised herself with her boldness.

He grinned. "No, you didn't, but I will wait and take you when you are mine, my love. We can wait for our wedding night, and I promise it will be worth the wait." He kissed her nose, then was gone.

CHAPTER ONE

See the dressmaker
Find just the right gift for Michael
Ask Mother for pin money
Write to Michael so he will know I am thinking of him

E linor had many more items to add to her morning list. A knock on her door forced her to put down her quill. "Yes."

Mother stepped inside. "Your father wishes to see you in his study, Elinor."

"Why so formal, Mother?"

"The matter is quite urgent." Virginia Burkenstock folded her hands and grimaced; her sour face much different from her normal serene expression.

Elinor placed her list inside her desk, stood, and shook out her skirts. When she reached her father's study, nerves twisted her stomach. She entered, her mother close at her heels

Rolf Burkenstock scratched his belly where it hung over his trousers, then tugged on his morning coat. He pointed at the chair near his desk. "Sit, daughter."

She obeyed.

"You will not marry Sir Michael Rollins." Clearing his throat, he fiddled with a document on his desk.

For a full thirty seconds, Elinor couldn't respond. It was so outrageous for him to be canceling her wedding a mere month before the much anticipated day, she was sure she had misunderstood. She stared at him for some sign that he would say more or make her understand. "Father?"

"We'll say no more on the subject, Elinor. It's bad enough

that we will have to deal with some gossip about breaking the engagement. The man should be left with some dignity." Her father's new earldom meant that Sir Michael Collins was now beneath her, but she never dreamed that either man would go back on their word. Recently raised to the rank of Earl of Malmsbury by the crown, Rolf had a new sense of his own worth. He stood prouder, had lost much of his natural modesty, and lived in fear of gossip and scandal.

Lady Virginia's eyes were puffy and her nose red. She bit her lip and sniffed, which she always did when trying to contain her tears. Several strands of her blond hair had escaped her usually neat chignon.

Father hadn't cried, of course. His imposing height and piercing pale blue eyes usually intimidated Elinor, but now he wouldn't make eye contact, looking from a spot on the wall to one on the carpet. As a diplomat for the crown, he met with kings and princes on a regular basis, but his own daughter made him uncomfortable.

"Has Sir Michael cried off?" Elinor was calmer than she would have thought possible.

Now neither of her parents would look her in the eye.

"Father, what is going on?" Her voice gained an edge.

Mother spoke. "He has been injured, Elinor."

"Injured? When? How? Why was I not summoned to care for him?" Panic rose in her chest. She rushed away to gather her wrap and have the carriage take her to Michael's townhouse.

Both of her parents shouted in unison, "Stop."

FOREVER BRIDES

Tainted Bride

Foolish Bride

Desperate Bride

Also by A.S. Fenichel

HISTORICAL ROMANCE

The Wallflowers of West Lane Series

The Earl Not Taken

Misleading A Duke

Capturing the Earl

Not Even For A Duke

The Everton Domestic Society Series

A Lady's Honor

A Lady's Escape

A Lady's Virtue

A Lady's Doubt

A Lady's Past

The Forever Brides Series

Tainted Bride

Foolish Bride

Desperate Bride

Single Title Books

Wishing Game

Christmas Bliss

HISTORICAL PARANORMAL ROMANCE

Witches of Windsor Series

Magic Touch

Magic Word

Pure Magic

The Demon Hunters Series

Ascension

Deception

Betrayal

Defiance

Vengeance

Visit A.S. Fenichel's website to view her full library.

www.asfenichel.com

Writing contemporary romance as Andie Fenichel

Christmas Lane

Dad Bod Handyman

Carnival Lane

Changing Lanes

Lane to Fame

Heavy Petting

Hero's Lane

Summer Lane

Icing It

Mountain Lane

~

Writing contemporary romance as A.S. Fenichel

CONTEMPORARY EROTIC ROMANCE

Alaskan Exposure

Revving Up the Holidays

CONTEMPORARY PARANORMAL EROTIC ROMANCE

The Psychic Mates Series

Kane's Bounty

Joshua's Mistake

Training Rain

The End of Days Series

Mayan Afterglow

Mayan Craving

Mayan Inferno

End of Days Trilogy

About the Author

 A.S. Fenichel also writes as contemporary romance author Andie Fenichel. After leaving a successful IT career in New York City, Andie followed her lifelong dream of becoming a professional writer. She's never looked back.

Originally from New York, Andie grew up in New Jersey, and now lives in Missouri with her real-life hero, her wonderful husband. When not buried in a book, she enjoys cooking, travel, history, and puttering in her garden. On the side she a master cat wrangler, and her fur babies keep her very busy.

Connect with Andie
www.asfenichel.com
www.andiefenichel.com